BIOGENESIS
FALLEN ANGELS – BOOK 2

Terence West

BIOGENESIS
FALLEN ANGELS – BOOK 2

DOUBLE DRAGON

Dedication

This book is dedicated to my wife, Shannon.

Acknowledgments

There are too many people to thank this time around. Everyone in my life, past and present, played a key part in helping me write and develop this book, whether they meant to or not. This book, more so than my first, was a bit of a personal journey. I needed to know that I had more stories to tell, and luckily I did. Thanks to all the people that kept pushing me to write this book. You know who you are.

Chapter One

The alien hung frantically at the end of the noose, the rope cutting into the soft gray flesh of its neck. Its already big black eyes were opened wide as its long, spindly fingers clawed at the rope. The alien's small slit like mouth was agape and emitting a horrid screech as the crowd looked on in horror. Suddenly, the alien's body lurched into an inhuman pose, and then fell silent. The only sound was the audible gasp from the alien's mouth as the last breath escaped his chest.

The once angry mob fell utterly silent. Their torches were still blazing brightly on this cold November night in 1589. A brisk North Carolina wind began to whip across Roanoke Island, twisting the alien's thin dead body back and forth at the end of the noose. One by one, the crowd began to fall back.

A large woman stepped out of the crowd holding her small infant girl. Her usually neat brown hair was flayed wildly about her head and shoulders. She had lost her bonnet in the fray. Swinging her oil lantern toward the alien, a look of horror crossed her face. "What's the matter with ya?" She turned to look at the body, "It's of the devil! It deserved to die!" she said in a British accent. Turning back, she stared angrily at the silent crowd while her baby cried. She looked down and tried to comfort her baby, "Hush, Virginia Dare. Be a good girl for Momma."

A tall, rugged man stepped out of the crowd. Lifting off his hat, he moved closer to the woman. "Elenore, I can't speak for the rest of us, but I don't think we did the right thing." His voice was low and gravelly, but filled with regret.

Elenore quickly turned and scowled at the man, "Don't you give me that, George. You were shouting to kill it just as loud as the rest of us. Don't you go and be gettin' sour on us."

"I ain't gettin sour," he stroked his thick brown beard. "I just think we should've thought this through a little better." The crowd responded with shouts of agreement. "I ain't ever seen anythin' like this before." George kicked at the dirt with his boots, "I don't think it's of the devil, Elenore."

Elenore took a step away from George and the crowd. She quickly pointed at the alien while coddling her child in her other arm. "Look at it! It ain't no person, and it sure as hell ain't no animal I ever seen! And have we all forgotten where we found it? It was sneakin' around Dan Anderson's farm! Terrorizin' his family!"

George dropped his head. "That still don't make it of the devil!"

Elenore stepped up to George, even though she was a full two feet shorter. "Dan's daughter said this thing came ev'ry night and took her away! It was takin' our children for god's sake!" Elenore swung around to face the crowd, "How many of you want this thing takin' our kids in the middle o' the night? I sure as hell don't!"

The crowd muttered in agreement with Elenore.

Elenore turned and pointed at the alien, "Now I say we cut this thing down and burn it!"

The crowd cheered and began to approach the alien. They suddenly stopped when a bright light appeared in the sky over them. The light exploded into a huge silver saucer. It hovered silently over them for what seemed like an eternity. The moment was shattered when a beam of light jetted from the hull of the ship and pinpointed the body of the alien. The beam then slowly moved along the ground, and before the crowd's eyes, three more gray aliens materialized. One of the aliens stepped forward and with a wave of his hand, the noose opened, allowing the dead alien to fall to the ground. The three aliens crouched down by their fallen comrade, apparently mourning their loss.

One of the aliens stood up and turned to address the crowd. They quickly fell back in terror.

Elenore could swear she saw anger in the alien's face. She mustered all the courage she had and stepped forward holding Virginia tightly against her chest. "Devil be gone!"

The alien made no motion toward her, instead it turned and stepped back into the circle of light. Picking up their fallen shipmate, the other two aliens joined the third in the circle of light, and were gone as quickly as they came. The crowd, still astonished at what they had just witnessed, turned their gazes skyward toward the craft.

Screams began to fill the air as the white light abruptly shifted to red and a smoke began to settle over the one hundred or so settlers in the crowd. The gas immediately went to work on the colonists' respiratory system, shutting it down. The gas also seemed to be acting like an acid, burning their flesh. The settlers writhed in agony as their flesh burned and their lungs began to produce thick yellow foam. They were drowning.

Summoning all his strength, George clawed his

way out of the light. Standing up, he looked through blurry eyes at his hands and arms, now covered by burns and blisters. Turning around, he watched his fellow colonists dropping to the ground one by one, their bodies beginning to melt into pools of fluid. He saw Elenore on the ground, her large frame covering her baby as she tried to protect her. George turned away, trying to block out the screams that filled his ears. He couldn't take anymore.

George knew he was about to die. Turning away from the horror behind him, he ran toward a small outcropping of trees. He needed to leave a clue to what had happened here. He didn't want all one hundred and seventeen settlers dying for nothing. He didn't want others to repeat their mistake.

Whipping out his knife, he started to carve a word on the tree. George searched his vocabulary for a word that closely meant "extra-terrestrial", and came up with "Croatoan". The Croatoan's were a tribe of Indians that had helped the settlers learn to fish and hunt when they reached the New World. Several of the settlers, upon first meeting the Croatoans, had remarked how unearthly they appeared compared to the English.

George had spelled out C-R-O when he saw the beam shift directions. Bolting off in a dead sprint, he weaved his way deep into the brush and trees. A tall wooden fence that cut through the thick foliage finally stopped George. Crouching down in terror, he watched the awful red light break through the treetops around him. He knew they were looking for him, and they would find him. Standing up, he carved the letters C-R-O-A-T- O-A-N in the wooden fence post behind him. He only hoped Governor John White would understand the message when he returned from England. When he returned to find the first colony of the New World had vanished without a trace.

Chapter Two

Every light tells a story, or so he had been told. The houses' lights below twinkled through a misty fog that filled the valley. He watched as people packed in cars made their way to work and home through the crowded streets. He tried to imagine what was happening in their lives. Were they having a good or bad day, were they fighting with their significant others, or were they simply on their way to a job they hated? So many things could be happening in these people's lives, it was hard for him to fathom.

His father had been a professional writer and had always tried to teach him how to find the story behind everything, but he was never really concerned with the plight of others, only his own.

A brisk wind whipped around him kicking up a patch of dust. He had parked his car on top of a hill that had a gorgeous view of Elko and Spring Creek, Nevada on both sides. For the past several days, they had seen a light snow fall, but most of it had melted away, leaving only the icy grip of winter.

He had parked his car facing north into Elko, and had seated himself on the hood. With his thick black boots and worn black leather jacket wrapped around him tightly, he stared into the partially clouded sky. The stars were shining brightly overhead, one of the assets of living outside a major city, but it didn't matter to him. They all looked dull and lifeless through his cynical eyes.

Tyler Mitchell's life was over, or so he thought. He had just been dumped by his girlfriend of three months. He had never been very good in school or been an athlete, so he'd never had much luck with women. Now in his senior year, Tyler felt as if his chances were beginning to dwindle. He had driven up to the Summit to clear his mind, but only found more pain. This is where they had always come to look at the lights. It had also been here where they had their first kiss, and first....

Tyler didn't want to think about that now, although she was great. Shaking the thought, he turned his attention toward the sky. Patches of stars were showing through the cloudy sky, but something else caught his attention, something bright. It looked like a star at first, until it started to move. He founded himself transfixed on the light as it swooped back and forth. A wave of anxiety passed over him as it paused above him.

He had read all the literature and watched all the documentaries; this was a UFO, and the moment he had been waiting for his entire life. Tyler knew it was crazy, but he had always hoped life really did exist outside of this planet, so they could come and take him away from his meaningless life. Tyler had always considered himself an outcast of society, electing not to attend parties or hang out with his friends on Saturday nights, but to diligently search the skies in hopes of catching a fleeting glimpse of aliens. This was it.

Standing up, Tyler walked around to the side of his blue late model sedan and opened the door. He grabbed his cell phone off the dashboard and quickly dialed a number. He listened as it rang. "Come on, come on. Pick up!" He kept his vision trained on the UFO.

"Hello?" an attractive female voice answered.

"Jessie!"

"What do you want, Tyler?" Her tone was harsh.

Tyler didn't know how to proceed. "I'm sorry, I just...well, I think I'm watching a UFO."

"Is this some sick ploy of yours to get back with me? You do realize it's over, don't you?"

"No, this is real! I'm watching it right now!" He waited as silence ensued on the other end of the line. "Jessie?"

"Look," he heard her sigh in exasperation. "It's over, Tyler. I'm not going to take you back. I've got to go, I'm going out tonight."

The click of the phone startled him. "Damn." Pressing the end button, he tossed the small black cellular phone back into his car. Glancing back up at the sky, he became alarmed when he couldn't find the light. He quickly whirled around scanning the sky for the UFO. *Where is it?*

A burst of cold wind caught him off-guard. Spinning around, Tyler came face-to- face with a huge craft. He stared in awe at its shimmering silver surface as it hovered silently in front of him. A wave of fear engulfed him. Taking several steps back, he unexpectedly caught his foot on a large rock and began to tumble end over end. Tyler fell awkwardly down the face of the hill. Finally hitting bottom, his right leg slammed against another rock, breaking it in several places. Tyler screamed in agony as blood spurted from the wound where the bone broke through his skin. Glancing up, he saw the huge craft maneuvering toward him, its bright red and blue collision lights blinding him. He tried to scream for help, but no one heard his cries; no one except the occupants of the craft.

***

The clinking sound of silverware against plates filled the room giving it an eerily musical sound. The large ballroom of the MGM Grand in Las Vegas, Nevada was lavishly decorated for this auspicious occasion. Crystal chandeliers accompanied by strands of gold garland adorned the ceiling and the corners of the walls. The floor was filled with several round tables occupied by well-dressed people of all ages. Laughter and conversation moved over the room as the guests spoke openly about politics and social standings amongst themselves.

A large wooden stage stood at the far side of the room. On it were two tables joined in the center by a tall wooden podium. On the right side of the podium, four well-dressed men were conversing and enjoying their dinner of smoked salmon. To the left of the podium, two men and two women sat anxiously waiting for the night's presentation to begin.

The room's attention was quickly drawn to center stage as the lights dimmed and a spotlight appeared. A middle-aged man dressed in a black tuxedo slowly stood up from the right and took a position behind the podium. Testing the mic, he tapped on it three times, filling the room with a dull thud from the speakers. His white hair shone in the harsh spotlight as his blue eyes twinkled. "First off, let me say thanks to all of you out there for making our dream become a reality." His opening remark was met with loud applause from the audience. "Thanks to your generosity, the Wills Foundation has raised well over one hundred thousand dollars to help our researchers combat cancer all over the world!" Applause erupted again. The man raised his hands to try and quiet the group. "Most of you know me," he scanned the audience, "and for those of you who don't, my name is Dan Wills, founder and CEO of the Wills Foundation." He stopped and smiled. "Now, what you've all been waiting for, our chief researcher here at the foundation," Wills turned to his left and gestured toward the man sitting next to the podium, "Robert Kincaid!" The crowd went wild.

Kincaid slowly stood up and turned to face Wills. Grabbing his outstretched hand, Kincaid shook Wills' hand, then moved past him to the podium. Reaching down to the table, he grabbed his glass of water and placed it on the podium in front of him. "Thank you."

Kincaid was a tall and wiry man with short, thinning brown hair. His thick dark rimmed glasses were the most outstanding feature of his long, plain face. Rubbing his hand across his forehead, he wiped the sweat off it. Taking a long sip of his water, he set the glass down and addressed the mic. "You'll have to forgive me, I've been feeling a little under the weather recently." He balled up his fist and held it in front of his mouth as he tried to stifle a cough. "As most of you know, it's flu season." A small laugh rippled through the audience. Taking a deep breath, he decided to jump into his speech. "As Dan said, I am the main researcher here at the Wills Foundation. For fifteen years, we've been striving to find a cure for cancer, to stop this deadly killer that fears no one. As some of you know—" He was cut off in midsentence by a wave of coughing. Trying to catch his breath, he took a long sip of water. Removing a handkerchief from his pocket, he dabbed it on his flushed face. Finally composing himself, he tried to continue. "Excuse me." He dabbed the handkerchief on the back of his neck and loosened the top button of his dress shirt. "As I was saying, cancer fears no one. It is a plague on the face of the Ea—" Another wave of coughing stopped him. A murmur of anxiety began to race through the audience. Placing his hand over the mic, he leaned over to Wills. "I'm sorry, Dan, I didn't know I was this sick."

Wills patted him on the shoulder encouragingly. "Do what you can, Rob. I think everyone will understand."

"Thanks, Dan."

Lifting himself back up behind the podium, Kincaid stared out into the audience. Raising his hand above his eyes, he tried to block out the spotlight so he could see the reactions of the crowd. Another coughing fit gripped his body. He felt his already tired muscles tense up as the dry heaves erupted. Looking into the crowd, his vision began to blur. Doubling over, he let out a gasp of pain.

Wills immediately jumped up and grabbed Kincaid to keep him from falling over. "Rob! Are you okay?"

Kincaid shook his head furiously as he tried to stop coughing.

Steadying Kincaid against the wall behind them, Wills grabbed the microphone. "We need a doctor!" Several people stood up in the audience and quickly made their way toward the podium. Turning around, Wills spotted Kincaid. He had slid down to the floor. Dropping to his knees, Wills grabbed Kincaid's face and turned it toward his. "Stay with me, Rob. Help's on the way."

A large black man pushed Wills aside. "I'm a doctor. I can help." Reaching down, the doctor pressed two fingers to the side of Kincaid's neck. "His pulse is very thready. We're losing him! Call 911! Now!" the doctor barked.

It was already too late for that; Robert Kincaid's life was quickly fading away as he lay on the floor behind the podium. The doctor ripped open his shirt and began to administer CPR. Looking down, the doctor watched Kincaid's eyes roll back into his head as another coughing fit gripped his body. Thick, yellow foam began to flow from his mouth, choking him.

The doctor reeled back in horror. "What the hell is that?"

The group that had gathered around Kincaid stood watching with their mouths agape as he died.

***

He awoke suddenly in a cold sweat. Sleep had been a luxury he hadn't enjoyed lately. Pulling off the sheets and sitting up, he looked around the stark motel room he was in. The light from the 'vacancy' sign outside his second floor window permeated the room giving everything a ghastly red glare.

It had been almost a year since he had helped destroy both of the top secret research facilities

18

deep in the Southern Nevada Desert, and Jake Silver was tired of running.

Grabbing the remote control off the nightstand next to his bed, Jake flipped on the television and stood up. Making his way into the cramped bathroom, he cranked on the faucet. Placing his hands on the counter, he stared at the exhausted man in the mirror. The beard he had grown to help disguise himself was starting to look very ragged since he hadn't trimmed it lately. Huge, dark bags hung under his deep blue eyes, and his usually short brownish-blonde hair now hung to his shoulders.

Putting his cupped hands under the running faucet, he splashed the cool water on his face. Turning off the light switch in the bathroom, he made his way through the room to the balcony. Throwing open the doors, he stepped out into the humid night air. It was June in New Orleans, and the streets were bustling with summer tourists. He stared down into the French Quarter at the old style buildings. He loved it here.

Before becoming a Private Investigator, he had been a Field Agent in the Federal Bureau of Investigation, stationed here in New Orleans. Originally from a small farming community in Kansas, he had never been in a major city until he came here. The city became a part of him during his fifteen years in the Bureau; he now called this place home.

It was also his first choice when he needed a place to lay low for a while. In the eleven months since he had helped destroy Area 51 and Site 4, agents of the government had been showing up everywhere he went. His mind wandered back to

19

that close call in Seattle, but he didn't want to think about that right now.

He was concerned with something else, or rather, someone else. It had been several months since he had last seen Alex Robinson. They had decided to split up, realizing that having the only two surviving people that knew what happened that fateful night in Nevada in the same place was dangerous. The logic behind the thought was that if one was caught or killed, the other would still be free. It was a good idea on paper.

He didn't know why, but in the time they had spent together running from the government, he had grown very attached to Alex. He had been married once, but his career had always come first. Jake remembered the morning he came home from an all-night stakeout and found a note from his wife that just said, "I'm sorry". She had left and taken his daughter without even attempting to work things out. This time, however, it was different. He couldn't explain why.

Alex had decided to stay with one of her colleagues at the University of Colorado in Boulder. She had insisted she needed time and a decent laboratory to work on the sample of the green liquid that the test subjects were being immersed in while they were at Area 51. Jake had agreed. He now regretted that decision, though. Jake now realized that even if they were in danger together, he needed her. Her continued belief in extra- terrestrials and the UFO phenomenon was the reason he kept running. Alex's passion was all consuming.

Taking one more look across his city, he stepped back into the air-conditioned room and closed the doors. Returning to the bathroom, he lifted a small brown travel bag off the floor and laid it on the sink. Turning on the tap, he held his hand beneath it waiting for the water to warm up. Unzipping the bag, he removed a small blue razor and dipped it in the water for a moment, then placed it next to the sink. Lifting a can of shaving cream out of the bag, he popped off the top and sprayed a generous helping of foam into his hand. He steadily began to smear it across his beard. Lifting the razor, he took one final look at his beard.

Trying to keep himself occupied as he shaved, he listened to the television playing in the background. Before he went to bed, he had been watching one of the twenty-four hour news stations.

"...*The President will return to work immediately after a week off spent with his family at Camp David. In other news, it seems the southwestern United States still seems to be having a stroke of bad luck.*" Jake stopped for a moment. Peeking his head around the edge of the bathroom door, he stared at the well-manicured anchorman. "*It was less than a year ago that the area around Las Vegas, Nevada was rocked by an earthquake measuring eight point two on the Richter scale. Thanks to federal aid, the area had just finally gotten back on its feet, but now, it seems an unknown contagion has hit the gaming capitol of the world. We now go live via satellite to Jill Marlens in Las Vegas.*"

The picture changed to a well-dressed woman standing in, what looked to Jake, like a hospital ward. Her long, brown hair was neatly tucked behind her ears and being held in place by a pair of wire rimmed glasses. She was wearing a germ mask over her face. *"Thanks, Bob. As you can see, the hospitals and doctors' offices are overflowing with patients. The first reported case of this mysterious illness was only reported about a week ago, when it claimed the life of world-renowned Wills Foundation cancer researcher Robert Kincaid, so it seems it's spreading very quickly. Researchers are still baffled by what's causing the outbreak. They do know one thing, if you are experiencing flulike symptoms and live in Southern Nevada, Southern California, or Northern Arizona, go see a doctor immediately. You may have contracted this deadly illness. The Federal Emergency Management Agency is on the scene, but so far, they have no answers either. This is Jill Marlens reporting live from Las Vegas, Nevada. Back to you, Bob."*

"Thanks for that report, Jill. In other news, the stock market hit an all-time high today. Most analysts think interest rates...."

Clicking off the TV, Jake sat down on the edge of the bed. The implications of that story were too big to just ignore. Reaching over to the nightstand, he grabbed his wallet and dug out a small business card. Lifting the phone off the hook next to him, he quickly began to dial the number printed on it.

After a few short rings, a female voice answered on the other end. "University of Colorado at Boulder. This is Suzanne, how can I help you?"

"I need to speak with Dr. Robinson. It's urgent."

***

22

It was a scorching hot day in the middle of the Southern Nevada desert. For the past few days, a patch of thunderstorms had moved through, but the rainfall wasn't enough to squelch the drought that gripped the entire area. The dry lakebed that the complex was built on was barren for miles. Surrounding the lakebed was a range of mountains littered with rocks, sagebrush and Joshua trees. It was a desolate place.

A tall, slender man with sandy blonde hair and deep blue eyes stood alone in the middle of the longest runway in the world. His dark blue uniform was neatly pressed and fit him perfectly. He adjusted his wire rimmed sunglasses as he stared at the newly rebuilt main hangar of Area 51. Crews had worked around the clock for ten months to rebuild the hangar and stabilize the underground portions of the base that had been damaged in the explosion.

He had read the files that dealt with the destruction of Area 51 and S-4, but was unable to fathom how two people could infiltrate, then destroy, two of the most top secret facilities in the world. He knew it would be no challenge to run this base more efficiently than either of his predecessors.

"General Foster?"

General Michael Foster spun around. "Yes?"

A slender woman with long brown hair and green eyes strode toward him. She extended her hand to him. "Sir, I'm Colonel Anne Carroll. I apologize, I wasn't informed of your visit until half an hour ago."

"Understood." He grabbed her hand and shook

it firmly. "Pleased to meet you, Colonel. You're in charge here?"

"Yes, sir. I was placed in charge of all base operations after General Perry was killed."

"I read in your report you were shot while defending S-4. Everyone in that base was presumed dead when it imploded, yet you survived. How?"

"My gunshot wound wasn't that severe. It missed all my major organs going straight through my side, but the pain I was in was excruciating. Using all my strength, I pulled myself up and made my way toward the exit. Once outside, I felt the first explosion tremor tear through the base. Moving as fast as I could, I tried to get as far away as possible before the second explosion." Her mind started to wander back to that horrible moment in time. "I wasn't far enough away when it happened, though. The shockwave from the explosion moved across the ground like a ripple in a pond, throwing me off my feet and slamming me into the face of the rock wall next to the access road." She grabbed her side, cradling her old wounds. Foster detected a small tremor in her voice. "I spent close to a week wandering in the desert before I finally found civilization."

"That's quite a story, Colonel," Foster admitted.

"Thank you, sir. The doctor that operated on me accredited my survival to my strong will to survive." Her voice returned to a more professional tone. Anne quickly directed Foster toward her waiting jeep.

Arriving at the jeep, Foster set his duffel bag in the back and unzipped it. He removed a large manila envelope and handed it to Anne. "Read this, Colonel."

Anne quickly opened the envelope and removed its contents. "Are these new orders?" she asked while scanning over the documents.

Foster paused for a long moment before answering. "I hate to do this to you, Colonel. I know this was your first command—"

Anne interrupted, "You're replacing me as the Commanding Officer of this base?" Foster nodded. "The President and Joint Chiefs felt it was wiser to have someone with more experience in charge of the facility, especially after what happened last year."

Anne began to flip through her new orders with disbelief. "Sir, I was given this assignment with the understanding that after we completed reconstruction, I would retain command."

"I am sorry, Colonel." Foster lifted himself into the passenger seat of the vehicle. Anne quickly composed herself and snapped to attention. "With all due respect, General, I deserve my own command." She thought for a moment. "What's my new assignment?"

Foster removed his sunglasses and stared at her. He slowly folded them and then slid them into the breast pocket on his jacket. "I need you here with me."

"Why is that, sir?"

"Your job here will still be one of command, I need you to help me get acquainted with the base and the men. I don't want to jump into this assignment blind."

"But, sir—"

25

"My final word has been given, Colonel Carroll," Foster replied sternly.

Anne crisply saluted. "Yes, sir." Moving around to the driver's side of the jeep, she climbed in and threw the vehicle into gear. Stepping on the accelerator, she piloted the white Jeep Cherokee toward the main hangar of the base.

***

Jim Durard was having a rough time traversing the rocky terrain wearing a pair of thick rubber boots. He stopped and began to wave a small silver device around himself, attempting to catalog the radiation throughout the area. Checking the meter, he let out an audible sigh. There was still no sign of anything.

He suddenly felt a twitch under his nose. Doing his best to stifle it, he felt it pass. Taking a few steps further, he suddenly sneezed inside his yellow contamination suit. Mucus splattered across his visor. He cursed under his breath as he vainly tried to wipe it off, even though it was on the inside. Reaching down, he worked his gloved hand over a small black transmitter on his belt. He flipped a small silver switch into the 'on' position. "Hey, Greg, are you there?"

The speaker crackled to life inside his helmet. "Yeah, go ahead, Jimmy."

"Where are you?"

"Down here! I'm waving at you," Greg Hollman replied with a bounce in his voice. Jim stared down into a huge hole in the Southern Nevada Desert that used to contain the top secret

26

underground base known only as 'S-4'. The crater had been estimated to be almost a mile deep and several miles in diameter. It was thought that when the base imploded, it disrupted the porous soil underneath that comprised most of the Great Basin area, creating a huge sinkhole.

Durard caught sight of Greg standing just outside a group of men in yellow contamination suits. "I see you. Hey, listen, I'm going to head back to base camp for a minute."

"What happened?" Greg asked.

Durard felt embarrassed at his rookie mistake. "I sneezed inside the suit. I need to wipe my face shield off." Laughter erupted from the speaker. "It's not funny," he stated very seriously.

"The hell it's not," Greg argued while still laughing.

"I'm heading back," Durard replied, trying to end the conversation.

"Okay," Greg was laughing as hard as he could. "Hey, you might want to grab some tissues when you come back next time."

Durard reached down and clicked off his transmitter. He enjoyed working with Greg, but sometimes, the man got on his nerves. Sliding the silver cylinder into its holster on his belt, he turned around and began to walk toward several white domes that stood near the top of the crater. They vaguely reminded him of gigantic igloos.

Reaching the nearest dome, he moved toward the entrance. He quickly grabbed the handle and twisted it, opening the door. Stepping inside, he stared at the large vents built into the floor and ceiling and another door in front of him. He tapped a glowing green button on a waist high console to his right that started two large fans in the vents.

After several minutes, the giant fans kicked off and a loud buzzer began to sound inside the small room. He slowly pulled off his thick rubber gloves and reached up to his helmet. Grabbing the zipper on his right shoulder, he pulled it down over his chest and slowly lifted off his helmet. Taking a deep breath of the fresh air, he slowly moved through the second door.

The inside of the dome wasn't as large as it seemed from the outside. It was filled with long tables that held scientific equipment of every kind. Lab technicians dressed in white jumpsuits with black gloves and boots moved about the equipment examining various samples attained from the site. Long ventilation shafts ran the entire length of the roof, giving it the feel of a warehouse.

Sitting down on a bench near the door, Durard began to peel off the contamination suit. Once the suit was off, he exhaled a long sigh of relief. Running his hand through his chin length blonde hair, he wiped the sweat off his forehead. It wasn't easy wearing a thick rubber suit in the middle of the desert.

He had only been employed by FEMA for a little over a year now. He had been recruited right after he'd graduated from Stanford. Being only twenty-six, Durard was one of the youngest men in the organization. Turning to his right, he spotted a dark- skinned man working at a computer terminal near him. "Steve!"

The man looked up from his experiment just long enough to acknowledge Durard. "What's up,

Jimmy?"

Steve Curtis was a lifelong scientist. He was one of those kids that pulled the legs off bugs to see what would happen, and the appliances around his parent's house never worked right again after he had taken them apart to see how they worked. Even though he was considered one of the friendliest people in the Federal Emergency Management Agency, he had an intimidating look to him. His dark hair was done in dreadlocks that hung to his shoulders. His lower face was covered with a thick black beard, while his light blue eyes set off his dark skin. He was a middle-aged man of about forty, but you couldn't tell by the way he conducted himself.

"I just needed to take a break for a minute. It's damn hot out there," Durard said, wiping the remaining beads of sweat off his face.

"Why do you have to lie to me?" Steve responded in a sarcastic tone, still concentrating on his work.

Durard was confused. "What?"

"Greg already radioed ahead and told us that you had a little 'accident' in your suit." Steve began to laugh, his deep voice echoing off the sides of the dome.

"I'm going to get that smart ass." Standing up, Durard made his way over to the table where Steve was working. "What are you looking at?" He quickly tried to change the subject.

Steve was delighted when anyone asked him about work. It was his passion. "I've found something really strange in a few of the soil samples we've recovered."

29

"Radiation?" Durard asked.

"No," Steve studied his notes for a moment. "I haven't even found the most minute traces of radiation at this site."

Durard was puzzled. "That's strange, considering the military told us this base suffered some kind of nuclear explosion."

"That may be what they told us, but that's not what happened."

"How do you know?"

Steve stood up. "Follow me." He quickly began to walk over to a section of the dome that was littered with large chunks of scrap metal. He pointed down to one of the bigger pieces, "See the scorching?"

Durard nodded. Long black char marks ran the length of the metal. "Okay, so that would still indicate there was an explosion of some kind."

"Right, but not a nuclear one. All these pieces tested negative for radiation." He began to walk back to his workstation. Hitting several keys on his laptop computer, the screen flickered to life with graphics. "You see this?" He pointed to his computer screen.

Durard studied the computer screen. "Yeah, it looks like your basic double helix."

"So you did study in college." Steve smiled at Durard. "This isn't your ordinary DNA strand, though. It contains code I have never seen before."

"And that means what?"

"It means this fragment of genetic material we found in the soil might not be terrestrial in origin."

Durard took a step back. He had never been one that believed in UFOs or aliens that visited Earth.

"Are you sure?"

"Yes."

"What was it doing there?"

"Apparently, the same thing it's doing now. Nothing. It's totally inactive." Steve thought for a moment, "It does remind me of bacteria, though."

"Why is that?"

"It's built the same way."

Durard began to chew on his fingernails, but quickly stopped. "How could something that might be extra-terrestrial look like bacteria here on Earth?"

"Hey, man, bacteria are one of the oldest forms of life on this planet. A lot of the big wigs at NASA are now theorizing that life on this planet may have started when a meteorite carrying alien bacteria crashed here billions of years ago. Once it landed on the fertile planet that was Earth, it began to flourish."

"I don't subscribe to that theory."

"Why not?" Steve asked. "It's completely plausible. That's a lot easier for me to believe than some omnipotent god came down and said, 'let there be life'."

Durard really didn't want to get into this debate with Steve. He had been known to argue his point until his opponent gave in or died, whichever came first. "So where did this particular strand come from?"

Steve shook his head. "I have no idea, but from my samples, it appears it's not contained to this area alone."

***

31

There was a long silence before someone picked up the phone. "This is Dr. Robinson," a female voice answered.

"Alex, it's Jake. How are you?"

"Jake! It's good to hear from you." Jake could hear Alex smile over the phone. "I'm great. How have you been?"

"Good, considering." Jake paused. "How's your work coming there?"

"With the help of Dr. Lucas, I've made some very big breakthroughs lately. It's been very exciting."

"Great." Jake didn't want to get to the point. He was just enjoying talking to Alex. "Have you been watching TV lately?"

"No, I haven't had much time to," Alex admitted. "Why?"

"Do you have a set near you?"

"Yeah."

"Turn it on. There's something I want you to see."

"Okay, hold on for a sec." Jake listened as Alex set down the phone and went to turn on her TV. Several moments past before he heard her gasp. She immediately picked up the phone. "What's going on in Las Vegas?"

"I don't know," Jake admitted, "but I have a sneaky suspicion that our friends at Area 51 do."

"Where do you want to meet?"

Jake felt a large smile cross his face. "Stay there. I'll come to you." Jake thought for a moment. "I'm in New Orleans right now, so I'll catch the next flight out. I should be there tonight."

Chapter Three

General Foster hung up his phone and sat quietly at his desk for several moments. Standing up, he paced around his spacious office, glancing at his various awards and decorations hanging on the walls. Clasping his hands behind his back, he stared out a huge picture window at the rear of his office.

To him, the Southern Nevada Desert was a horrid wasteland of sand, mountains and cactus. Foster hated it here. Before being assigned to Area 51, he had a cushy desk job in the Pentagon. He had done his time, seeing tours in both Vietnam and during Desert Storm. He knew he had earned the position in the Pentagon. *On the other hand*, he thought, *I've never failed at anything and this will not be the first time.*

A knock on his office door interrupted his thoughts. "Come."

Anne quickly moved into the room and stood in front of Foster's desk. Standing at attention, she quickly saluted. "You wanted to see me, sir?"

Foster spun around to address her. She was dressed in a tight fitting Air Force uniform. Her blue skirt and jacket hugged her curves and displayed her lovely, long legs. He quickly snapped his attention back to her face. "I've just gotten off the phone with the President." He took a seat behind his desk and motioned for her to do the same. "He has conveyed to me his unhappiness with the way this base has been run in the past. He also assured me that if anything like that happened on my watch, he would personally oversee my execution."

"Understood, sir," Anne replied, taking a seat.

Foster leaned forward on his desk. "This facility cost well over a billion dollars to repair. Do you realize that's more money than it cost to build this base originally?"

"I wasn't aware of that, sir."

Foster hated being blamed for something that wasn't his fault. Ever since he had accepted this position, he had been shouldering the weight of this base's demise. He stopped for a moment and waited for his anger to subside. "Moving on to our next issue," He adjusted a small stack of papers in front of him. "What the hell is going on in Las Vegas?"

The question caught Anne off-guard. "I don't understand, sir. What are you referring to?"

"This whole outbreak business. I want to know if we have anything to do with it." Anne thought for a moment. "Not that I'm aware of, sir."

Foster smiled as he leaned back into his chair. "We need to keep a low profile for a while. I want this base to quickly sink back into obscurity."

***

As Jake's flight circled over Denver International Airport on its final approach, he swore he was passing over several huge circus tents. Smiling at the thought, he reached down and buckled his seat belt. Glancing around the cabin, he noticed the flight was very empty. *The outbreak scare in the southwest must've stopped people from coming west completely*, he thought.

Jake hated to fly. He always joked to his friends that he felt safer in a sinking boat in shark infested waters than in an airplane. To this day, he couldn't understand his fear regarding flying. It had become a routine portion of his job when he was in the Bureau, but as many times as he had flown, he'd never come to grips with it. He usually solved this problem by getting drunk and passing out, but it was too late for that now.

Grabbing the window shade, he quickly slammed it closed and sank back into the seat. His knuckles began to turn white from squeezing the armrests so tightly. A knot welled up in his throat as the plane began to descend. He had read all the literature on flying. How one is more likely to be struck by lightning than to die in a plane crash, but he would still feel safer running through a thunderstorm wrapped in tin foil.

The plane jerked as the wheels hit the tarmac. Jake let out a long sigh of relief as the plane began to decelerate. Still holding the armrests tightly, he stared up as the 'buckle up' sign blinked off. He slowly unbuckled his belt and stood up, hitting his head on the stowaway compartment. Muttering obscenities under his breath, he rubbed his head knowing he would get a bump. Quickly opening the compartment, he removed a small suitcase that held all his belongings.

A single stewardess moved past him toward the front of the plane. The pilot, who was anxious to get home, met her there. The stewardess pulled hard on the lever to open the door. With a groan, it slid open. Standing to the side of the exit, the stewardess smiled and waved as each of the passengers walked past her.

Making his way up the ramp into the airport, Jake was in awe of the sheer size of it. He had been in a lot of airports, but this was by far the most awe-inspiring thing he had ever seen. Looking up, he began to follow the signs to the exit. Weaving his way through the crowds, Jake finally arrived at a bank of sliding doors. As the doors silently slid open, he stepped outside and was met by a cool gust of Colorado air. Stepping up to the curb, he waved his hand in the air for a taxi.

A sleek white mini-van screeched to a halt in front of him. The driver, a portly man probably in his early thirties wearing a black fedora, jumped out of the van and moved toward him. "Hey, buddy, can I take your luggage?"

Jake was bewildered. Setting down one of his bags, he grabbed the man's hand and shook it firmly. "Sure," Jake half muttered to himself.

The taxi driver reached down taking both of Jake's bags and quickly depositing them into his vehicle. "You know, the weatherman said we have a thirty percent chance of rain, but I don't think it will. I mean, look at those beautiful Rocky Mountain skies."

Jake didn't know what to do. Grabbing the man by the shoulder, he spun him around to face him. "Are you sure you're a taxi driver?"

The man laughed with a deep roar. "Pretty sure." Slapping a meaty paw on Jake's back, he guided him toward the van. "Come on, we need to get going if we're going to beat the rush." Jake nodded and slid into the passenger side of the vehicle. He watched in awe as the man puffed around the front of the van and finally pulled himself into the driver's seat. "Buckle up," he said with a wink. "It's the law." Grabbing the gear shifter with one of his huge hands, the man threw the van into drive and took off.

The g forces pressed Jake back into his seat. "Now, let me get this straight, you are a taxi cab driver, and not some insane terrorist trying to kidnap me, right?"

"Yeah, I'm a taxi driver. Why do you keep asking that?"

"It's just so odd. You're so…nice."

"Oh," the man began to chuckle. "I get that a lot." Slipping off his hat, he held it over his heart. "I pride myself on being quick and courteous. It's my calling in life."

Placing the hat back on his head, he patted Jake on the shoulder. "My name's Will, but everyone calls me 'Dunk'."

"I'm Jake." He began to feel a little more at ease. "Why do they call you 'Dunk', if you don't mind me asking?"

"It's all right." He quickly turned on his blinker and changed lanes, jarring Jake sideways in the seat. "I've been a little overweight all my life."

"Really? I hadn't noticed." Jake smiled.

"It's true. When I was a freshman in high school, my class took a field trip to the county fair. I was having the greatest time! I was winning at all the games and enjoying all the hot dogs I could handle. Then I saw it: the dunk tank. It looked like a lot of fun, so I paid my quarter and I got to throw three balls at the guy sitting above it. I dunked him on the first try." Dunk beamed with pride at his past accomplishment. "Well, as the man pulled himself out of the water, he told the barker he was taking a break. That was when the rest of my class showed up. Well, to make a long story short, push came to shove and I ended up being the one sitting above the dunk tank. All of my classmates took turns throwing the balls at the target trying to dunk me, but they were all pretty bad.

None of them could do it. That's when the class bully walked up to the target and pushed it. I fell into the tank...and got stuck. It took the fire department an hour to break open the tank with their axes. The whole time, my classmates watched mocking me. Finally, they pulled me out, but I've lived with that nickname ever since."

"Why do you still use it if it came from that traumatic an experience?" Jake asked. Dunk started to laugh. "Hell, I just made that up. People really call me 'Dunk' because I love 'Dunkin' Donuts'." Jake wasn't amused.

"I tell that story to everyone who rides in my cab, just to kind of lighten the mood." Jake found himself silently wishing for a rude cabby who wouldn't talk to him. "By the way, where can I take you? I know several five star hotels in Denver that—"

"That won't be necessary. Just take me to CU."

"The University of Colorado. You look a little old to be a college student."

"I'm not." Jake was beginning to get frustrated. "I just need to get there."

"Okay, you're the boss."

A long silence ensued between the two. Jake actually began to feel at ease and the idea of a quick nap crossed his mind. Staring out the window, he began to be mesmerized by the gently sloping hills and trees. His eyes began to slowly close.

"So, did you hear about that virus in the southwest?" Dunk's voice cut into Jake's daze.

Jake snapped straight up in his seat, his temper flaring. "I apologize if I'm being rude, but will you shut up?"

Chapter Four

The two deadly warriors were locked in combat. The man swathed in black spun around, whipping his red energy sword past the other man. The second warrior, wrapped in white and brown robes, easily countered the attack with his blue energy sword, then sent a lightning fast kick into his attacker's chest knocking him backwards.

The man dressed in black scowled through his grim red and black visage, then mounted a ruthless counterattack.

"I love this part! Watch how fast their reflexes are!" A thin young man grabbed his remote control off the couch and hit the rewind button. "Let's watch it again." Ray Copeland was seventeen, and a science fiction aficionado. He owned almost every piece of memorabilia from every sci-fi movie or show ever made. He brushed his long blonde hair out of his brown eyes. He was filled with excitement as he watched the movie intently. By all popular standards, he was a geek.

"Come on, Ray, we've already watched 'the duel' about fifteen times now. You've only had this video for three hours. You're going to wear it out." Ben tossed a handful of popcorn at his friend. "Let's go out and do something." Ben wasn't quite the fan Ray was. Standing a little over six foot tall, Ben Summers considered himself more of a musician and an artist. His long, wavy red hair hung to his shoulders and partially covered his hazel green eyes and red goatee. His monochrome style of dress always reminded Ray of the 'Fonze' on 'Happy Days'. Black jeans with a white t-shirt and black leather jacket. He was only sixteen and a year behind Ray in high school.

"Come on, let's watch it one more time." Ray hit the play button again.

Sighing, Ben stood in the dimly lit room and waded through the piles of unopened action figures and accessories toward the door to Ray's bedroom. "I gotta hit the can, be right back." Ray was too engrossed in the movie to even acknowledge Ben's statement. "Okay," Ben muttered to himself. He grabbed the door handle and flung the door open. The bright light from the hallway spilled into the room, temporarily blinding both. Closing his eyes, Ben walked blindly toward the bathroom door.

"Hey, Ben?" Ray asked without taking his eyes off the television screen.

"Yeah?"

"When you come back, can you grab me another soda out of the fridge?" Ben shook his head. "Yeah, sure."

Ray listened as the bathroom door closed. Turning around, he began to lose himself in that galaxy far, far away. Suddenly, the ring of the phone disturbed his enjoyment. Quickly weighing his options, he decided to answer it, just in case it was his mother. Reaching over, he grabbed the sleek black receiver out of the outstretched hands of a golden robot. "Hello?"

"Hi...is this Ray?" The female voice on the other end was filled with anxiety. "Yeah, who's this?" Ray asked with his attention still focused on the movie. "This is Janine Mitchell, Tyler's mom."

"Oh, hi, Ms. Mitchell."

There was a long pause. "Have you seen Tyler?

41

He's been gone an awfully long time."

Ray thought for a moment, "No, sorry. Have you tried Jessie's house?"

"Yes, she told me they broke up today at school." Ray could hear the anxiety in her voice. "That makes me even more worried about him."

"I didn't know they had broken up." Ray admitted.

That didn't make her feel any better. "If you see him, could you tell him to come home?"

"Sure, Ms. Mitchell."

Janine took a deep breath. "Thanks, Ray."

"Any time." Ray slowly returned the phone to its cradle in the robot's hands. Sitting back against the base of the couch, Ray was startled by the return of his friend. Grabbing his chest, Ray turned to Ben. "Jesus, you scared the hell out of me."

"Sorry," Ben said with a smile. "Here's your soda." Ben tossed the can toward Ray. Retaking his seat on the couch, Ben stared at Ray. "What's got you so spooked?" Ray shook his head. "Tyler's mom just called. She hasn't heard from him and she can't find him anywhere. She's worried about him because Jessie broke up with him at school today."

Ben smacked his hand against the back of the couch. "Dammit. I hate that hooker, Jessie." He quickly sat forward. "I say we go over to her place right now and give her a piece of our mind."

"Dude, shut up. You only want to go over there because you've got a thing for her," Ray quickly snapped.

"What are you talking about?" Ben asked defensively. "Everyone knows it. It's a wonder Tyler still talks to you."

Ben slowly slid back into the couch. He didn't want to admit it, but Ray's accusations were true.

Ray stood up. "Maybe we should go look for him."

***

"It's good to see you, Jake!" Alex threw her arms around Jake tightly and hugged him. Her long brown hair licked the collar of her white lab coat. Pulling away from the hug, Jake stepped back and admired her. She was wearing a dark blue blouse and a short white skirt that hung just above her knees. Her blue eyes shone in stark comparison to the deep red lip gloss she had on. She smiled and grabbed his hand. "Come on, let me show you around."

Jake nodded and followed. "Wow, this is a huge facility!" Jake stared at the tan tiling on the walls as he made his way past a plethora of microscopes and computers. The lab at the University of Colorado was lavishly filled with every scientific tool a researcher could ever need. Black topped tables spanned the entire length of the lab with high green stools flanking them.

"This is where they hold all the science classes," Alex said, admiring the lab. "I usually have to fight for lab time in here, even though I know the head of the science department."

Jake had missed the smoothness of her voice. Every time she spoke, it was like a wave of water washed over him. "You mean Dr. Lucas?"

"Yeah, he's been really great to me," Alex admitted. "Alan's allowed me to use all the equipment. That's usually restricted to just the students."

"Alan Lucas? If my name was Alan, I'd shoot myself." Jake joked, although he couldn't help sounding resentful.

"Be nice, Jake." Alex chuckled as she reprimanded him.

The two moved through a door into another smaller lab. Large rectangular computer systems occupied most of the wall space around the room. Three terminals stood at the far side. Alex led Jake to the middle one and sat down. Hitting several buttons on the keyboard, she logged into the system. "This is the main computer room for the science department. Every piece of information that goes through these labs is catalogued here."

"This is pretty impressive for a college," Jake admitted, looking around the room. Alex spun around in her chair to face Jake. "I realize that when you attended college, you had to fight off the dinosaurs for a good seat," Alex laughed. "Nowadays, most major universities have this kind of system."

"I'm not that old," Jake argued.

"I'm just teasing." She paused for a long moment, just staring at his face. "I have missed you, Silver." She lowered her head, "And Jason."

Jake placed his hand on her shoulder and tried to comfort her. "Major Griggs was a good man. If it weren't for him, we never would've succeeded in rescuing you. We owe him everything."

Alex looked up at Jake with an agonized smile on her face. Grabbing Jake's hand off her shoulder, she patted it several times, then tried to compose

44

herself. "I think about him a lot." She spun back around in her leather chair to face the computer screen. "He gave his life for ours."

Jake didn't want to sound like he didn't care, but he knew they needed to get to business. "I know." He wasn't sure how to proceed. "Have you found anything out about the green fluid that Jonathan Anderson gave us?"

Alex straightened up as she tried to pull her thoughts away from Griggs. "Yeah." She quickly moved her hand up to her eye to wipe away the tears. Clearing her throat, she hit several keys on her computer. The black screen jumped to life with brightly colored graphics.

"What am I looking at?"

"Well," Alex pointed to a bar chart in the upper right-hand corner of the screen. "The fluid is basically a very powerful anesthetic. It's main purpose is to relax the victim to the point where they can't fend for themselves. Now, the other part of the fluid," she paused, "that's the mystery."

"Why's that?"

"Alan and I can't figure out what it is." She grabbed a small white mouse to the left of the keyboard and maneuvered it around a gray mouse pad. Clicking the left button twice, another window appeared on her desktop. "See this?"

Jake leaned close and studied what looked to him like a sideways spiral staircase. "Yeah. What is it?"

"It's a DNA strand, except it's composed of three strands instead of two."

"So that means what?" Jake couldn't hide his confusion.

45

"It means this didn't come from any animal on this planet. Every DNA strand of everything on this planet, be it reptile, fish, or mammal, has only two strands." She lifted her right hand to her mouth and began to chew on her red polished nails out of habit. Realizing what she was doing, Alex pulled them out of her mouth and tapped the screen. "This can't be altered either."

"I don't understand," Jake admitted. "What do you mean 'altered'?"

"It means that even our most advanced geneticists haven't figured out a way to add a third strand to our basic DNA codes. This has to be the genuine article."

"So what you're telling me," Jake rolled the words around in his mouth for a moment, "is this is extra-terrestrial DNA?"

"I can't say for certain," Alex stared intently at the helix, "but it certainly could be."

Jake stood straight up and took a step back. "So what's it doing in this green fluid?"

Alex spun around in her chair to face Jake. "So far," she took a deep breath, "we have no idea."

Chapter Five

General Foster stood quietly in one of the many observation rooms that overlooked the main hangar of Area 51. He wondered how many times Presidents had stood in this very room overseeing the launch of one of the various experimental crafts designed and flown here.

The observation room was huge. Two beige couches sat side by side along the rear wall, while rows of benches occupied the remaining floor space. The front wall was one massive piece of glass that stretched from floor to ceiling. The dark brown floor was almost the same color as the walls, which were bare rock.

Before signing on for this mission, he had tried to read every document that dealt with The Groom Lake Complex, or Area 51, as it was better known. It was constructed in the early forties by the Atomic Energy Commission, now called the Department of Energy, to study the effects of an atomic attack. This base was essential in the dawn of the nuclear age.

It had been carved directly into a mountain range that ran through the Southern Nevada Desert. The area around the base was known as the Tonopah Test Range, and it dominated a major portion of Nye County, a county larger than the states of Maryland and Vermont combined. Later in its existence, the base was taken almost completely underground. Miles of passages and rooms were buried under tons of rock and soil, making this base impervious to a direct nuclear assault. Foster grimaced. *But not three terrorists who could walk in and effectively destroy everything.*

Foster slammed his fist against the window. He knew the base had been completely rebuilt and security measures had been tripled, but he also knew this base would always have a red mark in its permanent file. No longer was it the United States most top secret base. It had been deemed compromised.

Turning around, Foster began to stride toward the door. He was beginning to feel ashamed of working at this lackluster base. Area 51 used to be likened to a fierce animal, but now it had been effectively declawed and its teeth filed down. Tapping a small silver keypad next to the entrance, he waited as a thick steel door slid open. Stepping into the cool hallway, he began to make his way toward the control center.

During the down time, most of the major operations had been temporarily moved to an abandoned missile complex in Southern Utah. The Air Force had shifted its focus from dominating the airways to dominating space. Its next wave of attack ships were being designed to fly on the edge of the atmosphere and even in space, so they needed a facility to accommodate that change. Even now, preparations were underway to make the base in Utah the permanent home for all of the US' black projects.

Foster passed a small window. Stopping, he placed both his hands next to it and stared outside. He glimpsed one of Area 51's numerous runways. *The longest runway in the world,* he thought. *What the hell good is it now?*

Pulling away from the window, he turned and

continued his journey. The hallway he was in was the same drab color of brown as the rest of the base. It was wide enough to hold six people walking side by side so they would never touch the walls. Fluorescent lights littered the ceiling, while two-toned brown tiling weaved its way back and forth across the floor.

Along the way, Foster passed several empty offices. *Why did the Government even rebuild this base if they weren't going to fully staff it?*

Finally arriving at the doorway to the command center, Foster removed a rectangular piece of plastic resembling a credit card from his breast pocket. Holding it between his finger and thumb, he gently raised it toward a small black box on the left- hand side of the door. The box jutted out away from the wall at least six inches. It had a recessed keypad on the lower half of it, while the upper portion had only a thin two inch long slot and two lights on each side of it. Pushing the card into the slot, he waited for it to authenticate his access codes. A green light on the left blinked on and a loud buzzer sounded. Retrieving his card from the slot, he took a step back as the huge door swung open toward him. He waited for the door to open completely before entering the room.

The control room was immense. It was designed with thick steel walls so it could withstand a direct nuclear assault and continue to operate. Banks of computers stood on all sides, most of them unoccupied. All the silver surfaces were polished to a high gloss. Moving further into the room, Foster took his position in the command chair.

It was a high-backed seat with two control

panels on either side that monitored all the control room's operations. It stood on a platform at least a foot higher than the floor.

Leaning back in his seat, Foster rested his hands on the control panels as he surveyed the room. His sparse staff of ten was trying to do the job of at least fifty people.

Reaching over, Foster tapped several keys on his control panel. The banks sprang to life with the vital signs of the base. "Major O'Connell, report."

A young man of about twenty-eight years twisted around in his chair to face Foster. He was of medium height with short brown hair and brown eyes. "The perimeter is clear, General. The base is operating at peak performance." Major Kyle O'Connell had joined the Air Force a little over nine years ago. He was one of the few people left at Area 51 that was there before its downfall. After General Perry died, most of the personnel were turned over. They were either shipped off to other bases, or just mysteriously vanished.

"Very good, Major. Back to your duties."

"Yes, General." Major O'Connell swiveled around in his seat and returned to his work at his station.

Foster leaned over on his left elbow and began to rub his naked chin. *This is a great posting all right.*

***

Anne slowly slid the blade across the top of her arm. She watched as blood welled up around the cut and rolled away like water. Her mind was cluttered,

50

but she was enjoying the sensation of pain shooting through her body. Pulling the knife quickly out of the gash, she wiped the blood off onto her shirt, and then returned it to the sling on her belt.

Standing up, she looked around the dank room she was in. It was a huge room filled with long glass tubes that were, for the most part, empty. Gazing up, Anne stared at the flickering fluorescent light above her. It sounded to her like a hive of angry bees.

Pressing her hands against the side of her head, she tried to find a moment of clarity. She thought about General Foster sitting in the command chair looking smug as he oversaw *her* base, as he sat in *her* chair. *The Air Force must know what I'm trying to do,* she reasoned. *That's why they sent him, to spy on me.*

A noise caught her attention. Her soft eyes hardened as she scanned the room for intruders. She caught sight of a tall, slender man entering the room. Dropping to her knees, Anne quickly rolled under one of the tubes and waited. She listened quietly as the man's footsteps grew louder. A sinister grin crossed her face when the man stopped within arm's reach. With the speed of a cobra, she reached out and grabbed the man's leg. With one swift motion, she dropped him to the hard concrete floor. Slithering out from beneath the tube, she threw herself on top of him. Grabbing both his wrists, Anne held them firmly to the ground while she straddled him. "What are you doing in here?" she hissed.

The man was frightened out of his wits. "I...I just came in to check on the patients in stasis!"

51

Anne wasn't satisfied with his answer. Quickly letting go of his left wrist, she slapped him across the face as hard as she could. "I hate it when I'm lied to."

"What are you talking about?" he cried.

"*He* sent you to spy on me, didn't he?" Anne screamed. "Didn't he?"

"I swear I don't know anything!" The man was frantically trying to comprehend what was happening to him.

Anne leaned close to his face and rubbed her cheek across his. She let out a soft moan as their skin touched. Moving close to his ear, she flicked her tongue out like a snake and licked his ear lobe. She felt the man begin to relax under her grip. Letting go of his wrists, she moved her hands to his shirt. Slowly unbuttoning it, she caressed his throat with her lips. Pulling back, she smiled at the man. His face was a mixture of fear and pleasure. Grabbing his shirt, she ripped it open exposing his chest. She ran her hands over his pecs, then down to his stomach. Leaning over, she ran her tongue over his nipples.

Anne began to unzip her pants. Lifting herself onto the balls of her feet, she slid her hand down over his crotch and his hard penis. Standing, she sensually removed her pants, and then squatted back down on top of the man. He made no moves to escape. Unzipping his jeans, she lifted his member and took it into herself. She smiled as the man moaned with pleasure. He moved his hands up her thighs until he reached her waist. Anne forcefully grabbed his hands and threw them to the floor. Leaning over, she held him to the ground as she began to grind against his pelvic bone.

Several beads of sweat rolled down his forehead. "This isn't right. We shouldn't be—"

Anne pressed her hand over his mouth. "It's all right. It'll be over soon," she comforted.

Sitting up, Anne began to slowly unbutton her shirt. Letting it fall down past her shoulders, she pushed up her bra and ran her fingers over her erect nipples. The man stared at her supple breasts as she bounced on top of him. Her head fell backward as pleasure moved in waves along her body. Anne moaned loudly as she neared her orgasm. Holding her breasts in her hands, she felt it begin. She screamed with pleasure.

Lowering her body onto the man's, she pumped harder and harder. Wrapping her legs around him, she easily rolled over onto her back. Without hesitation, he began thrusting into her. Anne moved her hands up the man's back to his shoulders. She moaned again as she dug her nails in. The man tensed up as she broke skin.

"Faster!" she commanded him.

The man complied as best he could. Anne screamed again as her orgasm hit her with full force. Pulling the man close to her, she rolled over again. With her hands on his chest, Anne kept working until she was completely finished. Stopping, she let her head fall forward in exhaustion. The man looked up at her with confusion in his eyes. Anne stared right at him as she began to reach behind her. "I told you it would be over soon."

The man smiled and nodded at her.

With lightning reflexes, Anne grabbed her

pistol from its holster on her belt and trained it on the man. Startled, the man quickly tried to wriggle out from under her. "That was conduct unbecoming an officer. You took advantage of me."

"I did not!" the man screamed in horror. "What the hell are you doing?"

"For that, you deserve death." Without a second thought, Anne pulled the trigger and sent a bullet into the man's head. His body slumped on the ground. Laying her gun on the floor, Anne stared at the man's dead body. "You were really good, though."

Standing up, she began to make her way toward a door on the far wall. Reaching for the keypad next to it, she punched in her code and waited as the door hissed open.

Stepping inside, she looked around the room. It was smaller than the main room, with only one tube standing upright against the back wall. Everything was bathed in an unnatural green light. She smiled and began to walk toward the tube seductively. Removing the last of her clothing, she pressed her naked body against the tube. Goose bumps instantly began to rise as her flesh hit the cold glass. Looking up, she stared at a man's body floating inside a thick green liquid. "I just killed a man." She kissed the tube, "And I did it for you."

***

Jim Durard was roasting again, and being back outside in this thick, yellow rubber suit wasn't helping either. He stopped for a moment and looked up at the sun directly overhead. It was at least a hundred degrees today in the Nevada Desert. Redirecting his attention, he stared up at the rim of the crater. *The blast that created this thing must've been incredible.*

Dropping to his right knee, Durard reached into a small pack he was wearing around his waist. He removed a small silver object from it. It was about as long as his outstretched hand. It was thin and oval shaped with a small switch protruding from one side of it. Pressing the switch, the lid flipped open revealing an empty interior. Lowering it to the ground, he used it like a shovel, scooping a sample of soil into it. Durard let go of the switch allowing the lid to snap shut, sealing its precious cargo inside. Replacing the small silver device into his pouch, Durard was startled by a hand on his shoulder. Jumping up, Durard spun around to see who was behind him. "Jesus, you scared the hell out of me, Greg."

"Sorry, man." Greg Hollman stood close to five inches taller than Durard. He had short, dark hair with intense brown eyes, although you couldn't tell through the suit. From most accounts, Greg had been instrumental in the containment of a major outbreak of the Hanta Virus several years ago in the southwest. By his own admittance, he was a lifelong member of FEMA. "I was just wondering what you were up to."

"Oh," Durard relaxed. "Steve had just asked me to take some soil samples from the bottom of the crater."

"Steve, as in the big Rastafarian guy back at the lab?" Greg asked. "Yeah, why?"

"It just seems to me that you should be doing

55

your assigned job and not running errands for Steve."

"I was only doing him a favor," Durard admitted.

"Would our supervisor see it that way?" Greg asked gravely. "Or would he see you sloughing off your work?"

Durard was confused. Greg had never talked to him this way before. Greg had always seemed to be a major proponent of not working if he didn't have to. "What's wrong with you?"

"Nothing," Greg snapped. "I just think you should be very careful about who you trust in this place. No one is what they seem."

"What do you mean?"

"I mean your friend Steve may have ulterior motives behind asking you to come down here and collect soil. It's off limits." Greg placed his hand on Durard's shoulder. "You're doing his dirty work."

"When did this area become off limits to us?" Durard asked. "We were sent here to find out what happened, right?"

"Look," Greg glanced around checking to see if anyone was trying to listen in, "I like you, Jim. I think you have a lot of potential in the Federal Emergency Management Agency, but you need to learn how to take care of yourself."

"It was only a favor, Greg."

"Don't trust anyone." With that, Greg turned around and strode away.

Durard stood silently for a long time thinking about what Greg had just told him. He had no reason not to trust Greg, but then again, he didn't have any reason not to trust Steve either. Was this just office politics, or something more serious? Durard didn't know what to think. Retrieving the small silver device from his pouch, he contemplated dumping the sample out. Durard moved his thumb onto the button that activated the lid, but paused. *No,* he thought to himself. *I told Steve that I'd get this sample for him, and I'm not going back on my word.* Placing the silver device back in his pack, Durard turned and began the long trek back up the slope of the crater.

Chapter Six

Tyler awoke lying naked on a table. Instantly recognizing where he was, his mind began to panic. Tyler pulled frantically at the straps that were restraining him. They felt moist and elastic against his wrists and ankles. Trying to look around the dank room, he was blinded by the intense white light that seemed to cover only his body. Squinting his eyes, Tyler saw several dark forms moving back and forth just outside the ring of light.

Suddenly, his mind was flooded with terrible images. He saw a nuclear explosion over the middle of North America. Charred bodies filled the desolate landscape. Those who were lucky enough to escape the effects of the explosion and the radiation fallout, seemed to be stricken with an illness. In Tyler's mind, he watched entire families develop flulike symptoms and die within twenty-four hours. Tyler tried to close his eyes to block out the sights, but it was no use. They were coming faster now. He could see yellow foam running from the victims' mouths. A wave of nausea passed over him as he saw the rotting corpses being thrown into a huge pit, and then covered with dirt.

"Why are you showing me this?" Tyler screamed at the shadows. The shadows made no motions toward Tyler, but the images stopped. Tyler took a deep breath, and tried not to panic.

He had heard many stories of alien abductions. In some of them, the aliens were evil and tortured their subjects with horrifying medical experiments. Abductees had reported seeing other humans apparently "switched off" while the aliens cut open a live subject's chest and examined their internal organs. In others, the aliens were portrayed as peaceful and benevolent, and they were apparently concerned with the fate of humanity. From the reports, the aliens were artificially inseminating females with collected semen, and then harvesting the fetuses. The aliens then took the fetuses and raised them as their own, possibly preparing for a mass human extinction.

Out of the shadows, one of the creatures began to approach Tyler. Its huge black soulless eyes glistened in the light. Tyler's eyes widened at he stared at the being. The alien was horrible, and yet beautiful at the same time. Tyler watched it wrap its long spindly fingers around a silver tool that was sitting on a bench next to him and lift it into the light. Tyler could see the sharp serrated edges of the three pronged tool. He began to pray these aliens were the nice ones as the blades glimmered in the light.

A second being stepped out into the light and lifted a metallic bowl off the bench. Tyler watched the creature in awe as he slid his hand into the bowl and removed what looked like a small silver ball. Setting the bowl down, the creature slapped his left hand on Tyler's forehead. Lifting the silver ball above Tyler's face, the alien stared with its unblinking eyes up and down Tyler's body. With a movement that seemed much too swift for this gangly creature, it stuffed the silver ball into Tyler's mouth. Pressing an invisible button on the top of the ball, the alien watched the ball inflate to fill Tyler's whole mouth.

Tyler tried to scream, but nothing came out. He

watched as the first creature pressed one of his bony fingers on his sternum while bringing the silver tool's blade to rest on Tyler's chest. With one quick thrust, the three-pronged tool ripped into Tyler's chest and cracked his rib cage. Blood spilled from the wound over Tyler and the table. In that instant, he knew these were not the "nice" aliens.

***

Night had fallen on the University of Colorado. Shadows from the trees and buildings fell in all directions as the full moon loomed overhead. It was dead calm. Emerging from the shadows, two figures dressed in black quietly worked their way through the campus. Flattening themselves against the walls of the building that housed the student union, they carefully crept toward the courtyard. Finally reaching the edge of the structure, the lead man pulled a large pair of goggles over his eyes, making sure the other man followed suit. Flipping a switch on the side of them, a green glow filled their visors amplifying the light so they could see clearly.

Glancing around the corner, the lead man spotted one of the campus security vehicles pulling away from the building. Turning around, the lead man signaled to the other with his hand. Nodding, the two men quickly set off across the courtyard toward their goal. A random flash of light startled the two. Dropping to the ground, they waited to see what it was.

A lone woman on a bicycle emerged from behind a separate building. She slowly pedaled across the courtyard, the headlight on her bike slicing through the darkness. She reached down and lifted a small pair of headphones out of the basket on the front of her bike. Slipping them over her ears, she hit the play button on a small cassette deck. The two men, still hidden, laughed quietly as she began to sing to herself. Weaving around the courtyard, she passed within inches of the two men.

They watched patiently as she rode out of sight. Tapping the second man on the shoulder, the first man jumped to his feet and continued across the area. Weaving between several small bushes, they finally arrived at their destination.

The lead man dropped to his knees. Pulling off his pack, he laid it gently on the ground in front of him. Unzipping it, he dug inside and removed two small items: a flashlight and a lock picking kit. He handed the flashlight to the second man and moved around to the front doors of the science building. The lead man squatted down in front of the double glass doors and removed two thin picks from his kit. He inserted them into the lock and began trying to make the tumblers in the lock turn. With a resounding click, he knew he had succeeded. Standing up, he patted the second man on the shoulder. The second man grabbed the door handle and slowly opened the door. He knew there would be an alarm. Diving inside, he heard the tell-tale beep of an active alarm. Rushing toward the back wall, the man threw open the fuse box and kicked off all the fuses. The beep stopped. Breathing a sigh of relief, he signaled for his partner to come in.

The two men stealthily made their way through the science labs. They knew exactly where to go. There was no guesswork involved with this mission.

Both knew it was as simple as get in and get out.

Finding their way to the main lab, they moved toward a large set of lockers on the sidewall. All the lockers were thin and stood almost as tall as the ceiling. The first man quickly moved three lockers over and stopped. A heavy silver padlock hung from the handle. The first man scoffed to himself. Pulling a small black Dremel out of his pocket, he clicked it on and went to work on the lock. Moments later, it fell to the floor and they were in. They began to root through the locker, pulling out papers and books. They stopped. The first man pulled out a vial of fluid. Shining the light through it, he saw it matched the description of the target: one vial of thick green liquid.

Slipping the vial into his pocket, the two began to systematically tear up the lab. They knocked over chairs and destroyed entire experiments. They destroyed everything they could get their hands on. After only a moment, the two men stepped back to assess their work. The lab was in a shambles. Their work was done. Then, as quickly and as quietly as they had come, they disappeared back into the darkness.

***

"They took it, Jake." Alex was a mess. She had been awakened at three in the morning and called down to the lab. She was wearing a pair of jeans and a baggy button up shirt, with an old tattered blue ski jacket wrapped around her. Her hair was pulled back in a ponytail, and her mascara was running down her face because she was crying.

62

"Took what, Alex?" Jake didn't look much different than usual; a pair of worn blue jeans, a t-shirt and his battered brown leather jacket. It was six o'clock in the morning. The police had been there since five.

"The vial. The one Jonathan Anderson gave you." Alex's voice was weak. Jake's eyes widened. "What?"

"It's gone. Mine was the only locker they opened last night." Alex shook her head, "The worst part is the police have no idea who did this."

Jake turned away from her and stared out the large windows at the sunrise. "I do." Turning back around, he scooped Alex into his arms and tried to comfort her.

***

"Where does Tyler usually go when he's depressed?" Ray asked.

"Jessie's house," Ben answered dryly. "Maybe he went to one of the casinos downtown to have coffee."

"Nah," Ray denied the idea. "He doesn't really like to do that anymore."

Ben easily guided his mid-sized pick-up truck through traffic on Idaho Street. It always made Ben laugh that the main street in Elko, Nevada was named Idaho Street.

Laughing, he turned his truck into the parking lot of the biggest casino in town. Ben spotted a parking spot near the door. "All right! Front row seats!" he exclaimed. Turning off the ignition, Ben and Ray climbed out.

The neon lights above them were casting an odd pink hue on the ground, even though the sign was done in red and blue. It made Ray's shadow appear to be lighter than the other shadows next to him. Looking up at the entrance, he grabbed the handle of the door and pulled it open. Stepping into the casino, their senses were immediately assaulted by the sounds of hundreds of slot machines and cheesy music being piped into the gaming pit. The carpet on the floor was a horrid mixture of red and dark blue with the occasional vomit stain thrown in. Pushing past the flood of shimmering lights and cocktail waitresses, they made their way toward the coffee shop in the back.

It was basically still part of the casino, but it had a four foot tall retaining wall all the way around it. This was to discourage the practice of not paying for your meal. Ben started to scan for Tyler. Tapping Ray on the shoulder, Ben pointed toward a woman sitting in a booth near the wall.

"Oh, no," Ray sighed.

"She might know where Tyler is," Ben said delightedly. "We need to ask her."

"Okay." Ray knew it was better not to argue. Ben was going to go and talk to her, whether he wanted to or not.

Ben casually made his way up to her booth. "Mind if we join you for a moment, Jessie?"

She smiled and nodded. "Whatever rings your bell."

Ben slid into the booth next to her with Ray on the opposite side. Ray quickly gave her the once over. He never understood what Tyler, or Ben for that matter, saw in her. She was about five and a half feet tall with wiry black hair and green eyes. She never really took care of herself, always showing up in a dirty pair of jeans, a wrinkled t-shirt and a pair of sandals she wore even in the dead of winter. Even if she did dress herself up, Ray always thought she looked like a prostitute. On this particular night, she had opted for her usual messy attire.

"So, what've you been up to, Jessie?" Ben asked, trying to make small talk. "Just having a cup of coffee," Jessie said in a scratchy voice, cultivated after years of smoking. "My date just left, and I don't want to go home yet."

Ray was outraged. "You had a date tonight? You and Tyler have only been broken up for about five hours!"

Jessie shrugged nonchalantly. "And?"

Ben tried to intervene. "Whoa, hold up Ray. That's not what we're here for."

"So how did your date go?" Ray asked angrily.

"He got what he wanted." She smirked. Jessie knew she was egging Ray on. "You bitch!"

"Stop it, Ray!" Ben slammed his fist down on the table.

All three sat in silence for a moment while tempers cooled.

"Sorry. It's none of my business who you screw, as long as it's not Tyler." Ray hated apologizing to this trashy woman. He would rather bite off his own fingers and then dip the bloody stumps into a glass of lemon juice.

"Speaking of Tyler," Ben continued, "have you seen him?"

"No, and why should I care what happens to

that little bitch?" Jessie asked spitefully.

"Now hold on, Tyler was never anything but good to you. You're the one who treated him like shit." Ray stopped and smiled. He just realized what she was doing. "Let me guess, you dumped him today, just so you could bed down your new boyfriend with a clear conscience."

Jessie snapped her fingers. "Contestants, we have a winner!" She took another sip of her coffee. "Now, if you don't mind, would you both piss off?"

"Fine with me." Ray scooted out of the booth and began to walk off.

Ben seized the opportunity. Sliding his hand onto her shoulder, he leaned close to her ear. "Since you're finished with Tyler, how about giving a real man a try?"

Jessie pulled away and began to laugh. "You show me a real man and I will." Ben shot her a dejected look. "I meant me."

"I know what you meant," Jessie replied still laughing. "Get the fuck out of here." Sitting up straight, Ben stood up and walked away. Walking out the exit, he found Ray waiting for him and giving him an extremely dirty look. "Don't even say it. She shot me down, again."

Ray and Ben stepped out into the cool Nevada night. Following the sidewalk, they reached Ben's truck and got in. Ben quickly slid his key into the ignition and started up the truck. Hitting play on his CD player, he put the truck into reverse.

"Hold on a minute." Ray pressed the eject button, stopping the music. "Why would you do that?"

"What are you talking about?"

"Don't give me that shit," Ray yelled. "You know exactly what I'm talking about. Why would you hit on Tyler's ex like that?"

"I don't know, man. It's a sickness," Ben joked.

"Damn right it is. We're out looking for our friend, and you're hitting on his woman."

"Ex-girlfriend," Ben quickly corrected.

"I don't give a shit. That's cold, man." Ray chose his next words carefully. He knew Ben was more of a sensitive person than anyone gave him credit for. Ray didn't want to crush him, only wound him. "Some fucking friend you are."

Ben's hand fell off the gear shifter. Slowly turning toward Ray, anger crossed his face. "Listen here, Tyler is one of my best friends, and I don't want to see anything happen to him."

Ray smiled. He knew he had achieved the emotion he wanted out of Ben. "Then let's go find him."

"Damn straight. Where do we look?"

Ray shrugged. "Beat's the hell out of..." Ray stopped in midsentence and snapped his fingers. "I've got it!"

"Are you going to share?"

"Where does he always go when he's upset?" Ray waited for Ben to answer. When he didn't, Ray finished the question. "Up on 'E Hill'. He likes to go up there and look at the stars!"

"That's right." Pulling the truck out of its parking spot, Ben kicked it into first gear. "We're on our way."

Chapter Seven

Jake led Alex into an unoccupied office in the science building. Sitting her down in a chair that stood in the corner, he grabbed the leather one behind the small wooden desk. The office was lavishly decorated with artifacts apparently gathered from all over the world. On one wall, several long black masks hung in a group. They were surrounded by what looked like green and blue peacock feathers. A large bookcase sat against the opposite wall that housed several volumes of anthropology textbooks, and more artifacts. A long wooden spear and several arrows hung over the window behind Jake. *Nice,* Jake thought.

Sitting down in the chair, Jake laid his left hand on his knee, while he rubbed the stubble on his face with the other. "I know who broke into the lab and took your sample," Jake admitted dryly.

Alex perked up. "Who?"

"The same men who have been tracking us for almost a year now," Jake paused, "the government."

Alex's eyes lit up with rage. "I think you're right. That makes perfect sense. To make sure we couldn't prove they were doing unethical experiments at Area 51 and S-4, they needed to get back the only piece of evidence we had."

"The vial of fluid." Jake leaned back in the leather chair. "The question now is how do we get it back?"

Both sat silently for a long time.

"I haven't the first clue," Alex admitted.

"I don't either, but I may know someone who would." Reaching toward the desk, Jake picked up the phone and started to dial.

"You can't use that, Jake. That's University property."

Jake waved a hand in front of Alex's face, dismissing her worries. He listened intently as the phone rang. *Come on, it's Wednesday morning. I know someone's there.*

"Federal Bureau of Investigation, New Orleans Field Office." A gruff male's voice answered on the other end.

"Hi, I need to speak to Special Agent Connor please," Jake said. "Speaking," the gruff voice replied.

Jake was startled by his response. "Sam? This is Jake!"

"Hey, Jake! How are you doing?" The gruff voice changed to a happier tone almost instantaneously.

"Good, how about yourself?"

"Not too bad."

Jake cut to the chase. "Hey, listen, I need a favor."

"I knew it had to be something," Sam replied. "You never call unless you want something."

Jake chuckled. "Hey, I sent you a card last Christmas."

"No you didn't," Sam responded jokingly. "The last card you gave me was in 1985 for my birthday."

"Oh, I must've forgotten."

Sam laughed. "What can I do for my ex-partner?" Jake paused. "Is this line secure?"

"As secure as it's going to get. Come on, what do you need?"

"I need some info on Area 51," Jake said

seriously.

Sam started laughing again. "Despite what you've seen on TV, my friend, there is no office in the basement with files on aliens, ghosts and goblins."

"I know that," Jake snapped. "I'm asking you to dig up some info for me."

Sam became very serious. "The bureau doesn't like us sticking our noses into the affairs of the government. It's very taboo. Hell, I shouldn't even be talking to you."

"Why's that?"

Sam paused, reluctant to answer. "You've been added to the FBI's ten most wanted list. You and that scientist Alex Robinson are wanted for terrorism."

"No shit?" Jake didn't even know it had gone that far. "I could get arrested for aiding a known felon."

Jake was stunned. "Sam, you know I didn't do anything like that."

"I don't know anything."

"Good man. Will you help me?" Jake asked again.

Silence ensued on the other end of the phone for a long moment. "I'll see what I can get for you, but no promises."

"Thank you, Sam, you're beautiful." Jake hung up the phone. Turning back around to Alex, he placed a hand on her leg to reassure her. "Everything's going to be all right."

***

"Colonel Carroll, I've called you into my office for a specific reason."

Anne stood in front of Foster's desk with her hands clasped behind her back. His spacious office hadn't been fully decorated yet. The walls were solid gray, with several awards and photos, plus a picture of the current president on the wall behind him. "Yes, sir. What can I do for you?"

"Please be seated." Foster motioned to a chair next to her.

Anne slid into the chair, but remained at attention. "Yes, sir. Thank you, sir."

"I just want to make sure you're all right with our arrangement. I never intended to steal this command from you." Foster was trying to play nice. He didn't want to step on anyone's toes. He knew from years of experience that egos can be very frail at times.

"Permission to speak freely, sir?" Anne asked. Foster nodded.

"I am a little disappointed. This was my first command, but I'll work through it. The goals of the United States Government come before anything else."

"I'm glad to hear that, Colonel." He pulled a yellow folder out of the top drawer of his desk and tossed it to Anne. "That aside, it seems we have a problem."

"What's that, sir?" Anne tried to sound genuinely concerned.

Foster stood up and turned around to look out the window behind his desk. "Read the file I've handed you."

Anne flipped open the folder and was shocked

71

to see pictures of a dead body. She instantly recognized the man. "What is this, sir?"

"That was Captain John Parker. He's a researcher here at the base attached to the 'Uber-Soldier' Project."

"I wasn't aware the project was still underway." Another lie. She had headed up the team that reinitiated the project over six months ago.

"Not to the level it was a year ago, but yes."

"What happened?" Anne was trying her best to feign ignorance.

Foster stared out the window. "One of our patrols found his body stuffed into a ventilation shaft on D level. No autopsy has been performed as of yet, but the cause of death is pretty clear. He took a bullet to the head."

"You mean someone killed him?"

"I'm afraid so," Foster replied gravely.

Anne closed the folder and laid it on Foster's desk. "What does this mean?"

"Well," Foster turned around and sat on the edge of his desk. "We either have a spy amongst us, or this poor bastard just pissed someone off and got himself killed. The strangest thing about this is that Parker's middle finger on his left hand had been removed." Foster shook his head. "Either way, I will find out who did it and make sure they are prosecuted to the fullest extent of the law." Foster stood up, then anxiously sat down in his chair. "That's the main reason I've called you in here."

"Why's that, sir?" Anne felt a twinge of anxiety pass over her.

"You know the men better than I do, so I was

hoping maybe you know if one of them fits the description of spy or hothead."

"Not to the best of my knowledge, sir." Anne thought for a moment, "We have a very select group of men here at the facility. All of them have gone through rigorous psychological profiles before being assigned here."

Foster tapped his fingers on his desk. "Have the base security cameras been fully installed yet?"

"No, sir. They are being finished as we speak. Do we have any eye witnesses?"

"None that have come forward yet, but it's still early."

"I understand, sir."

"If you find anything out, I want to be the first to know."

"Yes, sir."

"Dismissed," Foster stood and retook his position in front of the window.

Anne stood, saluted, then walked toward the door. Once outside, she allowed herself to smile broadly. She was going to get away with this and she knew it. Reaching down into her shirt, she grabbed her dog tags and lifted them out. On her necklace, she had attached her newest trophy, one severed human finger.

***

Sitting outside the science building on a green wooden bench, Jake was trying to enjoy a cigar. Denver had seen a light sprinkling of rain throughout the day, leaving a beautiful dusting of dew on the grass and plants. Staring into the west, he watched the sun setting behind the Rocky Mountains creating a beautiful mixture of pink, red and orange in the sky. Taking a long drag of the cigar, he exhaled it slowly savoring the taste.

It had been several months since the government had tried to bring them in. Jake had finally been able to catch his breath, until now. He knew it was the brass at Area 51 that ordered the break-in. They wanted the vial back, so they wouldn't have any incriminating evidence against them. Although, even if they did, Jake knew it wouldn't stop them. They had too many allies with lofty positions in the government.

Jake watched the sun slowly sinking behind the mountains. He couldn't remember the last time he had been able to watch the sun set. His life for the past year only consisted of running, sleeping and more running.

Staring at the horizon, Jake caught sight of a strange silhouette on top of a nearby building. He squinted trying to make it out. Setting down the cigar next to him on the bench, Jake slowly stood up. A strange red glimmer sliced through the night. A feeling of anxiety settled in the pit of his stomach. Looking down, he saw a red dot hovering in the middle of his chest.

"Shit!" Jake dove to his left just as the crack of a high-powered rifle echoed through the night. Turning around quickly, Jake stared at the hole carved into the bench by the bullet. Rolling into a nearby patch of bushes, Jake heard the weapon fire again. Chunks of plaster from the wall sprayed everywhere, leaving a fine, white powder all over him. Rolling onto his back, Jake unzipped his jacket and pulled his silver forty-five out of his shoulder holster. Cradling it in both his hands, he contemplated his next move. He knew if he jumped up, the sniper could easily pick him off. He heard another gunshot ricochet off the wall behind him. It was now or never. Jumping up, Jake felt a bullet whiz past his head. He knew the sniper was trying to unnerve him.

It was never. Pushing aside the bushes, he tried to get a bead on the shooter. Unfortunately, the sun had finally sunk behind the mountains, leaving only shadows to work in. Trying to estimate where the sniper was, Jake squeezed off several shots toward the roof. Silence ensued for a moment, followed by another shot in the dark. *Damn, I missed him. I need a new plan of attack.*

Dropping to his stomach, Jake began to army crawl toward the end of the bushes. He stopped. Between the bushes was a gap at least three feet wide. Jake knew the sniper had to be using some kind of night vision technology, and that he would be very vulnerable for that brief moment he would be exposed.

Deciding to roll the dice, Jake lifted himself to his knees. Taking a deep breath, he jumped. Landing on the other side, he felt a bullet graze his exposed ankle. Quickly pulling his legs into the safety of the bushes, Jake grabbed his leg and put pressure on it to stop the bleeding.

Rolling onto his back, Jake waited. He knew he was in no condition to try and stop the shooter. His only option was getting into the safety of the science building. Crawling as fast as he could, he came to the edge of the bushes. It was five feet from there to the front of the door. Lifting up into a three-point stance, Jake momentarily tried to drown out the pain in his leg. Gathering all his strength, he bolted for the door. A spray of bullets tore up the ground behind him. Grabbing the door handle, Jake threw open the door and tossed himself inside. He landed hard on the white tile, momentarily getting the wind knocked out of him. Jake gasped for air as he skittered across the floor. He knew he had to get away from the glass doors. Another bullet shattered the glass door, sending shards of glass into the lab.

Standing up, Jake caught sight of his solution. Running toward the wall, he grabbed the lever on a fire alarm. Pulling it down, he heard the alarms start to sound. Putting his back against the wall, Jake slowly slid down to the floor. He knew the fire department would be here any minute.

From out of the corner of his eye, Jake saw a figure moving toward him out of the shadows. He quickly brought his gun to bear. "Hold it right there! You move and I blow your head off!"

"Jake, it's me!"

Alex's voice calmed him. "I thought you were someone else. Sorry." Jake took a deep breath.

"I heard the alarm and came running!"

Jake slowly lifted himself off the floor and began to limp toward Alex. "There was a sniper—"

"Jesus, Jake. What happened to you?" Alex rushed to Jake's side and helped him across the floor toward a chair.

"A bullet grazed my leg, nothing serious," Jake said, playing the hero.

"Well, stay put," she said in a sympathetic tone. "I'll go get some bandages and an ice pack." Alex turned to leave when one of the campus guards burst through what was left of the front doors.

"Freeze!" The man shouted in a frightened voice. Alex quickly spun around. "I'm Dr. Robinson!"

"I need to see some ID!" The guard moved closer. He was wearing a tan uniform with a dark brown jacket. His gold rent-a-cop badge was proudly displayed on it. He was trembling as he held his gun. Both Alex and Jake could see that.

Alex slowly began to reach into her lab coat. "I'm reaching for my ID, okay?" The guard nodded for her to continue.

Alex slowly moved her hand down to a pocket on her lab coat. Reaching inside, she pulled out a laminated badge and handed it to the guard. "Here."

The guard snatched the badge from her hand and quickly glanced over it. "Sorry about all the trouble, Dr. Robinson, I had to be sure. We had reports of gunshots in this area."

Alex nodded. "We need you to call 911. Jake's been hurt. He needs an ambulance."

"I'm not sure that's necessary," Jake replied dryly.

The guard quickly pulled out his radio and called dispatch. "Dr. Robinson?"

Alex turned toward the guard. "Yeah?"

"Dispatch says the fire department is already on the way. They're bringing a meat wagon."

"Excuse me?" Jake asked.

"Sorry, figure of speech," the guard said while placing his radio back on his belt. Alex stared at the guard and shook her head. "I'll be right back, Jake." Alex turned and walked out of the room.

Jake snickered to himself. "I think you can stand down, deputy. The situation's under control."

The guard suddenly realized he was still standing with his gun aimed at Jake. "Oh, sorry." The guard holstered his weapon. "I haven't had this job for long."

"What's your name, son?"

"My name's Dan, but everyone calls me Danny." Jake could see the youth in his face.

"Well, Deputy Danny, why did you want to become a security guard?" Jake was trying to ignore the pain in his leg.

Danny smiled. "I'm just doing this to work my way through college."

"Well, at least you have a goal."

Alex returned with a handful of bandages. "Let me see the wound, Jake."

"Can't we just wait until the EMTs get here?" Jake asked uneasily.

"I think that would be best," Danny chimed in. "I'm a doctor!" Alex argued.

"A doctor of anthropology," Jake snickered.

The crack of a rifle sounded again. Jake and Alex snapped their heads toward Danny. He had doubled over with his hands wrapped around his stomach. "Danny?" Alex began to rush to his side when Jake grabbed her. "No! Get back!" Jake yelled.

"Damn it, Jake! What about the guard?"

"Do you want to die?" Jake was shouting frantically.

"No, but the guard!" They watched Danny drop to his knees, then fall face first on to the ground.

The room was suddenly filled with the flash of

red and blue lights. "The Fire Department is here. We'll be safe now."

"Yeah," Alex stopped struggling and slid to the floor next to Jake, "but for how long?"

***

"How long are we going be out here?" Ben asked impatiently.

"I have no idea. I just thought maybe Tyler would be up here," Ray answered with a sigh.

The two had driven up to the top of 'E Hill', so named because the town had inscribed a giant 'E' facing into the town. Ray had never understood this practice. *It was one thing to have town pride, but a giant letter on a hill?*

They had parked Ben's truck facing north into Elko. The summit had two distinctive sections. The first was a small turnaround area the local kids used to park and make out, while the second, larger part, was an access area for a microwave tower.

Zipping up his coat, Ray began to walk along the narrow access road that led to the second area. A tall outcropping of jagged granite rocks separated them. Rounding the corner, Ray stopped. "Ben, over here! I found Tyler's car!" Running up to the blue car, Ray stopped and peeked inside.

Ben quickly rounded the corner. "Hey, Tyler! Where you been, man?"

"He's not here," Ray said with disappointment. "Just his car."

"Where the hell is he?" Ben turned around, "Tyler! Hey, Tyler!"

"What are you doing?" Ray asked sarcastically.

79

Ben shrugged. "I just figured he might be around here if his car was. You know he doesn't like to get that far away from his ride."

"Yeah." Ray opened the driver's side door and climbed in. "Hey, look at this." Ben stepped closer to the car and peered inside. "What?"

"The keys are still in the ignition." Ray reached over to the passenger seat, "And his cell phone is still on. He couldn't have been gone long."

"Hey, look at that." Ben pointed to the base of the rocks.

"That is strange." Pulling the keys out of the ignition, Ray jumped out and made his way toward the rear of the car. Sifting through the dozen keys on Tyler's set, Ray tried to find the key for the trunk.

"What are you doing?"

"Tyler always came prepared. He keeps what he calls a 'Jessie Emergency Kit' in his trunk. It consists of a few blankets, a sleeping bag, a few candles, and if we're lucky, a flashlight." Ray slid the key into the lock and popped the trunk.

"A 'Jessie Emergency Kit'?" Ben asked amusedly.

"Yeah," Ray laughed. "He always wanted to be prepared if he and Jessie got the 'urge', if you know what I'm talking about."

"They went at it more than rabbits do."

"Ah-ha!" Ray pulled out a bulky black flashlight. "Here we go." Clicking on the light, Ray was stunned. "What the hell happened here?" Ray slowly shined the light around the area. It looked to them like all the plants and weeds had been burned in a perfect circle pattern around the car. Char marks extended around the perimeter and through it.

"Jesus," Ben muttered to himself.

"Hey, look at this." Ray swung the light around toward the car.

"How do you think that happened?" Ben stared at the roof and hood. The paint had bubbled and started to peel, while the metal showed signs of warping.

"I have no idea, but whatever warped the steel in the roof of this car had to be damn hot." Ray ran his hand over the top. "This is weird."

"Take a look at this!"

Ray rushed to Ben's side. "What is it?"

"Footsteps." Ben pointed to the ground, "And they head off in that direction." He pointed toward the edge of the bluff.

Ray followed the footsteps toward the edge. "Whatever happened here, it kind of looks like there was a struggle."

"What the hell are you? Holmes' junior detective?" Ben joked.

"Smart ass." Ray pointed toward the ground, "Look here. The footsteps move in this direction, then there's a large skid mark, probably caused by someone knocking Tyler over, or him tripping."

Ben was amazed. "How do you know all this?"

"I read a lot of detective novels."

"So what are your conclusions, Sherlock?" Ben asked snidely.

Ray shot Ben a warning glance. "From what I can tell," he paused, "he must've...." Ray stopped to reconsider. "He may have...." Ray sighed. "I have no idea. This whole thing beats the hell out of me."

"Great conclusion, detective."

"I don't see you helping here," Ray shot back, finally tired of Ben's insults.

"I'm sorry, man," Ben hung his head. "I'm just really starting to get worried about Tyler."

"Me, too," Ray patted Ben on the shoulder. "Me, too."

Chapter Eight

Tyler came to in total darkness. He couldn't tell where he was, but he knew he wasn't in the examination room anymore. His mind was groggy. It felt like he was recovering from a powerful anesthetic. Trying to stretch out his arms, he felt around the smooth confined space he was in. He couldn't extend his arms fully in any direction, and it felt like his legs were being held in position by some unknown force. Reaching in front of him, he ran his fingers over a small indentation, with what felt like buttons in it in the front wall.

Tyler quickly removed his hand from the buttons and grabbed his chest. Flashes of the aliens cutting into this chest rampaged through his mind. He could still see the blood spilling out of the gaping wound. Tyler saw an image of one of the aliens with his long fingers wrapped around his heart while holding it above his chest. Trying to shake the images, Tyler quickly ran his hands over his chest searching for the wound, but found nothing. His mind became frantic. He began to claw at the walls with his fingernails. He stopped suddenly when he felt a trickle of blood run down from his nose over his lip.

Using his hand, Tyler tried to wipe the blood from his nose, but only succeeded in wiping it all over his lower face and hands. He felt one of his elbows bump the recess that housed the group of buttons, and stopped. Lifting his hand, he ran it slowly over the group of three bumps arranged in a vertical line. Next to the bumps, were a series of small ridges. Tyler couldn't understand what they were, but felt they might be writing of some sort. Placing his finger on the first button, Tyler tried to quiet his mind for a moment. He wanted to be fully ready for whatever happened next. He began to push the button, then stopped. Tyler didn't know why, but he just knew not to press that button. Sliding his fingers down to the second button, he waited to see if he would have the same sensation as before. Nothing.

Taking a deep breath, Tyler applied pressure to the end of his finger and pressed. The cold rounded button sank slowly into the recess. Moments felt like hours as Tyler waited for something to happen. Suddenly, a bright light clicked on below his feet. Finally exhaling, Tyler breathed a sigh of relief.

Looking around him, he noticed the space he was in was shaped very similarly to a coffin and was about as big. Tyler glanced over at the recess in the coffin's lid. He was surprised to see words written in English next to each button. The second button was clearly marked "light". The first and third button had "death" and "pain" written next to them. He became suddenly very happy he'd followed his instincts and not pressed the first button.

"You have done well," a deep voice boomed inside his head. "This was a test of your psychic ability, and you have done very well." The voice sounded human, but somehow not. It was both human and mechanical at the same time.

Tyler looked around the coffin. He could see no speakers anywhere, and from what he could tell, the box was tightly sealed to make it soundproof. "Why are you doing this to me?" Tyler cried in frustration.

"We must make certain," the voice responded unemotionally.

"I just want to go home!" Tyler felt his salty tears running down his face. The voice did not reply.

Tyler felt alone inside the small box. Crossing his arms over his chest, he tried to make himself take deep breaths to stop crying. Tears still ran down his face. His thoughts shifted to his friends and family. He had never realized how important something like saying "goodbye" or "I love you" was until he wasn't able to say them anymore. Jessie's picture appeared in his thoughts. He missed her. He needed her. If he ever got out of here, he swore he would tell her what he felt. He needed to get out of here.

Tired, lonely, and beaten down by his alien captors, Tyler allowed himself a moment of rest. Taking a deep breath and slowly exhaling it, he closed his eyes and thought of home. He hated the town he was from, but anywhere was better than where he was currently.

He heard a click inside the box. Tyler opened his eyes to see the leg restraints unlatch and being pulled out of the box. Lifting his legs one at a time, he stretched them the best he could. A cramp had started in his left calf, and was steadily growing worse.

The lights went out in the box, leaving Tyler blanketed in darkness again. He slammed his fists against the coffin's walls. "No more tests!" Tyler shouted at the top of his lungs.

He heard another click somewhere outside the coffin. A bead of sweat rolled down his forehead.

For a brief moment, Tyler suddenly felt himself floating in space with no floor below him. The bottom of the box had dropped open, sending Tyler screaming into the darkness.

***

The nurse dabbed the sweat off Dr. Eric Brooks' brow. The emergency room was a nightmare, full of sick patients all suffering from what the staff had taken to calling 'The Yellow Death'. Brooks, dressed in green hospital scrubs, was barking orders like a drill sergeant. The patient, a Hispanic female of about forty-five, was severely dehydrated and suffering from flulike symptoms. One of the nurses hurriedly tried to insert an IV needle into her arm, but was having trouble finding a vein. The patient screamed in agony as her body temperature surged above one hundred degrees.

"Give this woman a shot of muscle relaxer. Her throat muscles are beginning to constrict, shutting off her airways." Brooks moved with trained efficiency about the ER. He was a tall, lanky man with a thick, brown beard and receding hair. His wire rimmed glasses glimmered in the bright surgical lights. He had been a doctor for as long as he cared to remember. During that time, he had seen all manners of emergencies, but this new strain of virus scared the hell out of him.

A nurse quickly replied and began giving the patient an injection. "Doctor, she's not responding to the treatment!"

"Give it a minute to start working!" Brooks yelled.

The head nurse looked up at the doctor, "We don't have a minute. We're losing her!"

"I don't know what else to do! I've tried everything!" Brooks replied chillingly.

The patient's heart monitor began to race while her temperature shot up another ten degrees. Her body arched up in pain. A gurgling noise erupted from her throat. "What's happening?" one of the nurses asked.

"I have no idea," Brooks answered grimly.

All the hands stepped back as the patient began coughing up a thick yellow fluid. They watched in horror as her eyes began to roll back in her head.

"Doctor! Do something!"

"Do what?" Brooks asked bewildered.

The woman's body went into convulsions. The thick yellow foam oozed out of her mouth and onto the gurney. Her hands clawed at the sheets, tearing them. She was dying, and there was nothing anyone could do for her. Her body seized one final time, and then stopped. Everyone in the ER slowly turned to look at the solid flat line that was crossing her heart monitor. The room became still as the constant beep of the heart monitor filled the room.

Brooks stepped close to the woman. "Announce the time of death."

A nurse stepped forward and checked her watch. "Time of death is—" The doors to the ER burst open and several men dressed in yellow contamination suits marched in. "We need this area cleared," the leader announced unsympathetically.

Brooks pulled off his mask and stepped in front of them. "What the hell is going on here? You're not allowed to be in here!"

The men pushed Brooks aside and began prepping the body for removal. "We need this patient ready to move in two minutes, people!"

"As Chief Surgeon, I demand to know what's going on here!"

One of the men in the environmental suits pushed Brooks away from the patient. "I'm Greg Hollman with FEMA. We are officially making this area part of our quarantine zone. We have full authority to do so, and I'll have you arrested if you don't comply with my orders."

Brooks was too shocked to speak.

Pulling a large black body bag out of his pack, one of the men laid it on a separate gurney that he rolled toward the patient. The men quickly lifted the woman onto the second gurney and began to zip her up in the bag. Two men took opposite positions and pushed the body through the ER's doors.

As the men began to exit, Greg stopped and looked back. "We need all these people in quarantine immediately! They've been exposed to the pathogen."

***

"How are you feeling, Danny?" Alex asked caringly.

Danny shook his head. The oxygen mask strapped to his face wasn't allowing him to talk. Two emergency medical technicians on either side of his gurney were working frantically. They pushed past Alex. "Ma'am, we're going to need you to step back so we can do our job."

Alex looked at the EMT, and then nodded. "Is

he going to be all right?"

"We're going to do everything we can."

Turning around, Alex made her way through the crowds of police officers and emergency technicians toward the front doors of the science building. She heard the crack of broken glass under her feet as she walked through the lobby. A small pool of blood stood in the center of the floor where Danny had hit the ground. She felt her stomach begin to churn at the sight. Holding her hand over her mouth, Alex quickly moved through the front doors and into the cool Colorado night.

"Alex!"

Alex turned to see Jake sitting in the back of the ambulance. An EMT was applying bandages to his leg. "How are you doing?" She tried to compose herself while she walked toward the ambulance.

"I'm fine. How's Deputy Danny?"

"They're still not sure. They need to get him to a hospital."

Jake grunted as the EMT accidentally brushed against his wound. "Be careful down there!"

The EMT looked up at Jake and smiled. "You're all done, you big baby."

Jake stood and slowly applied pressure to his leg. Placing his hand on Alex's back, Jake quickly moved out of earshot. "We need to get out of here," he whispered.

"Where are we going to go? They always find us," Alex warned him.

"We need to get back to Las Vegas. I know the military is behind this outbreak. I know we can find a way to stop them," Jake argued.

"Why is it our problem?" Alex asked cynically.

Jake was stunned. He had always figured Alex as a crusader like himself. "I don't understand."

"I'm saying, why is the virus our problem? We've done our bit for the rebel crusade. We brought down Area 51 and S-4," Alex let out a long sigh. "I'm sick of running." Alex grabbed Jake by the shoulders and turned him toward her. She looked deep into his weary eyes. "Aren't you tired of the chase? We've been running for a year now! I can't take it anymore," she confessed.

"Yeah, I'm tired of running. That's why we have to bring those sons a bitches down! We won't need to run anymore." Jake reached up and grabbed Alex's hands and held them. "You're absolutely right, the outbreak isn't our problem, but tonight proved something to me. We're never going to be safe until we stop them."

Tears began to stream from Alex's eyes. "I just don't have it in me anymore. I can't do this with you." She turned away from Jake. "I can't change your mind?"

"No," Alex replied meekly.

"Fine," Jake answered angrily. "I need to get going." He turned and began to walk away.

Alex quickly grabbed Jake's shoulder and spun him around. "Stop, please."

"Why?" Jake asked in an icy tone.

She let her hand slowly slip off Jake's shoulder. "I don't want you to hate me," Alex lowered her eyes away from Jake's anger filled gaze. "Before I got involved with this whole Area 51 thing, I was a scientist. I'm not cut out for this. I just want you to understand."

"I understand one thing," Jake began to raise

his voice, but stopped. "I am sick of running, and I want to do something about it. If you're too much of a coward to be a part of that, fine." Jake turned away from Alex. "You keep on hiding, Alex, but I want my life back."

Chapter Nine

"It's exactly the same." Steve stood up and turned toward Durard. "It has the same genetic matrix as the other samples I've tested." He leaned over and stared into the black lenses of his microscope. The lab was quiet. Most of the other researchers had already gone home, or to the hotels where they were staying. Steve had wanted to stay late and work on these new samples.

"What does that mean?" Durard stood anxiously behind Steve, his yellow environmental suit hanging around his waist.

"The whole crater has this same genetic material through it. I've had soil samples taken from all around the crater, and the only place I can find this genetic material is inside it."

"So it must've been scattered here by the explosion."

"Right, but some of this material should've been tossed away from the blast. We should've been able to find some in the surrounding area," Steve added.

"Not necessarily," Durard theorized. "From what I understand about the explosion, it was more of an implosion."

Steve nodded. "Yeah, that's right."

"So, most of the material could've stayed right here in the crater."

Steve shook his head; his long dread locks swaying back and forth. "Even if it was an implosion, massive amounts of debris and dust would've been thrown into the air as S-4 went under."

"So, we should still be able to find trace amounts of the genetic material around the crater," Durard deduced.

"That would be my guess," Steve answered sternly.

A hissing sound startled Steve and Durard. The two spun around to see two armed guards dressed in green camouflage standing in the doorway. The guards had their weapons trained on Steve and Durard. "Excuse me, sirs, but I'm going to have to ask you to step away from the table."

Durard stared at the guards. "What the hell are you talking about?"

A tall well-built black man dressed in Air Force blues stepped through the guards toward Steve and Durard. "Good evening, gentlemen. My name is Captain Gordon, I'm with the US Air Force." Even though his black goatee was perfectly trimmed, it still gave him an air of danger. His steely dark eyes showed no hint of emotion as he looked over Steve and Durard.

Durard stepped out from behind the desk and approached the captain. "What can I do for you?" Durard was trying to play it cool.

"Let me jump right to the point. This site has now become off limits to all personnel, except for qualified Air Force scientists. I need to ask you to turn over all research material and data immediately." Gordon spoke in a flat tone.

"What the hell are you talking about, Captain?" Steve leaned forward onto the table, his hulking form still impressive. "We were led to understand FEMA had full autonomy here. We have no intention of allowing you access to our workroom materials."

"I'm sorry you feel that way." Gordon turned to his men and nodded.

The two massive guards quickly moved toward Durard and Steve. Without a struggle, the guards handcuffed the two men and began escorting them out of the building.

Turning toward the table, Gordon swiftly moved toward it. Looking over its contents, he found the samples Steve had been working on. He picked up a small vial of soil and slipped it into his pocket. Sliding a small piece of glass out from under Steve's microscope, Gordon dropped it on the floor and crushed it under his foot. Gordon reared back and slid his arm across the table, sending all the equipment crashing to the floor. Stepping back, Gordon pulled a small radio out of his back pocket and held it up to his mouth. "Sir, the two suspects have been removed from the premises and their samples destroyed."

"Very good, Captain," a female voice crackled through the radio's speaker. "I want them to be detained. They both present very serious threats to my plans."

***

Jake's hotel room was cold and dark. He had left the campus over an hour ago and checked into a Hilton in Denver. Since he had arrived, he had been sitting quietly in the dark waiting for the phone to ring. He had hoped that Alex would come to her senses and call, but so far, nothing. Kicking off his boots, Jake settled back into the queen-size bed in

94

his room. He looked around. This was one of the nicer hotel rooms he had ever stayed in. The walls were lavishly decorated with expensive paintings and were covered in white wallpaper with gold pinstripes. A large red couch sat against the far wall under a huge picture window. He had left the curtains open so he could look across the sleeping city. He was used to New Orleans, where no one ever slept. After dark, it cooled off enough for people to come out and enjoy the town. During the night, the French Quarter came alive. It was too quiet here.

Even now, he could see splinters of orange and pink colors cutting through the eastern sky. Jake had no idea why he rented such an expensive room when he knew he would only have a few hours until check-out time. Pulling up the covers, Jake let his head fall back into the thick down pillows. He needed sleep. He had been awake since five yesterday morning. During the past year, Jake had learned to survive on less sleep, but now, he just felt exhausted. His soul was weak, and he knew why. He was now alone. The journey had begun with Christina Anderson, then Major Griggs had joined in. Then there was only Alex and himself. Now, there was only Jake. The world had suddenly become a very cold and empty place.

***

"We've searched the entire mountain, Ray. I think it's time we call it a night," Ben moaned.

"No, we can't give up until we find out what happened to Tyler." Ray was standing at the bottom of 'E Hill' in the beams of Ben's headlights. The night had rolled in like a fog through the valley. Makeshift trails had been blazed through the entire area. This was a favorite spot of off-roaders and hormonally driven teenagers. The main access road stood in between two small hills. This place was one of the most secluded spots just outside town. Looking up, Ray admired the vault of heaven. The stars were shining brightly in the great western sky, and the moon filled it like a huge silver platter. Ray turned around with his head hung in shame. Kicking his feet, he knocked over a small pile of rocks. His eyes suddenly widened.

"Man, I need a drink. Can we head back? I hear Dan's throwing a huge party at his house tonight." Ben's comments went unheard as Ray knelt down in the rocks. Ben shook his head and stepped closer to Ray. "What are you doing now?"

Ray flipped over one of the rocks. "Look at this." He lifted the rock up into the headlights of Ben's trucks. "It looks like it's covered with blood."

Ben wiped his finger across the rock, "And it looks like it's still fresh."

Ray suddenly dropped the rock and stood up. "Oh my god, I hope that's not Tyler's blood."

"It's probably not."

"What if it is? He could've been murdered! I mean, we found his car up there," Ray pointed to the top of the hill, "and obvious signs of a struggle!" He was frantic. His mind hadn't gone through the full possibilities of what could've transpired here. "What if he's dead?"

Ben tried to calm him down. "Just relax, man, he's not dead. He probably just fell."

"Then where the hell did he go?"

"Who knows," Ben suggested. "He might've just hit his head and lost his memory. I've heard about cases where people have gotten amnessisoa. You know," Ben struggled to explain his thought process, "that thing where you can't remember who you are?"

"Amnesia," Ray corrected him.

"Right, amnesia. They forget who they are and just wander off aimlessly into the desert."

"Come on, you don't really think that happened. I mean, what are the odds?" Ray returned his attention to the bloody pile of rocks. Something else caught his eye. "Hey, look at that."

"It looks like the same burn marks we found up on the top of the hill."

"Yeah," Ray jogged over to Ben's truck and climbed in. Kicking it into reverse, Ray cranked the steering wheel hard and pointed the lights toward the hill. Climbing out, he looked up at the hill in awe. "Look at it."

Ben's jaw dropped as he stared at the well-defined trail of scorched sagebrush and earth that extended all the way to the bottom and ended in a huge circle. The soil was darkened a horrible shade of black that Ben had only seen during some of the worst brush fires. "What do you think caused that?"

Ray shook his head. "It looks like the same burn marks we found on the top of the hill."

"Excuse me!" A voice boomed from behind the two. Ben spun around startled, "Huh?"

"I'm going to need you two gentlemen to come with me." A large man dressed in black fatigues stepped out from behind Ben's truck and stopped.

He had dark brown eyes, a shaved head, and a long scar that ran from the corner of his right eye to his mouth. His body was huge. Ray could see the man's rippling muscles even underneath his uniform.

Ray took an uneasy step backward. "Who are you?"

The soldier raised a hand into the air and pointed toward the two teenagers. Suddenly, the night was flooded with bright white light from several vehicles parked just behind Ben's truck. "Who I am is not important."

Ben held his hand above his eyes to shade them. "Why should we go with you?"

"Because I said so."

Ray snickered, "That's a great reason."

"Get them," the soldier commanded as two more men joined the group. The two newest soldiers sprinted toward Ray and Ben. Ray was quickly apprehended. The soldier pulled a pair of handcuffs from his belt and slapped them on Ray's wrists.

"What the hell is this?" Ben wriggled free of the second soldier's grip. "I'm not going anywhere with you fuck heads!" Ben began to sprint away.

The second soldier raised his weapon to bear on Ben. "Stop or I'll fire!" The soldier pointed his rifle up and fired a shot into the air.

Ben didn't stop. He tried to weave between the bushes of sagebrush, but there was nowhere to go. His only choice was to follow the road.

"I am authorized to use deadly force!" Lowering his rifle, the soldier squeezed the trigger and fired.

Ray watched in horror as his friend crumbled to the ground. "No!"

The soldier turned to his commanding officer. "He left me no choice, Captain Jannis."

"Understood. Wrap up the body and get it in the truck." He pointed at Ray, "And put that one in with it."

"You fuckers! You killed Ben!" Ray was hysterical. "He was my best friend!" The soldier began to push him toward the vehicle. "I hope you fucking rot in hell, you bastards!"

Jannis walked up to Ray. "He was warned. Now, unless you want to be next, I suggest you shut your mouth, son."

Ray reared back and spat at the man. "You can't scare me with your Nazi tactics! You can go to hell!"

Jannis wiped the spit from his eyes, then sent a punch into Ray's jaw, knocking him to the ground. "You'll pay for that, you little bastard."

Ray looked up at the man as blood dripped from his split lip. "You won't get away with this. People know we're out here. They'll come looking for us!"

Jannis pulled a pistol from his belt and rammed the barrel into Ray's temple. "After tonight, people won't even know you existed."

Another soldier interrupted him, "Sir, we've just gotten word that the local law enforcement is on its way."

Jannis uncocked the hammer and lowered his gun. "Looks like you've just got a reprieve." He turned to the soldier behind Ray, "Get this little bitch into the truck and pack up. We're leaving."

"It's almost time, precious." Anne slid her hand along the long glass tube. She could feel the coolness emanating from inside. "Then we will finally have our revenge."

The man inside the cylinder stood silently watching over the room. His blue unblinking eyes looked eerie through the thick green substance. His toned body almost completely developed after months of gene therapy.

Anne was dressed in her formal blues. Her long slender legs were tanned a wonderful shade of brown after spending months in the sun. *One of the few benefits of living in the desert,* she thought. Turning away from the tube, she moved toward a set of monitors wired into a control panel next to the cylinder. Tapping several buttons on the keypad, the man's vitals were instantly displayed on the monitors. "Your stats are very strong. You'll be out in no time, love."

Chapter Ten

Alex was sitting quietly in Dr. Lucas' office in the science building. It was a disgusting mixture of crumpled papers and old fast food containers. Several pizza boxes stood in the corner, complete with uneaten crusts, while old textbooks and science journals littered the desk and the floor. Alex had to push a load of old hamburger wrappers and stale french fries off the chair before she could even sit down.

Leaning back in the cushioned leather seat, Alex stared at the bookshelves on the far wall. They were overflowing with papers and ancient scientific equipment. *How can Alan live in this dump?*

Alex ran her hand over Dr. Lucas' white phone. She had hoped Jake would call. Alex wanted to hear Jake apologize for what he'd said to her. Just like Jake, she was also tired of running. She wasn't sure why, but she needed his blessing to move on. She knew how Jake felt. Alex wanted her life back too, but she didn't want to assault another base to get it. This outbreak in the southwest wasn't her problem. It couldn't be her problem.

Alex stood up and began to stare out the window. She lifted her hands to the panes of glass, then pressed her left cheek against it feeling the cool air outside. After a few moments, she leaned back and watched the sun rising on the horizon. It had been a long night for her and she was feeling it. Her eyes were becoming weary. She tried to stifle a yawn as it began to well up from her chest. Lifting her arms up, she arched her back and stretched her sore muscles. Alex quickly spun around when she heard the office door open. "Oh, Alan." She breathed a sigh of relief.

"Hey, Alex, how are you this morning?" Dr. Alan Lucas was a short, pudgy man. His messy black hair was plastered to his head in stark contrast to his neatly trimmed beard. The brown blazer and tan slacks he was wearing were wrinkled, looking as if he had just woke up in them and come to work. Even though he was now entering his late forties, he still wanted to be a kid. He had never been out of college, choosing instead to become a professor rather than accepting a better paying job at a prestigious research and development company.

"It's been a long night. How about you?" Alex stood up and moved around to the front of Lucas' desk.

Lucas swiftly moved past her and dumped his duffel bag on the floor. Taking his seat, he leaned back and looked out the window. "I've been up all night. I got the call about the shooting early this morning, and I haven't been able to get back to sleep since. What happened this morning?"

"It's a long story, Alan, and I don't want to go into it right now," Alex admitted wearily.

Alan understood. "I'll probably get the report from the security people later today anyway." He began to shuffle through the piles of papers on his desk. "Damn, I thought I left my lesson plan for today here last night," he stopped and looked up at Alex. "Have you seen it?"

Alex shook her head. "Hey, Alan," she paused, "can I ask you a question?"

"Sure, shoot," Alan replied, still shuffling through his papers.

102

Alex turned around and walked toward the door. "Nah, never mind." She waved her hand in a dismissive gesture.

Alan leaned back in his chair and rubbed his beard, "Come on, you can ask me." He smiled, "I'm a good listener."

Alex mustered a small laugh. "All right." She turned around and leaned against the door. "Do you think I'm a coward?"

Alan's face became suddenly serious. "Why would you think that?" He stood up and stepped toward Alex.

Alex shook her head. "It's something someone told me last night." Alan grabbed Alex's hand. "Who would tell you that?"

"A friend of mine." Alex made no move to pull her hand away. She wanted to be comforted.

"Must not be much of a friend," Alan consoled.

"He's one of my best friends, and I owe everything to him." Alex felt her voice begin to falter.

"Then why would he say that to you?" Alan asked sympathetically. Alex lowered her head, "Because, I think he's right."

Alan placed his hand on her face and lifted it. He looked into her eyes, "Look, I haven't known you for very long, but I think you're one of the most courageous women I've ever known."

Alex smiled. "Thanks, Alan."

Alan nodded and stepped back. "Now, if you'll excuse me, I need to get a cup of coffee."

Alex stepped aside. "Thanks for listening."

"Anytime." Alan shot her a smile as he grabbed for the door handle. Opening it, Alan stepped out.

103

Turning around, Alex made her way back to the window. The sun had risen above the horizon and was casting a beautiful warm orange light across the landscape. She looked up at the building across from theirs. Its black silhouette no more than a blotch against the colors of the sunrise. *Jake's wrong,* Alex told herself. *I'm not a coward; I just want to live my life again.*

The crack of a rifle and the crash of glass startled her. Pain shot through her chest as she felt a bullet rip through her midsection. Falling to the ground, her head crashed into the leg of Alan's desk knocking her unconscious. Blood poured from her mouth onto the hardwood floors, pooling around her head.

Alan suddenly burst through the door. "Alex? I thought I heard a...." He saw the broken window. Rushing over to his desk, he spotted Alex's body lying on the floor. "Dear God!" Reaching down, he lifted Alex off the ground and held her in his arms. His phone startled him as it began to ring. Frantically, Alan answered the phone. "I need help!" he screamed into the receiver. "She's been shot! I need an ambulance right now!"

A long shadow crept along the floor, then across Alan and Alex. Alan slowly looked up to see a tall man wearing a ski mask dressed entirely in black. He was holding a high-powered rifle with a massive scope on it. Alan slowly let the phone fall to the floor.

Chapter Eleven

Tyler had been sitting in ankle deep water for longer than he cared to think about. He was still completely naked, but at least there were a few rays of light filtering into this huge room through several grates along the ceiling. Every once in a while, he would see one of the aliens walk past one of the grates, and sometimes, they would even stop to look at him. Tyler hated their eyes; their big, black, unblinking, almond-shaped eyes that seemed to just stare right through him.

Standing up, he began to walk around the large room in the murky water. From what he could tell, the walls and floor were a dirty brown and seemed to be made of an organic substance. Tyler felt very uncomfortable in this room.

On the far side of the room, he saw a portal open that was about ten feet above the ground. An intense white light shone into the area casting strange reflections off the water. Tyler saw a dark form come through the light, then a splash.

Silence ensued as the water began to calm. Tyler couldn't see who, or what had fallen into the water with him. He was sure of one thing though, it was humanoid in shape. Sliding silently out of the light, Tyler tried not to make any sudden movements. He began to hear a very familiar soft weeping emanating from the direction of the splash. "Hello?" Tyler asked weakly.

"Tyler?" a soft female voice echoed out of the distance. "Jessie?" Tyler stepped into the light.

"Oh, my God!"

Tyler heard splashing coming his direction.

Relief washed over his body. He wasn't alone anymore. Jessie ran into the light, completely naked and scared to death. Tyler wrapped his arms around her and held her tightly. "Are you all right?"

Jessie looked up at him with her soft green eyes. "No," she said softly. "I'm in a place I don't recognize, I'm cold, I'm wet," she started to sob, "and there are monsters here!"

Tyler ran his hand over the back of her head. "It's going to be okay, Jess, we're together now." He tried to comfort Jessie by rubbing her back as she cried in his arms. "How did you get here?"

"I don't know." Goose bumps began to rise on Jessie's skin. "One minute I'm getting ready for bed, the next thing I know, I'm lying naked on a cold table and there are these...things standing around me! I don't like their eyes!"

Tyler began to slowly let down his guard. Even though these weren't exactly the circumstances he had hoped for, Jessie was back in his arms again. "Don't worry, from what I've read about alien abductions, they never keep anyone indefinitely. They always return the abductees."

"I just want to go home," Jessie sobbed.

"I know," Tyler was doing his best to comfort her. "I know." Jessie moved her head up and kissed Tyler's neck. Moving her hands down his back, Jessie began to caress Tyler's body. Tyler stopped her. "What are you doing, Jess?" He looked at her with confusion.

"I was just trying to relax us both," Jessie said with a smile. "This always seems to work."

"I don't think this is the time for...." Tyler let his sentence trail off as Jessie ran her hand between his legs.

Jessie moaned softly as she kissed down his neck. "I think it's working."

Tyler gave in. Running his hands over Jessie's shoulders, he cupped her soft white breasts. Leaning in, he kissed her passionately. "I think you're right," Tyler admitted while staring into her deep green eyes. He knew every curve of her body. He knew how her skin felt against his, the way her body tasted, and the way her green eyes could light up a darkened room. Pulling his hands away from her breasts, he pressed his body against hers and kissed her again. He held his hands firmly on her hips, and then slowly moved them up to her waist.

The two dropped to their knees, the energy building between them. As they embraced each other, Tyler saw an alien's eyes flash through his mind. Stopping suddenly, Tyler pulled away from Jessie. Looking up, he checked all the grates for aliens.

Jessie looked confused. "What's the matter?"

"I can't." Tyler looked around. "Something's not right here."

Jessie leaned back into the water and rested on her elbows. "Come on, Tyler."

Her body was inviting. Her curves looked even better as water lapped against them. Jessie began to run her fingertips sensually over her breasts, and then slowly moved down between her spread legs. "You know you want to."

Tyler was too aroused to say no. Leaning over her, he kissed Jessie's nipples as he pushed his erect penis into her vagina. Jessie moaned with exquisite pleasure. Tyler began to work away, slowly at first.

All thoughts and worries began to melt from his mind. He closed his eyes and tilted his head back as a wave of pleasure run up his spine. Lowering his head, Tyler opened his eyes to look at Jessie. He was horrified to see one of the aliens beneath him.

Jumping back, Tyler stared at the alien in the same position Jessie had been. "What the hell?" The alien slowly lifted itself out of the water, then stopped. It made no movements while it stared silently at Tyler. Suddenly, Jessie was standing before him again and the alien was gone. Tyler dropped to his knees, slamming his hands to the side of his head. "What the hell is happening?"

Jessie came to his side and began to caress his body again. "What's the matter? Don't you want me?" she asked seductively.

Tyler pushed her away. "You're not Jessie! Get away from me!"

"What are you talking about?" Jessie knelt down next to Tyler. "Of course I'm Jessie. Who else would I be?"

"You're not Jessie! You're a fucking alien!" Tyler stood up and staggered backwards. "You get away from me!" Tyler stared at Jessie as she stood up. Instantly, he was looking at an alien again, then Jessie. "This is one of you tests again, isn't it?" Tyler yelled. "Somehow, you picked the image of Jessie out of my head and used it against me!" Tyler shook his fists toward the grates in the ceiling. "I won't let you do this to me anymore!"

Tyler charged, knocking Jessie splashing to the ground. Stopping, Tyler looked down at Jessie.

A trickle of blood ran down her lip as she stared angrily at him. "How dare you hit a woman?"

Tyler kicked Jessie hard in the ribs. The young woman cried in pain as she rolled over onto her hands and knees. "You're not a woman!" Tyler kicked her again, sending her flying off her knees and onto her back.

"You bastard, Tyler!" Jessie started to wipe the blood off her mouth.

Tyler quickly dropped to his knees next to her. "I know what you really are." He threw a right hook into her nose. Jessie fell back into the water, grabbing her broken nose. Tyler grabbed Jessie's arms and pinned them down under his knees. He delivered four quick jabs to her face, then pulled back and threw a vicious left hook across her jaw. He watched as Jessie's eyes became blurry and she passed out. Suddenly, Tyler found himself sitting on top of an alien, it's huge black eyes closed and a green fluid dripping from its slit like mouth.

"I knew it," Tyler reassured himself. Standing up, he kicked the alien hard in the head with his bare foot. Turning around, he looked up at the grates in the roof. Dozens of pairs of black eyes were staring at him. "Was this another test, you sons a bitches?" Tyler screamed.

"You have done great harm to one of us," a voice sounded in his head. "We offered you pleasure to repay you for your time in our tests. You have disappointed us greatly."

"You wanted me to fuck an alien?" Tyler yelled at his captors. "I don't care if I've disappointed you," Tyler said in a spiteful tone. "You are doing this to me against my will! I will snap each and every one of your scrawny little necks if I have to until you let me go!"

The pairs of eyes peering at Tyler through the grates began to disappear until only one pair remained. "You will not be released until you meet our criteria. You don't realize your importance to us, and to the human species."

***

"Dr. Lucas!" Jake was screaming into the phone. The sound of a gunshot shocked him. He could hear another man's voice in the background shouting as the phone went dead. "Damn!"

Jumping up, Jake grabbed his leather jacket and pulled it on. Snatching his keys off the nightstand, he dumped them into his pocket and was out the door.

The day had dawned into a beautiful Colorado morning. Dew sparkled as it clung to the leaves of bushes and trees. A cool morning breeze was blowing through the city, but most of the long-time residents knew that soon, it would be very hot and humid.

Jake sent his rental car skidding around a corner. Cranking the steering wheel hard, he pinned the accelerator to the floor, gunning the engine. He suddenly became aware he was heading the wrong way down a one-way street. Keeping a cool head, he weaved in and out of traffic, trying to make it down the road. Jake quickly glanced up into his rear view mirror as he came to the head of the street. He saw the familiar flashing of red and blue lights. "Damn police," he muttered under his breath.

Tearing around the corner, Jake saw the University of Boulder looming in the distance. He checked his mirror again; the black and white police cruiser was closing in. Turning his attention back to the road, Jake's eyes widened when he saw another car merging into his lane directly in front of him.

"Shit!" Jake twisted the wheel hard and mashed on the breaks. He felt the police cruiser slam into the rear-end of his car, sending his vehicle sailing into the side of the one in front of him. Hitting the gas pedal, Jake maneuvered around the car beside him and continued on his way.

Twisting around, Jake looked behind him. The police car's hood was crunched, and the officer had climbed out and was checking on the driver of the vehicle Jake smashed into. Sliding around a final corner, Jake sent his black sedan careening across the lawn of the college. His sedan dug deep ruts into the grass as he floored it. Piloting the car up onto the concrete of the parking lot, he popped it into park and jumped out, leaving the car running. His mind was numb as he hit a dead sprint toward the science building. He couldn't feel his legs, but he knew he was running as fast as he could.

Bursting through the front door to the science building, Jake skidded to a stop.

He didn't know where Dr. Lucas' office was. Rolling the dice, he cut left and raced down a long hallway. He moved past several closed doors until he heard Lucas' pleas for help. Stopping, he held his breath and tried to figure out where the cries were coming from. He heard them again. Jake sprinted toward the end of the hall. Charging blindly around a corner, he slammed into Lucas, knocking both of them down.

"Don't kill me!" Lucas screamed.

Jake lifted himself off the injured man, "I'm not going to hurt you! My name's Jake Silver and I'm here to help!"

Lucas was crossing his arms across his face. "Leave me alone!" His chest and face were splattered with blood, and he had a bullet wound in his left thigh. Jake couldn't determine if the blood on his shirt and face was Lucas' or not.

"I'm a friend of Dr. Robinson! Where is she?"

"Alex," Lucas was babbling almost incoherently. "They took her!" he said in a moment of clarity.

Jake grabbed the man by his shirt and lifted him up. "What did you say?"

"They shot her, then took her! They came in here and took her!" Tears were streaming from Lucas' eyes.

"Who took her?" Jake shook Lucas. "Who?" Jake couldn't wait for a response. Letting go of him, Lucas slumped to the floor. Jumping up, Jake trotted the rest of the way down the hall to Lucas' office. Stepping inside, he immediately saw the broken window. Moving closer, he discovered a pool of blood on the floor. Dropping down to his knee, he ran his fingers through the blood. "Damn!" He slammed his fist against the wall. "I knew I shouldn't have left her here alone." Anger began to well up inside him. "We have the building surrounded. Come out with your hands up!" Jake heard the slightly distorted sound of a police bullhorn echo through the campus. "I repeat, we have the building surrounded, surrender now!"

"Shit! They think I did it! Lucas must've called the cops." Jake wiped his hand across his face. "I've got to get out of here."

***

Ray stared at Ben's lifeless corpse lying next to him on the bed of the truck. They had been loaded into a large covered rig that could easily hold twenty men sitting side by side. It was dark inside, with only random rays of lights bleeding in through the canvas top. His stomach was churning with acids. An hour ago, he was looking for one of his friends, now, his best friend was dead and he was being hauled off to God knew where.

He had no idea how much time had passed since he had been taken. All Ray knew was that it was now daylight. He had forgotten to wear a watch, and he had left his cell phone lying on the passenger seat of Ben's truck.

He glanced down at Ben's body again. He couldn't stop it this time. Leaning over, he vomited on the floor. All the muscles in his body tensed up as he pushed all the nastiness out of his mouth. Lifting up, he took a deep breath and wiped the vomit off his lips.

A silver pair of handcuffs bound his hands while his feet were tied and strapped to the edge of his seat. He wasn't going anywhere.

Leaning his head back, he closed his eyes. He was exhausted. He had been going since yesterday morning without any sleep. Blackness washed over him as his mind drifted off. It was a listless sleep. He kept replaying the previous night's events in his head. Over and over, he saw the soldier pull the trigger and Ben's body fall to the ground. Regret gripped him. If he had said something, if he had done something differently, would Ben still be alive?

His mind suddenly snapped back to consciousness as a soldier dressed in black fatigues slapped him hard across the face. "I'm going to untie your feet," the soldier announced. "If you so much as twitch, I'll blow your head off. Do you understand?"

Terrified, Ray nodded at the soldier.

As the man crouched down, two other soldiers climbed into the truck and began to pull Ben's body out. Ray watched as they grabbed him by the feet and drug him along the dirty floor. Ben's head made a sickening crunching sound as it hit the bumper on its way down. The soldier stood up and grabbed Ray by his shirt lifting him up. He tossed Ray forward toward the edge of the truck. Ray stumbled over a loose floorboard and fell, hitting his jaw and sending his teeth slicing into his tongue. Ray rolled over in pain, blood spurting from his mouth.

The soldier kicked Ray in the ribs. "Get up, you little maggot!" Ray shook his head. "Fuck off!"

Another soldier grabbed Ray by his shoulders and pulled him out of the truck. Ray hit the ground hard. Twisting onto his side, he tried to catch his breath. The soldier reached down and grabbed the small piece of chain that connected the metal cuffs on Ray's wrist, and lifted him up. Ray moaned in pain as the cuffs dug into his flesh. Letting go, the soldier grabbed Ray's shoulder and shoved him toward a dirt path that was surrounded by sagebrush. Fighting through the pain, Ray quickly scanned the terrain. *This still looks like Nevada,* he thought. The soldier shoved him again, starting him down the path. They were in a flat area with hills on all sides. The path wound its way down a small slope toward several large white tents. Guards were positioned all along the trail and around the tents. Ray watched as men in white environmental suits scurried around base camp.

What the hell is going on here? As Ray neared the first tent, he watched as Jannis stepped out. He towered over Ray by at least a foot. "Well, how's our little spy?" Jannis asked in a sarcastic tone.

"What the hell are you talking about?" Ray shouted. "I'm not a spy!"

Jannis studied the young man for a moment. "How can you explain being in an area quarantined by the United States Air Force?"

"Quarantined? Since when?" Ray was shocked.

"Since yesterday at nineteen hundred hours," Jannis replied matter-of-factly. Jannis snapped his fingers twice. A soldier standing behind Ray grabbed him and slid his arm around Ray's neck. "I want this man placed in lock-up."

"Yes, sir." The soldier pulled Ray toward the second tent.

"You can't do this to me! I'm an American citizen!" Ray was yelling frantically. "I have rights, you sons a bitches!" Ray was scrambling to get free.

Jannis pulled a cigarette out of his breast pocket and slid it into his mouth. Pulling a silver lighter out of his pant pocket, he flicked open the lid. "Not anymore, kid." Igniting the lighter, Jannis lifted the flame to his cigarette and took a long drag, allowing the tendrils of smoke to wrap around him like fingers from an unseen hand. He hoped she knew what she was doing. She was taking an awful risk having him grab people off the street like this.

Chapter Twelve

Jake remained crouched in front of the window. He knew that if he stood up, a police sniper would pick him off. He needed to get out of the building, and fast. Dropping to his hands and knees, Jake crawled toward the door. Stopping, he carefully peeked around the corner. To his surprise, the hallway was empty. Jumping to his feet, he moved cautiously toward the main doors. He knew they would be heavily guarded, but Jake wanted to see what he was up against.

Flattening himself against the wall, he slowly poked his head around the corner. His eyes widened. There were at least six squad cars and dozens of police officers, all with their weapons trained on the front door. He wasn't going out that way, but he needed to get to his car. Turning around, he quickly made his way back down the hall toward Lucas' office.

Turning around the corner, he glimpsed two officers and immediately ducked back out of sight. Two SWAT team members had come in through a window and were slowly moving in his direction. Looking to his left, he saw another open door. Making a split second decision, Jake pushed off the wall and sprinted toward the door.

"Stop!" He heard the officers yell.

Jake dove for the door just as machine gun fire tore through the door's frame. Slamming the door shut, Jake scanned the office. There was a desk situated in the center of the room with two large bookcases on either side of the door and a small window to the rear. Grabbing one of the bookcases, he toppled it over in front of the door. Doing the same with the other, he knew he had bought himself a little time. He heard the officers banging on the door behind him. Running toward the window, he cautiously looked around. No sign of any police.

Throwing open the window, he squeezed through and toppled to the ground. Lifting himself up, Jake dashed off toward a nearby building. He guessed he was on the north side of campus, while his car was in the parking lot on the south side. He needed to circle around.

Working his way in and around the buildings, he came to a clearing where he could see his car. He cursed under his breath when he noticed three officers were surrounding it. He recognized one of the officers as the one who rear-ended him. Jake knew that by now, they had broken through his makeshift barricade into the office and found him gone. Time was short. Sneaking up to the rear of the car, he waited for the right moment to jump.

"Freeze!"

Jake felt his heart drop into his stomach. Lifting his hands above his head, he slowly stood up. One of the soldiers was standing over Jake with his pistol aimed at his head.

"Turn around."

Jake complied. Two of the officers standing on either side of his car had their weapons drawn, and the other was quickly making his way around to Jake.

"I didn't do anything," Jake argued as the cop snapped a cuff around his wrist. "Sure, that's what they all say," the cop joked.

"No, I mean it!" Jake ripped his hand away

from the cop and sent an elbow into the man's stomach. Dropping to the ground, Jake yanked his pistol from its holster and fired on the other cop, hitting him in the knee. The officer fell to the ground in agony. Rolling over on to his back, Jake sighted the third officer's foot and fired. The officer hit the ground swearing. Jumping up, Jake ran around his car toward the third officer. "I hate to do this, but...." He kicked the man in the head, knocking him out cold. Holstering his weapon, Jake jumped into the car. The battered car sputtered to life. "I don't think I'm going to get my security deposit back on this one," Jake laughed.

Dropping the gear shifter into drive, he smashed the accelerator to the floor and tore out of the parking lot just as several other cops rushed onto the scene. They immediately started firing at the black rental car. Jake ducked his head down as he sped away from the University of Colorado.

***

"Testing of the virus is going well. Patient Zero has unfortunately died, but not before we had a complete blood work-up done. We should have an antidote within two days."

"Very good, Dr. Hollman." Anne sat motionless in her chair in the far corner. The room they were in was oddly lit. The light emanating from the many containment tubes was creating an unnatural green glow across the room. Only random shafts of bright white light sliced through the green haze. The few times Greg had been in these labs, he had always felt uneasy. The cylinders made this

119

room feel like a morgue.

"We do have one problem, though," Greg admitted nervously.

Anne stood up and began to move toward Greg. Her dress blues were neatly pressed, and her long brown hair was braided behind her head. Her hips swayed seductively back and forth as she walked. "What's the problem?"

Hollman paused. "Jannis was only able to secure Dr. Robinson. He missed Silver."

Anne slapped Greg across his face. "I said I wanted both of them!" She turned away from Greg, "Where is Dr. Robinson being held?"

Greg felt a trickle of blood run down from his lip. "At our camp in Southern Utah."

"I want Dr. Robinson brought to me immediately, and as for Mr. Silver, I want him here within forty-eight hours." She turned back to face him, "And I want him alive.

***

Durard's eyes began to dilate as the tent flap was thrown open. The bright daylight was stark in contrast to the blackness he had been kept in. Looking up into the light, he saw the blurry form of two men entering the tent, then the flap snapped shut again, engulfing them in darkness. Feeling along the bare ground, he scooped a medium-sized rock into his hand. He readied himself for whatever came next. Suddenly, there was another brief flash of light, and a thud.

"Hello? Is anyone here?" a weak voice called from the darkness.

120

Durard said nothing. Gripping the rock tightly in his hand, he lifted himself into a crouching position.

"Please, I don't know what's going on," the voice pleaded.

Durard could hear the fear in the young man's voice. Dropping the rock, he sat back down in the dirt. "Yeah, over here, kid."

"Who are you, and where am I?"

"My name's Jim, and lying unconscious over there in the corner is Steve. What's your name?"

"Ray."

"So," Durard began in a joking tone, "what brings you to Club Med?"

"What?"

"Sorry, just a little joke," Durard apologized.

"I don't think that's very funny," Ray scolded him.

Durard wished he could see the young man, to know what emotions he was feeling. "Sorry, kid, joking is my natural defense mechanism. I was just trying to lighten the mood a little."

Ray sighed. "I apologize, I'm just a little on edge, you know?"

"I understand." Durard let the conversation fall into an uncomfortable silence. Ray couldn't stand being in the dark, he needed to talk to someone. "Do you know why we're here?"

"Beats the hell out of me. Steve and I were just working in the lab. Then some goons came in, roughed us up and brought us here."

"Do you know where here is?" Ray asked. Durard thought for a moment. "Best guess?"

"Yeah."

"Well, estimating from the time I traveled in the truck, I think we're somewhere in Northern Arizona, or in the middle of nowhere." Durard rubbed his head, "Hell, I don't know."

"I don't know how we got here, I just want to go home," Ray said with pain in his voice.

"So do I." Durard kicked at the dirt. "You said 'we'. Where's the other person you're with?"

Ray didn't want to answer, but he had a strong sense it really didn't matter anymore. "He's dead."

"I'm sorry, kid, I had no idea."

"They shot him when he tried to get away. I had to ride all the way here with his body lying in front of me." Tears erupted from his eyes. Ray didn't know how to handle this. "They fucking shot him, man!"

"Jesus," Durard muttered under his breath. "How old was he?"

"Ben had just turned seventeen last May."

"Christ," anger began to well up inside Durard. "They killed a baby."

"This was our senior year. We had plans to go to college together." Ray wiped the tears from his eyes.

"What were you two doing when they came for you?"

"We were looking for our friend, Tyler."

"What happened to him?"

"I don't know. He just disappeared. We found his car and some blood, but nothing else." Ray lowered his head. "Wait, we did find some really strange burn marks around the area."

"What kind of burn marks?"

"That's the really weird part, they were in a

122

perfect circle around his car, and in two symmetrical lines heading down the hill toward where we found the blood."

"Strange." Durard picked up a handful of pebbles off the ground and played with them in his hand. "Could the marks have been caused by a fire?"

"I don't think so. They were too perfect. The wildfires in Nevada always burn out of control because of the dryness."

Another flash of light blinded the two. They heard a thump and a moan from behind them. Ray felt his way toward the new person in the tent. "It's a woman." Ray lifted his hand and rubbed his fingers together, "And it feels like she's hurt. I have blood on my hand."

Durard quickly made his way toward the woman. Finding her neck, he checked for a pulse. "Her heartbeat is very weak." Rolling her over onto her back, Durard placed his hand on her forehead. "She's burning up. We need to get her to a doctor."

"I am a doctor," she said in a weak voice.

Durard and Ray were surprised when she spoke. "Can you tell us your name?" Ray asked.

"Alex, Dr. Alex Robinson."

Chapter Thirteen

"Sam, I need your help again." Jake cradled the payphone's receiver snugly between his hand and face.

"What now, Jake?" Special Agent Sam Connor was exhausted. He had just gotten back to his office after an all-night stake-out in the Garden District.

Jake glanced through the windows of the phone booth. "I'm at a payphone in Steamboat Springs, Colorado, so I don't have much time."

"I thought you were in Denver."

"That was before Alex was taken."

"Taken? By whom?"

Jake sighed, "I think you know who, Sam."

"Jesus, Jake. I think you're going a little overboard with this conspiracy shit."

"Damn it, Sam! Just listen for a moment!" Jake cautiously turned to look around him again. "I need you to tell me what you dug up on Area 51."

"I didn't find much," Sam admitted.

"Anything will help."

"Well," Jake could hear Sam rustling through some papers. "After it was destroyed a year ago, Congress divvied up several billion dollars for repairs and upgrading of the facility, but here's the strange thing, Congress also set aside another huge sum of capital to refurbish a second base."

"A second base?"

"Yeah, but I don't know where this one is. From most reports, it's somewhere in Southern Utah, but I don't have any hard facts on it."

"Is it another Area 51?" Jake asked.

"I'm not sure. It just seems odd to me that the

government would spend all that money to rebuild Area 51, then create a new one."

"Maybe they rebuilt Area 51 as a decoy," Jake theorized.

"I see what you're saying. So while everyone is still focused on Area 51, they can build and test all their new black projects at this new base in Utah." Sam snapped his fingers. "That does hold water."

"So where was Alex taken? To Area 51, or this new base?"

"I couldn't honestly say."

"Thanks, Sam." Jake hung up the phone and stepped out of the phone booth. He looked down the main street of Steamboat Springs. Little specialty shops and boutiques littered the streets of this tourist town. Lifting up the collar on his leather jacket, he wrapped it tightly around his neck. Even though it was spring in the Rocky Mountains, it was still cold. A brisk wind whipped around him as he began to walk toward his battered rental car. Opening the driver's side door, he quickly climbed in and slid his keys into the ignition. Looking out his window, he noticed four white Jeep Cherokees drive past him. The windows were heavily tinted, hiding the identity of the passengers. "Damn." Jake recognized the vehicles as the ones commonly used at Area 51. *They must be on to me,* he assumed. Twisting his keys in the ignition, he waited as the car's engine chugged to life. Luckily, he had filled the car with gas just before he had stopped to make the phone call. Putting the car into gear, Jake maneuvered it into traffic.

He had lost sight of the small convoy of jeeps. The traffic was too dense. Slowly traveling west, he made his way out of town. He had to get to Southern Nevada. This was his only lead on Alex's location. Jake's mind wandered from paranoia to fear. He was heading headlong into the unknown. *Last time I had help from Major Griggs and General Davis. I'm on my own this time.*

***

Jannis ripped open the tent flap and let the sunshine flood in. "Rise and shine, fuck heads!" Ray, Durard and Steve all tried to cover their eyes. After living in the inky blackness for days now, their eyes had become accustomed to it. Squinting, they watched several soldiers stride in with their weapons drawn. "We're all going for a little ride. Cooperate with my soldiers, or you will die." Jannis looked over at Alex. She was lying unconscious on her back. He pointed at Alex, "Pick her up. We need to take special care of her."

The soldiers moved in and grabbed Alex, Durard, Ray and Steve. The four put up little resistance to the soldiers. They all knew Jannis wasn't bluffing when he said he would kill them. Ray had learned that lesson all too well.

The soldiers led their prisoners out into the daylight. Durard stared off into the distance. He knew the sun would be setting soon. It had already begun to dip down behind the horizon. Durard glanced over at his friend Steve. He had a cut over his left eye from when he had been tossed into the truck. It had caused the eye to swell shut. Looking to his left, he stared at Ray. He was only seventeen and he looked as if he had been beaten down by the world. His eyes looked hollow, without that glimmer all teenagers had. Jannis had taken Ray's soul when he killed his friend. Looking behind him, Durard caught site of Alex. She was stumbling along, trying to keep her balance while a soldier kept shoving her in the back. It looked to Durard like she had a bullet wound in her stomach. Blood had permeated her white shirt and lab coat, staining it a dull brown. Her face and neck had numerous lacerations, while a long gash ran from her elbow to the middle of her hand. She was a mess. Durard knew if she didn't receive medical attention soon, she would die.

"Keep moving." One of the soldiers jabbed his rifle into Durard's back.

Looking ahead, Durard saw they were being escorted toward a caravan of trucks. Stopping short, Jannis pulled a cigarette out of a pack in his breast pocket and lit it. He took a long drag and slowly exhaled it through his nose. "Put them all in one truck," he commanded. The soldiers placed the prisoners one by one in the trucks. Once inside, Jannis stepped up onto the bumper and leaned over. He took another drag off his cigarette and blew it toward his prisoners. "Get comfortable," Jannis joked. "It's going to be a long trip, and more than likely, it's going to be the last trip you ever take." He stepped back as his men dropped the canvas door on the truck. The four prisoners were once again swallowed by the darkness. They could hear Jannis laughing outside the truck.

"I hate that bastard," Ray confessed.

"I second that emotion," Steve added groggily.

Durard knelt down and laid his hand on Alex's

back. She was lying flat on the wooden floor with her face buried in her arms. "Are you okay, Dr. Robinson?"

"No," Alex moaned. "I'm bleeding internally. I'm going to die."

"No you're not," Durard argued. "I'm going to make sure that you don't."

"How are you going to do that?" Ray asked.

"I don't know," Durard admitted. "I just can't sit back and watch her die."

"I'm with you, Jim." Ray dropped to his knees next to Durard. "I've already lost someone, I'm not going to let it happen again."

They felt the truck rumble to life and begin to roll forward. The four lurched back, but quickly regained their balance.

"Where are they taking us?" Alex asked weakly.

"We don't know. Hopefully to a place with a doctor that can help you." Durard was softly rubbing Alex's back.

"Famous last words of a fool," Steve laughed.

***

"It's time." Anne slid her hand along the tube. Turning around, she glanced over her small staff of researchers in the room. They were scurrying about in their white lab coats, readying for this momentous occasion. A human being had never been resurrected from the dead before, and they wanted to make sure they had gotten it right.

A short balding man with a thick gray beard waddled up to Anne. "We're ready to begin,

Colonel."

"Very good, Dr. Emerson." Anne turned around and looked at the man in the tube. "Proceed."

"Preparing to unthaw." Paul Emerson had requested assignment at Area 51. He had done his time in the Air Force while stationed at White Sands. He craved something more exciting. Something that was a little more cutting edge. Emerson had always felt he was wasting his talents designing rockets and spy satellites. He walked around the cylinder to a small bank of controls and monitors. Tapping several keys, the man's stats were displayed on the monitors. "Vitals looking strong. Beginning unthawing process." Emerson hit a final key and stepped back. He had never seen someone brought out of stasis before. He didn't know what to expect.

A blue wave of electricity surged through the tube from top to bottom. Anne watched as the muscles in the man's chest began to twitch. Steadily, the fluid in the tube began to liquidify.

"Removing the fluid." Emerson tapped in a set of instructions on the keyboard. Hoses connected to the top and bottom of the cylinder began to pump out the green fluid. After it had been completely drained, a fine mist began to wash through the tube. "Beginning decontamination of the subject." The mist slowly evaporated. A loud hiss filled the room as the lid of the tube snapped open.

Anne and Emerson stepped toward the tube. Reaching in, Anne slid her hand along the man's chest, then to his face. "Clear the room," Anne commanded. Her staff quickly complied.

The man's eyes suddenly shot open. "Where

am I?"

"You're fine. You've just been brought out of stasis," Anne reassured him. "Let me help you out of the tube."

The man lifted his arm and wrapped his hand on Anne's shoulder. "Why does my body hurt?"

"You haven't used it in almost a year. It'll pass as soon as you're up and around again." Anne grabbed the man's hand and helped him out of the tube. "Here, sit down," she said while grabbing a nearby chair. "I'll get you some clothes." Turning around, Anne walked toward a small closet at the rear of the room. Opening the door, she removed a black jumpsuit, a towel and a pair of standard issue boots.

"I can't remember who I am," the man said, rubbing his head.

Anne tossed him the towel. "Your name is Jason Griggs. You hold the rank of Major in the United States Air Force."

Griggs began to dry off with the towel, but stopped to look at Anne. A strange look crossed his face, "I remember you, but I can't remember from where."

"I'm Colonel Caroll. I was your CO." She handed him the uniform. Griggs jumped up and saluted. "Sorry, sir. I don't seem to be myself."

Anne was amazed he saluted and called her "sir". She hadn't expected this much of his memory to remain intact. Her team of researchers had assured her that he would probably be a complete blank after coming out of the tube, if he survived the process at all. "At ease, soldier. Get dressed." She hated to tell him that because she loved to stare at his naked body. "There will be a debriefing shortly."

"Yes, sir."

Anne turned to leave the room. She paused just before leaving to look at him again. Smiling, she closed the door behind her.

Griggs stood up and tried to steady himself. His equilibrium was still reeling. Slipping on the jumpsuit, he zipped it up and sat down again. Placing his feet in the boots, he began to slowly lace them up. He didn't know how he knew to do this, it just seemed right. Leaning back in the chair, he ran his hand through his long, blonde hair. That didn't feel right, he knew his hair was shorter. Closing his eyes, he tried to cut through the fog that hung over his memories. He knew they were there; he just couldn't get to them. Suddenly, a flash of the past shot through his mind. He could see a woman and a man kneeling over him. He didn't recognize either of them. The woman was pumping his chest, and the man was trying to stop her. Griggs could see the woman crying, but he didn't know why. Leaning forward in the chair, Griggs grabbed the sides of his head. *Why can't I remember?*

Chapter Fourteen

Tyler had been forced to endure endless hours of tests. He had finally been moved out of the water chamber and into a much smaller circular room. During that time, he had been sitting in a solitary chair for longer than he cared to think about. The chair really reminded him of the kind you would find in the dentist's office. It reclined and had a long footrest, but unlike a dentist's chair, this one seemed to be made of metal and offered little comfort at all.

Tyler's hands and ankles were strapped to the chair and a large metallic object had been lowered from the ceiling that covered his genitals. A fine mist, that actually felt warm on his skin, was falling from the roof. It reminded him of standing in the bathroom just after taking a hot shower with the steam still on the mirror.

A tall, gangly alien suddenly appeared in the room. Its oversized head was bobbing like that of a bird's. In its hand, the alien held a small, silver, circular device. Moving slowly to the right, it gently placed the object on Tyler's forehead. "This will ease most of your pain," the alien said without speaking. Using its long spindly fingers, the alien tapped a small gold button in the center of it. The device began to shudder as it whirred to life. There was a sudden, sharp pain directly below it. Tyler stared up at the alien with a worried look on his face.

"It has sent what you would call a needle directly into the pleasure center of your brain. It will hurt only for a moment," the alien reassured him.

A sudden sense of euphoria passed over Tyler. "Thank you."

The alien nodded its bulbous head. "It is the least we could do for the savior." The alien turned to leave.

"Wait, what do you mean, the savior?" Tyler asked, but the alien had vanished through the door without another word.

***

They felt the truck lurch to a halt. The four occupants in the rear sat quietly, not knowing what to expect next. The rear flap of the canvas was thrown open and three soldiers dressed in black fatigues quickly climbed in. With their rifles trained on the occupants, they led them out into the cool desert night.

Ray, Durard and Steve were all moved into a line near the rear of the truck. They watched as two more guards climbed in and began to drag Alex's almost lifeless body out. Durard turned his attention away from the soldiers, trying to get a fix on where they were. His eyes widened when he caught site of a huge hangar bay that seemed to be built into the side of a mountain. Looking away, he noticed a dark streak of asphalt that seemed to stretch off endlessly into the desert.

Ray leaned close to Durard. "Oh my God," Ray whispered. "I think this is Area 51! We're screwed. Everyone knows once you go inside, you're never seen again!" Another soldier slammed the butt of his weapon into the back of Ray's head, knocking him to the concrete. "No talking, or you all die," the

133

man announced. "You son of a bitch," Durard shouted and leapt at the soldier.

The soldier quickly dropped Durard to the ground and delivered a quick kick to his midsection, knocking the wind out of him. Training his rifle on Durard's head, the man's face was filled with rage. "That was dumb."

"Stop!" A voice cut through the darkness. "I want them all alive," Anne said while slowly emerging from the shadows.

The soldier quickly snapped to attention. "Sorry, Colonel. He attacked me."

Anne walked up to the soldier. "I don't give a fuck if he pissed in your eye. I want them alive. Is that understood?"

"Yes, Colonel," the soldier replied sternly.

"Very good." Turning her attention away from the soldier, she addressed her four prisoners. "Let me welcome you to the Groom Lake Complex, or better known as Area 51." She took a step closer to Durard, who was lifting himself and Ray off the ground. "My, we're a spunky one, aren't we? And what is your name?"

Durard spat at Anne.

Wiping the spit off her face, she reared back and slapped Durard hard across the face. "You ever do that again and you won't live long enough to regret it. Is that understood?"

Durard turned away from Anne. "Fuck off. If you're going to kill me, then just do it!"

"In good time." Anne turned and began to walk toward the two soldiers that were holding Alex. "Let go of her." The two soldiers quickly complied and dropped Alex on the ground. Kneeling down,

Anne tucked a piece of her brown hair behind her ear. Studying Alex for several seconds, Anne reached down and grabbed a handful of Alex's hair and her head lifted up. "Hello, Dr. Robinson." Alex tried to focus her eyes. Blood spilled from her mouth as she tried to breathe. "I'm so glad you could make it. I hope my men weren't too rough on you." Anne smiled, "There's someone I want you to meet, so don't die just yet." Anne let go of Alex's hair, allowing her head to slam into the ground with a thud. Standing up, Anne adjusted her uniform. "Get all these prisoners inside right now!"

"Belay that order!"

"What?" Anne screamed. "Who the fuck do you think you are?"

General Foster stepped into the light and stood face to face with Anne. Foster glanced quickly over the group of prisoners that stood behind him. "What the hell do you think you're doing, Colonel?"

"This is none of your concern, General. I apprehended—"

"None of my fucking concern?" Foster asked in a low dangerous voice. "Who the hell do you think you are? I give the orders here, and I did not sanction this!" Foster leaned close to Anne's face, "I will have you court-martialed for this, Colonel! Your career is over!" Foster signaled to one of the soldiers standing with Anne, "I am placing you under arrest and relieving you of duty. Apprehend this woman!" The soldiers did nothing. Anne smiled broadly. "God damn it! I said, apprehend this woman!"

Anne pushed Foster away laughing. "You're an idiot!"

Foster's anger turned to disbelief. "What the hell is going on here?"

"This facility is once again under my command, and you are no longer needed here." Anne turned to the soldier behind her and grabbed his pistol. Swinging around, she quickly drew a bead on Foster. "So instead of one of those long drawn out military ceremonies, I'll just relieve *you* of duty right here."

"You're insane!" Foster began to stumble away from Anne, but was quickly stopped by one of the soldiers.

"I resent that," Anne smirked. She began to pull the trigger.

Thinking quickly, Durard threw himself at Anne, knocking them both to the ground. The pistol skittered away as it hit the hard concrete. Foster seized the moment and delivered two quick punches to the nearest soldier's face. Grabbing the soldier's rifle, Foster easily picked off two of the four guards. The third guard leapt to the ground and returned fire. Foster cried out in pain as one of the bullets tore through his shoulder.

Steve quickly threw himself on the fourth guard. Using his huge frame, Steve sent them both sprawling to the concrete. Steve pulled back and threw several right hooks across the soldier's chin. The soldier reached up and grabbed Steve by the throat and tossed him off. Leaping onto Steve, the soldier sent his knee into Steve's midsection. Steve heard several of his ribs crack. The soldier sneered as he punched Steve's throat, effectively collapsing his windpipe. As Steve struggled on the ground trying to breathe, the guard scrambled to retrieve his weapon. Lifting it off the ground, the guard stabbed the barrel of his rifle into Steve's temple. Steve's eyes widened. Twisting hard, he tried to toss the guard off him, but the guard held fast and pulled the trigger.

Durard grabbed Ray by the shoulder and threw him behind the truck just as a spray of wild bullets tore across the concrete in front of them.

Anne began to lift herself off the ground just as the bullet slammed into Foster's shoulder. Standing up, she smiled as her superior officer crumpled to the ground. Retrieving the pistol, she strode over to Foster and looked him in the eye. Raising the gun, she aimed for his heart. "This base is mine." She fired. Anne turned to look at the chaos behind her. She caught a glimpse of Durard and Ray standing behind the truck. "Come out right now, or I'll kill you both."

Durard and Ray looked at each other, then stepped out with their hands raised. "All right, we give up," Durard announced.

Anne watched as two of her four soldiers picked Alex up and propped her against the side of the truck. Her two other soldiers lay silently on the ground. "Take everyone down to the main lab. We need to attend to Dr. Robinson. She needs to be well when she meets an old friend."

***

His eyes gradually adjusted to the almost pitch blackness of the cell he was occupying. Durard had been the last one thrown into a cell. He had to watch as all his fellow prisoners were thrown inside, then violently beaten by the guards. Ray had received the worst of it. Durard kept seeing the image of Ray lying on the hard concrete floor with blood pooling around his head. *They had no reason to do this to us*, Durard thought, *to do that to Ray.*

Standing up, he rested himself against one of the cold concrete walls. The coolness felt good on his bruised and battered body. His mind was still reeling from the fact that just days before he had been performing his job, and now he was stuck in this cell. *Too bad the rest of the Government doesn't work as efficiently as this branch does,* he joked to himself, finding some strange comfort in it.

Durard heard footsteps approaching his cell. Steeling his nerves, he flattened his body against the wall. He wanted to exact some justice for what they had done to Ray, even if it meant his own death. The sharp click of boots drew closer. Durard slowly crept back into the shadows, hoping they would conceal him from whoever was there.

Two soldiers stopped in front of Durard's cell. One pulled a key card out of his pocket, while the other stepped back and trained his weapon into the darkness of the cell. "All right," the first soldier spoke. "Step out where we can see you." Durard made no movement. The soldier slid his key card through a slit next to the cell door. The lock instantly snapped open, and the bars began to slide to the side.

Durard made his move. Summoning all the focus and strength he had, he leapt at the first soldier and threw a solid punch into his stomach. The first soldier fell to the floor with the wind knocked out of him. Rolling onto the floor, he tried to bark an order at the second soldier, but Durard had already disarmed him and was pounding on his face.

Durard's focus began to fade as rage enveloped his mind and body. Punch after punch, he kept pounding until the second soldier's face was a bloody mess. Reeling back in horror, he lifted himself off the man. Durard watched as his body lay motionless on the floor. Spinning around, Durard was caught off-guard by the first soldier. This one, a taller and much bigger man with a jagged scar that ran down from his right temple to the corner of his mouth, grabbed Durard by the throat and began to squeeze. Durard gasped for air as he struggled to loosen the man's grip.

The soldier smiled as he squeezed tighter. "I could kill you right now. Do you understand?"

Durard continued to try and loosen the man's grip on his throat.

"You're lucky, though. Colonel Carroll wants to see you, and unfortunately, she did specify you had to be alive." The man loosened his grip allowing Durard to fall to the floor. Pulling his pistol from its holster, the soldier trained it on Durard. "Now get up." Durard complied unwillingly, still trying to catch his breath.

Chapter Fifteen

Twelve hours later, Jake saw Las Vegas looming in the distance. He had been driving non-stop through the day and well into the night, obsessed with finding Alex. His mind began to wander as he stared at the desolate landscape rushing by his window. It was a stroke of irony that he had spent almost a year away from Alex with the hopes they would be safer apart, only to return to her side and his fears become realized. Jake slammed his fist on the steering wheel. *Damn,* he thought. *I can't even protect Alex.*

How the hell am I going to get into one of the most secure military bases in the world?

As Jake cruised into the city limits, an odd feeling of isolation swept over him. The city seemed abandoned. Everywhere he looked, he saw only buildings and flashing lights. No people anywhere. Reaching over to his glove compartment, he popped open the door and snatched a small surgical mask. Slipping it over his face, he made sure his windows were tightly sealed.

Taking a right, Jake was awed at the sheer magnitude of the virus' devastation. Not a single living soul was left to walk the streets. Glancing up into the windows of the hotels, he saw nothing. It seemed as if Las Vegas had been deserted.

Pulling his attention back to the road, Jake quickly slammed on the breaks. A middle-aged black man had wandered out into the middle of the street. The man staggered toward Jake's car and began to pound on the driver's side window. A thick yellow fluid was oozing from his mouth and nose.

"Help...." the man could barely mouth the words.

Jake stared in horror as the man's eyes rolled back and his body slumped against the side of Jake's car. Fear shot through Jake's body. *What a horrible way to die.* Pressing his foot slowly on the accelerator, Jake could hear the man's body sliding down the side of the car, and finally crumple to the ground. He knew he couldn't help the man and he couldn't risk infection.

He needed to get out of Las Vegas. The desolation was too intense. Driving his car quickly through the streets, he made his way up an on-ramp and back onto the interstate. He stared at the empty streets as he passed them. Suddenly, his attention was caught by a large, black helicopter swooping overhead. He followed the helicopter's flight path until it was out of sight. Jake quickly took the next connection to the north, following the helicopter.

***

Alex slowly came to. Her eyes slowly opened to see a bright blur. *Where am I?* Gradually, her eyes began to focus. Lying flat on her back, she stared at several banks of lights in the ceiling. Sitting up, she felt a surge of pain shoot up her back. There was an IV needle inserted into her right hand, along with several electrodes attached to her head and chest. She quickly noticed she was only wearing her bra and panties.

Looking down at her stomach, she saw large white bandages wrapped around the area where she

141

had been shot. Running her hand over it, she detected no pain and no wound. Quickly unwrapping the bandages, her eyes widened. The bullet wound was gone. Alex swung her legs over the side of the metal table she was on and looked around.

The room appeared to be an operating room. Banks of monitors sat alongside the table with a bright examination light directly overhead. No one was in the room with her.

Standing up, Alex quickly grabbed the side of the table as a wave of nausea and disorientation flowed over her. She knew she was in no condition to be up and around. Lifting herself back onto the table, she rested as her mind cleared. The sudden hiss of the door startled her.

"So, you're finally awake?"

Alex turned her head toward the door. She could've sworn she was looking at a ghost. "I killed you," Alex's voice trailed off as she remembered that day deep in the heart of S-4.

Anne walked slowly into the room and twirled around in front of Alex. "As you can see," Anne ran her hands seductively over her body, "I am very much alive." Stepping close to Alex, Anne placed a hand on the metal examination table. "I've been thinking about this day for a very long time, you know."

"Fuck off," Alex responded harshly.

"Now, is that any way to treat an old friend?" Anne replied smugly. Alex turned away, refusing to talk.

"Did you know I spent several days wandering through the desert with a bullet wound in my

142

midsection? Do you know what I thought about during that time?"

Alex shook her head.

"Your death." Anne sneered, "and the death of Jake Silver. It was all that kept me going." Anne lifted herself onto the metal table next to Alex. "Now I have you." She placed a hand on Alex's shoulder, "And I'm going to make your death very slow and painful."

Alex jumped off the table and turned to face Anne, "Then why the hell did you heal my wounds?"

Anne smiled as she crossed her legs. "It's all part of the fun! First, I fix you up so you're in perfect condition, then I get to kill you! This way, it will last longer. After all, the state you were in when you arrived, you wouldn't have lived very long at all."

"You nursed me back to life, just to kill me? You're one sick bitch." Alex ripped the IV needle from her hand and began to quickly remove the electrodes from her body. "Either kill me right now, or get out of my way, because I'm leaving."

Anne shrugged. "Suit yourself. The door is over there."

Alex turned and quickly raced toward the door but stopped short. The door had no handle or keypad, just a slot for a key card.

"Oh," Anne pulled her card out of her pocket and tossed it to Alex. "You'll need this."

Alex caught the card. "What are you doing?"

"I'm giving you a chance to leave, if that's what you really want." Anne stood up and walked over to Alex. "Look at yourself. All you're wearing

143

is your bra and panties, you can barely stand as is and you're in the middle of the desert. Where are you going to go?"

"Away from you." Alex turned and slid the card through the slot. The door hissed and opened. Three armed soldiers were standing outside the Medical Ward. The middle soldier was standing with his back to the door.

"Before you go, I want to show you something." Anne smiled broadly. She snapped her fingers, "Major!"

The middle soldier turned around to face Alex. Her mouth fell open and she almost tumbled to the ground. "Jason!" She stared at Griggs' face. This made two ghosts she had seen today. She threw herself on Griggs, wrapping her arms around his neck. "Oh my God, Griggs! You're alive!"

Griggs tried to break out of the embrace. Grabbing Alex's arm, he forcefully tossed her to the floor and quickly drew his weapon. "Stay where you are. I am authorized to use deadly force."

Alex's eyes began to tear up. "What the are you doing, Jason? Don't you remember me? It's Alex! Dr. Alex Robinson? You and Jake rescued me from Area 51 over a year ago!"

"I have no idea who you are," Griggs answered sternly. "Jason! It's me, Alex!" Tears rolled down Alex's face.

Griggs stepped forward and slapped Alex. "Shut up! If you speak again, I will kill you! On your feet, prisoner!"

Anne stepped in. "At ease, Major. Good work."

Griggs snapped to attention. "Yes, Colonel. Thank you, Colonel."

Anne motioned for the two other guards to pick Alex up and take her to a cell. Anne moved closer to Griggs. "You've done well. Much better than I had anticipated."

"Thank you, Colonel, I—"

"You can drop the 'Colonel' now. We're alone."

Anne ran her hand down Griggs' chest. "Anne."

Griggs scooped her up into his arms and kissed her. "You're too good to me."

"I know." Anne caressed his face.

"Do you mind if I ask you a question?"

"Sure," Anne answered in a very soft voice.

"Who was that woman? How did she know my name?"

Anne shook her head. "Don't worry about it, Jason. She was one of the whackos we picked up trying to get into the base." Anne kissed Griggs again before he had time to ask another question. "Now take me back to my quarters and show me how much you love me."

Griggs smiled. "My pleasure, Colonel."

***

General Foster crawled to the top of a sand dune and stopped. A full moon was out, throwing too much light around. Lifting himself into a sitting position, he opened his jacket and checked his wound. Blood had soaked through the cloth again. Tossing the tattered piece of fabric aside, he reached down and tore another swatch off his jacket. After applying it to the wound, he buttoned his jacket tightly to try and keep it in place.

It had been almost two hours since Colonel Caroll had shot him at Area 51. After they had taken the prisoners inside, no one had come to check on him. Foster had seized the opportunity and escaped. *I'll be damned if I let a mutiny happen on my watch.*

Standing, he scanned the horizon. He knew he was heading in a vaguely eastern direction toward Las Vegas, but he couldn't be sure. The landscape was very unfamiliar to him. Placing his hand over his makeshift bandages, he set off across the desert.

Chapter Sixteen

Greg Hollman stood over an electron microscope. Wearing a blue level five decontamination suit, he carefully worked his thick rubber gloves over a sample of the virus. Twisting the cork off the vial, he slid an eyedropper into the tube and extracted a small amount of the yellow fluid. He smiled with delight. *This should do it. This should give me the antidote.*

He carefully placed a bit of the yellow fluid into a Petri dish and set the eyedropper aside for a moment. Grabbing a syringe from the table on his right, he injected a few drops of the clear fluid into the Petri dish.

Setting down the syringe, he slid the dish carefully under the microscope. "Now, I should see a chemical reaction as the virus begins to break down."

He watched the virus carefully. The constant movement of the bacteria gave way to stillness in the sample. Hollman threw his hands up into the air, "I've done it! I've created the antidote!" He picked up the syringe, "You're going to make us a lot of money. Especially when all the world leaders come running to us for the antidote to the virus."

He peered down into his microscope again. There was still no activity. Just as he was about to look away, several of the bacteria twitched. "What the hell?" Hollman increased the magnification. To his horror, the virus slowly began to resume their normal activity. "The virus has adapted, and evolved to include the antidote as part of its genetic makeup!"

Hollman knew the implications of this event. He stood up and moved toward the airlock. Quickly unlocking the air hose from his suit, he opened the door and stepped into the decontamination room. Unzipping his suit, he stepped out of it and made his way to the second door. Once outside in the main lab, he grabbed a phone off a nearby table. Lifting the receiver, he punched in a three digit number and waited. He listened as the phone rang on the other end.

"Caroll, go ahead."

"Colonel, this is Hollman. We have a problem," he said frantically into the receiver.

"What's the problem?" Anne asked. "The vaccine doesn't work!"

***

Anne paced back and forth in her office. There was a major flaw in her plan. If the antidote didn't work, she would have no bargaining chip, and the virus might run rampant over the world. It could conceivably decimate the entire human race. This was unacceptable. She couldn't rule, if there was no one left.

There was a knock at her door. "Come."

Greg Hollman stepped inside, still wearing his light blue scrubs. "I don't know what happened, Colonel."

Anne turned and scowled. "Sit down." Hollman quickly complied. Seating himself in a chair in front of Anne's desk, he waited patiently. "This is a major setback for us."

"Yes Colonel, I—"

"Shut up." Anne strode around the side of her desk and took a seat in her high- backed leather chair. "Why didn't the vaccine work?"

"I have a few theories," Hollman admitted. "Give me the most plausible one."

"Well," Hollman rubbed his chin. "The virus sample we found in the Southern Nevada desert is so mutated, it can conquer anything it comes in contact with." He sat up in his chair, "Look at it this way, right now, the virus has mutated to include strands of the common cold and influenza in it. What happens when it finds a strand of AIDS to include in itself? Or Ebola? Or the Hanta Virus?" Hollman leaned back in his chair considering the ramifications he had just set forth. "The virus is evolving."

"How do we contain it?"

"I don't think we can. From the moment we let it loose, it was out of our control." Anne leaned back in her chair and crossed her legs. "What do we need?" Hollman leaned forward and placed his hands on Anne's desk. "I need a sample of the original virus. The samples I've been using have all been mutated thus far. If I can get my hands on an untainted sample, I think I could have a better shot at neutralizing it."

"Where do we get an 'untainted' sample of the virus?" Anne asked.

Hollman shook his head. "I'm not sure. The only sample I knew of was the one contained inside S-4...."

"And now, S-4 is nothing more than a big crater in the Earth."

"Right." Hollman leaned back in his chair. "Do

149

we have any way of knowing where the scientists at S-4 got the sample in the first place?"

"From what I know, it was contained within one of the recovered alien spacecrafts."

Hollman's eyes lit up, "Then can't we just go down to the hangar and pull out another sample?"

Anne shook her head. "All the alien crafts housed inside Area 51 vanished during the raid over a year ago."

Hollman slammed his hand down on the armrest of his chair. "Damn." He thought for a moment. "Doesn't the Air Force have detailed records on this sort of thing?"

"Yes," Anne acknowledged. "I'll have a team start combing through them right now." Anne stood up, "Dismissed."

Hollman stood up to leave, but stopped short of the door. "I'm also going to need a subject to test the virus and vaccine on."

Anne smiled. "I know just the person for that job."

***

Jake sat alone near the 'Black Mailbox'. The Black Mailbox was one of the last places outside Area 51 where civilians could congregate without fearing a reprimand from the military. The mailbox itself was white and battered, standing alone next to a desolate road. Many strange UFO sightings had occurred while waiting at the Black Mailbox.

Jake's car was idling with the heater running. It was the early hours of the morning with the sun not yet up in the sky, so the desert was a cold and lonely place. He had removed the germ mask and was taking long drags off one of the few cigars he had remaining. He was carefully considering his plan of attack.

Taking a long drag off his cigar, he tossed it out the window, then closed it. He stared off into the quiet night skies. *How did it ever come to this? I used to have a normal life. Now I'm reduced to one crusade after another.*

***

"Colonel, we've spotted a black car parked just outside the Area 51 property line," one of the board ops reported.

"Can you identify the car and driver?" Anne asked.

"Yes, Colonel," a board operator replied. "It's the same vehicle Jake Silver was driving when our team spotted him in Colorado."

Anne stood from her seat in the command center, "I want that man apprehended and brought to me. Send Captain Jannis. I want this done right."

The board op turned around to face Anne. "Colonel, he's still outside our jurisdiction."

Anne lashed out. "Did you hear my orders, Lieutenant?" The board op nodded. "Then do it, God damn it!"

"Yes, Colonel." The board op turned and began to work feverishly.

Despite Anne's outburst, she smiled broadly. As she began to walk toward the door, a lone thought crossed her mind. *This was a lot easier than I thought it would be.*

***

Jake pushed his gearshift down three notches into the drive position. Pulling onto the road, he stepped on the breaks and prepared himself. It was less than a mile to the Area 51 border. Letting his foot off the break, he smashed his foot down on the gas pedal. It was now or never and he really didn't have a plan.

His car fishtailed along the dirt road as a cloud of dust collected behind him. Jake saw the guard shack looming in the distance. Wrapping his hands tightly around the steering wheel, his knuckles began to turn white.

Jake pressed himself into the driver's seat as he approached the guard shack. A wooden guardrail was being lowered across the road. Two soldiers dressed in black jumped out of the shack and aimed their weapons at Jake's car. He floored it as he neared the guardrail. The two soldiers quickly jumped out of the way just as the vehicle crashed through the rail, sending splinters of wood sailing in all directions. Rolling into a firing position, the two guards fired. The rear window shattered as bullets tore through the cab of the car. Ducking down while covering his head, Jake tried to keep his vehicle on the road.

In the distance, Jake spotted several pairs of headlights. Looking around, he saw nothing but hills in either direction, and he knew his car wouldn't survive an off-road trip. Slamming his foot on the break, Jake sent his car skidding sideways toward the roadblock ahead of him. A cloud of dust rolled by as his car finally lurched to a stop.

All at once, several armed soldiers had surrounded the car. "Hands where we can see them!" one soldier shouted.

Jake slowly lifted his hands. "Damn," he muttered under his breath.

A second soldier stepped to the driver's side door and opened it. He was a man of medium height, and in Jake's estimate, built like a brick wall. His green eyes burned like fire in his eye sockets. A long scar cut from the man's right temple, to the corner of his mouth. "Get out of the car now and lay flat on the ground!"

Jake slowly complied. Unbuckling his seat belt, he got out of the car. Dropping down to his knees, he laced his fingers behind his head. "Hey, I'm just a lost tourist. Isn't this the way to Vegas?" Jake asked coyly.

"Don't fuck with us, or we will kill you," the soldier answered sternly. "Come on, guys, I was just looking for a gas sta—"

The nearest soldier whipped the butt of his rifle around and jabbed it into Jake's ribs. "Down on your stomach, now!" Jake buckled over in pain. He quickly dropped down to his hands and knees. The soldier leaned over Jake, pressing the barrel of his rifle into the back of Jake's neck. "You have entered a restricted area. Use of deadly force is authorized here. Do you deny you entered this area willingly?"

Jake moaned. "It was just an accident. I was looking for a gas—"

The tall soldier kicked Jake hard in the ribs,

153

knocking him flat to the ground. "Do you deny you entered this area willingly?" he asked again.

"I'm just lost," Jake said, gasping for air.

The soldier began to squeeze the trigger, when another soldier interrupted him. Jake couldn't hear the substance of the conversation; he just knew he was glad to be alive. He heard the other soldier refer to the man as Captain Jannis. "On your feet!" Jannis instructed. Jake pulled himself up and leaned against the hood of his car. "It seems you've been granted a reprieve from above," Jake could hear disappointment in Jannis' voice. Jannis turned to a different man and began to bark orders. "The Colonel wants to see the prisoner ASAP! Let's move!"

Jannis grabbed Jake and forced him into the back seat of his battered black car. Sliding into the driver's seat, he quickly instructed another soldier to get in the passenger's seat and keep watch on the prisoner. The soldier quickly complied. While waiting for the other men to return to their vehicles, Jannis kicked the car into drive. Once the last vehicle had moved out, he pressed the gas pedal to the floor and sent the car barreling toward Area 51.

***

Durard sat quietly in an empty room. A lone light hung from the ceiling directly over him, spilling white light over the gray stone room. Durard's arms and legs had been lashed to a thick steel chair. Only a single black door could be seen at the far right of the room. Durard had no concept of time in this small room, but if felt like he had

154

been sitting there for hours.

Durard was alarmed by the sound of the door handle clicking. Two soldiers strode into the room, followed closely by the woman he had seen before on the tarmac. She was still wearing her dress blues, her brown hair wrapped tightly behind her head.

She walked quickly up to Durard and slapped him hard across the face. "Why were you taking unauthorized soil samples from the FEMA dig in the Southern Nevada Desert?" Her tone was low and harsh.

"I was just following orders," Durard replied meekly.

"Bullshit!" Anne slapped him again. "No one ordered you to take that sample. Why were you taking the soil sample?"

"I was following orders!"

Anne pulled her hand back to slap Durard again, but stopped and took a step back. "Okay, Mr. Durard, we're going to play a little game," Anne chose her next words very carefully. "I'm going to ask you a question. If you answer it correctly, nothing happens to you, but if you lie to me, I have my men cut off one of your fingers." Anne watched terror flash through Durard's eyes. "Are you ready, Mr. Durard?"

Durard was too terrified to answer.

"Good. Let's begin." Anne motioned for her soldiers to take their position. Durard watched one of the soldiers unsheathe a large knife from his belt as he walked toward him. Kneeling down, the soldier grabbed Durard's left hand and held it tightly to the arm of the chair. Lowering his blade, he pressed it against Durard's index finger. Beads of sweat began to roll down Durard's forehead.

Anne stood at the rear of the room, the light barely glancing off her body. Her face was concealed by the darkness. "How long have you been employed by the Federal Emergency Management Agency, Mr. Durard?"

Durard swallowed hard. "Over a year."

Anne smiled. "See how easy that was? You didn't even lose a finger." Anne stepped fully into the light, "Shall we continue?" She walked around and placed a slender hand on Durard's shoulder. "What do you know about the nature of the genetic material found at Site-4?"

"I don't know anything. I'm just a field op—" Durard stopped as the soldier began to slice into his finger. Blood spilled onto the arm of the chair as pain shot up his arm.

"See what happens when we don't answer the question truthfully?" Anne asked smugly.

Chapter Seventeen

Tyler awoke still sitting in the same chair in the same room. After the alien had attached the device to his head, Tyler had fallen fast asleep. He didn't know for how long. Two aliens entering the room suddenly startled him. They both moved quickly, as if with a purpose. One was carrying a large gray box, and the other had several multicolored cords hanging from his hands. Setting the box down on a small table next to Tyler's chair, the alien touched a switch with one of his long, bony fingers. The box's lid flipped open to reveal a bank of controls and monitors. The other alien laid the cords on Tyler's chest and began to unwind them.

Attached to one end of each colored cord was a long silver needle. On the other end, there was what resembled a standard audio jack. The alien began handing the sides of the cords with the jacks to the second alien, who, in turn, began to plug them into the gray box.

"What are you going to do to me?" Tyler asked.

The aliens didn't respond. They just kept on with their tasks. The second alien lifted a blue cord and steadied himself. Lowering the chord to Tyler's temple, it inserted the needle into Tyler's brain. The alien continued the process over and over until Tyler's upper body was covered with implanted needles and wires.

"What's happening to me?" Tyler asked.

The aliens looked at Tyler, "We need to alter your genetic make-up."

"Why?" The device on Tyler's head whirred loudly as it tried to cancel out the pain he was in.

His mind remained clear and sharp.

One of the aliens adjusted several of the needles in Tyler's chest. "We need to make you immune to the effects of the virus."

"What virus?" Tyler asked.

The aliens didn't respond. Tyler turned his head to the left and watched the alien operating the gray box. He saw the alien connect the last cord into the box. Flipping a small red switch, the box crackled to life. Dozens of lights and dials lit as it powered up.

Tyler began to feel static electricity jump needle to needle over his body. The two aliens looked at each other to signal their readiness. The alien operating the gray box flipped three blue switches along the front panel, sending waves of electricity flooding into Tyler's body. His spine arched up toward the ceiling as his muscles began to convulse.

"What's happening to me?" Without warning, the device on Tyler's head overloaded and exploded in a shower of sparks. Without the device, his pain receptors snapped into action allowing pain to surge throughout his body. Tyler screamed out as his muscles tensed, twisting his body into strange positions.

The two aliens looked at each other for a moment, then proceeded. One of them tapped the small round device on Tyler's head with his fingers. Pressing the gold button, the device slowly struggled to life again.

Tyler's screams slowly subsided as euphoria passed over his body once more. "That's much better."

Tyler's body began to slowly relax as the aliens

turned down the power on the machine. The one controlling the box flipped another set of switches. Strange warmth began to pass through Tyler's body. The warmth flared into a steady heat. Tyler felt like his body was burning up from the inside. Beads of sweat rolled off his body as his temperature kept rising.

"I feel like I'm on fire!" Tyler shouted.

The alien on the right side pressed his hand to Tyler's chest, then quickly removed it. He nodded to the second alien to begin reducing the heat. "The transformation is almost complete," the aliens stated. "Endure the heat for a bit longer. It will be over soon."

"I can't take it anymore!" Tyler screamed. Even though he wasn't in any pain, he could feel his organs beginning to boil.

The two aliens nodded at each other. "We are complete." The alien snapped off the switches on the box. Tyler's temperature began to return to normal. "You have now been genetically altered. You are now immune to the virus, no matter what form it takes."

"Why have you done this to me?" Tyler asked.

"You are going to be the savior of all mankind," the alien's voice boomed sinisterly in Tyler's head. Quickly, the alien on the left pressed a silver tube to Tyler's neck. A haze rolled over Tyler's mind as the chemical swiftly took effect. As Tyler's eyes began to involuntarily close, he saw the aliens removing the dozens of needles from his body. Tyler slowly closed his eyes and drifted back into an uncomfortable sleep.

Jake was being drug along a brightly lit corridor by his feet. Two soldiers, under the instructions of Jannis, had pulled Jake out by his boots when he refused to leave his car. He could feel the bruises and knots forming on the back of his head from the abuse.

Jake's feet dropped to the floor as the two guards stopped in front of a cell. After sliding their key card through, the door of the cell slid open with a clang.

Jannis, who was following behind, stepped over Jake. "On your feet and into the cell! Now!" he barked at Jake.

Rolling onto his stomach, Jake tried to lift himself up. A rush of blood went to his head sending his equilibrium off kilter. Jake stumbled from his feet back down to his knees. Searing pain shot up the back of his head and neck. He knew he had a concussion.

"You're wasting my time," Jannis announced. Pointing at Jake, he ordered the two guards to toss him into the cell.

The two soldiers quickly complied and grabbed Jake by the arms. With one quick heft, Jake found himself lying flat on his back in the middle of the cold concrete cell.

Jake tried to lift his head, but another wave of shooting pain stopped him.

Jannis stepped close to the door and watched it close tightly. He reached out and shook the cell door once, just to make sure it was locked. Turning around, he ordered the two soldiers back to normal duty. Glancing down at Jake one more time, Jannis shook his head and strode off.

Jake looked around the gray concrete cell. *This all seems very familiar,* he thought.

***

Durard stumbled back into his cell, his hands a bloody mess, but with all of his digits still intact. After watching the cell door slam shut and the two guards leave, Durard quickly tore two strips of fabric from his shirt and wrapped them around his still bleeding hands. He knew he needed stitches to properly close the wounds in his hands and fingers.

Standing up, Durard moved over to the front of the cell and tried to peer around the bars. He couldn't see any guards stationed nearby. "Hello?" Durard hoped that Steve and Ray had been put in cells near his own. He needed to know they were all right, especially Ray.

No one answered.

"Steve? Ray? Are you guys down there?" Durard heard a groan from the next cell. "Who's there?"

"Jake."

"Jake who?" Durard asked.

Jake grumbled. "Jake the fellow prisoner, that's who."

"Is there anyone in your cell with you?"

"No."

"Do you know if there's anyone in any of the cells around you?" Durard asked. "Don't know. Just checked in," Jake replied dryly. Lifting himself into a sitting position, Jake propped himself up against

161

the cold, gray wall. "Hey, I never caught your name."

"Jim. My name's Jim."

"What are you in for, Jim?" Jake asked as he dug through his jacket pockets.

"I don't have any idea," Durard said. "One minute, I'm just doing my job, the next, I'm on a truck bound here."

"Our tax dollars hard at work," Jake complained under his breath. "How'd you get here, Jake?"

"Long story." Jake found what he was looking for. Pulling his last cigar out of his pocket, he placed it in his mouth. Extracting a small blue lighter from his other pocket, he slid his thumb over the igniter. Nothing. He tried again. Still nothing. Holding the lighter close to his ear, he shook it hard. *Just my luck, it's out of fluid.*

"We seem to have plenty of time."

Jake groaned again. He felt like he had been beaten with a wet sack of doorknobs. "Long story short, I'm here to rescue a friend of mine."

"Looks like your rescue mission went a little awry," Durard commented. "You could say that."

Durard stared down and his hands. The bandages were already soaked with blood. "Must be some friend."

"Pardon?"

"I mean your friend," Durard tried to clarify, "the one you came here looking for. He must be very important to you."

Jake nodded. "She."

"I'm sorry?"

"My friend is a she, and yes, she's more

162

important than I even realized."

"What's her name?"

"Alex."

Durard stood straight up. "Dr. Alex Robinson?"

Jake's eyes widened, "Yeah, that's her! How do you know her?"

"She was one of the prisoners I was transferred here with."

"How is she?" Jake quickly stood up. A rush of nausea passed over him. Grabbing the cell bars, Jake tried to steady himself. In his excitement, he had forgotten about his concussion.

"When I saw her last, she...." Durard hesitated.

"Tell me!" Jake demanded.

"She wasn't in the greatest condition. Alex had a gunshot wound to her lower abdomen, as well as several lacerations on her face and arms. For most of the trip, she floated in and out of consciousness."

"Oh, Christ." Jake felt his heart drop. "Did she survive the trip?"

"As far as I know," Durard answered. "The last time I saw her, some insane military Colonel was beating her on the tarmac."

"Military Colonel? Do you know what his name was?" Anger began to well up in Jake.

"She never said her name."

"She?"

"Yeah, it was a woman, the same bitch that just tried to cut off my fucking fingers as she interrogated me."

"What did she look like?" Jake asked.

"She was about medium height, with long brown hair and green eyes. She was wearing a blue Air Force uniform."

163

Jake instantly recognized the description, but it couldn't be. She was dead. Jake shook his head. It wasn't her. "What did they ask you about in the interrogation?"

"Some bullshit about unauthorized soil samples, and genetic material at a FEMA dig I was at." Durard looked down at his bloody hands. "Where was the dig?" Jake asked inquisitively. "Southern Nevada."

Jake's eyes widened. He had the sinking feeling that events were all starting to come full circle. "You don't mean S-4, do you?"

"I'm afraid I can't divulge—" Durard started to quote FEMA regulations, then remembered where he had gotten by following orders. "Yeah, it was the hole in the ground that used to be Site-4."

"Why were they asking you about genetic material?"

"One of the guys I work with, Steve, found some interesting genetic samples in the dirt at the site."

Jake began to form a theory. "What kind of genetic material?" Durard didn't answer.

"What kind of material was it, Jim?"

"Man, I'm not going to talk about this with a complete stranger. You're going to think I'm nuts."

"I wouldn't worry about that. You're talking to the man who brought down S-4 in the first place."

"You're Jake Silver? Did you know you're on the FBI's ten most wanted list right now for domestic terrorism?"

Jake nodded, "Yeah, I heard that somewhere." Leaning close to the cell bars, Jake lowered his voice. "I need to know what you found. I want to

164

finally bring these sons a bitches down, so I need all the evidence I can get."

Durard understood. "The genetic material...well, it wasn't...." Durard was interrupted by the sound of a door opening. Captain Jannis strode into the detention block and stopped in front of Jake's cell. "Time to go see the colonel, Silver." Jannis spoke in a low gravelly voice. Sliding his key card through the slot. Jake heard the cell door unlock. "If you so much as breathe wrong, Silver, I will kill you." Jannis pulled his pistol from its holster and took two steps back from the cell. "Now step out slowly, and put your hands on top of your head." Jake opened the cell door, and slowly moved out. Lifting his hands up, he turned his back toward Jannis. "Very good, maggot. Now move. We don't want to keep the colonel waiting, now do we?"

Chapter Eighteen

Jake was handcuffed to a gray metal chair inside Anne's office. Anne was sitting behind her desk in front of a huge picture window, her long brown hair hanging loosely over her shoulders. Two soldiers stood at attention beside the entrance. Jannis loomed over Jake, casting his evil shadow across him.

Anne leaned forward and reset her elbows on her desk. She gazed ominously at Jake. "I have a very interesting proposition for you, Mr. Silver."

Jake smiled. "I thought you were dead. I watched Alex kill you."

Anne shook her head. "All that's irrelevant now. Obviously, I'm alive and well."

"You bitch," Jake laughed. "I liked you better when you were dead."

Anne smiled. "Would you like to hear my offer?"

"Sure," Jake answered sarcastically. "Hit me with it."

Jannis leaned over and grabbed Jake by the throat. "I'd advise you to show some respect." Letting go, Jannis retook his position behind Jake.

"You've heard of the virus that's hit the Southern United States?" Jake took a deep breath. "I remember hearing something about it."

Anne stood up, "Well, you get a chance to see it first-hand." Walking around her desk, she leaned against the front of it. "I need a patient to test our new antidote on, and the only way we can do that is by infecting you with the virus."

Jake's face distorted with rage. "You bitch. I

just realized what this is all about."

An evil smile flashed across Anne's face. "Why don't you tell me what you think is going on, Mr. Silver?"

"You staged this whole thing, the virus, kidnapping her and destroying Alex's lab, just so you could get me here and kill me."

"Well, someone has a bit of an overinflated ego. You honestly think I wiped out a third of the population in the Southwestern United States just to get your attention?" Anne laughed out loud. Standing up, she walked over to Jake. "I missed you, Jake. You always made me laugh." She leaned over and kissed him gently on the cheek. Straightening up, she moved back to her leather chair and sat down. "You are correct on one count, though."

"What's that?" Jake asked.

Anne crossed her legs. "I am going to kill you."

***

Alex sat up on her cell cot with sweat covering her body. She had tried to get some sleep, but images of Griggs kept flashing through her mind. She remembered the look of peace on his face as he died almost a year ago in S-4. She remembered the blank expression he had as he looked at her only hours before. Pain welled up inside her as tears streamed down from her eyes. *What has she done to my Jason?*

Alex heard the clank of another cell door opening. Quickly wiping the tears from her eyes, she curled herself up in the corner between the cot

167

and the wall.

A large guard stepped in front of her cell door. He tossed a small bundle of clothing into her cell. "Put these on, we'll be leaving in about an hour."

The pack of clothing landed right in front of her. Waiting until the guard had left, Alex scrambled down the floor and opened the bundle. It contained one black jumpsuit and a pair of standard issue military combat boots. Standing, she slid the jumpsuit on and zipped it up. *Anything is better than walking around the base in my underwear,* she thought. Sitting down on the edge of her cot, she pulled on the boots one foot at a time. She laced them up tightly, then slid back onto the cot to lie down.

Before she had time to delve into her thoughts, she again heard the clank of a cell door opening. Looking to her right, she stared out through the black steel bars and waited. A guard passed by the cell with a prisoner in tow. Alex jumped up and ran to the cell door. "Jake!"

Jake glanced to his left and saw Alex. "Oh my God, Alex! Are you all right?" Jake ran to Alex's cell and grabbed her hands. "They told me you had been shot!"

Alex nodded, "I was, but—"

The guard interrupted her. "Shut the fuck up, and get in your cell." He grabbed Jake by the back of the collar and pulled him away from Alex. "Jake, what's happening?"

"I don't know," Jake shouted as the guard pulled him down the hall.

"Jake! Major Griggs is alive!" Alex shouted. She waited. No response. *The guard must have put*

168

Jake in his cell already, she thought. At least she knew he was alive. She took great comfort in that fact.

***

"Pack your bags, Mr. Hollman."

"Pardon me, Colonel?" Hollman answered sheepishly.

"Our boys in research have found exactly what we're looking for." Anne strode into Hollman's personal quarters without even knocking. Hollman had been dead asleep on his bunk with all the lights out.

"What did they find, Colonel?" Hollman sat up.

"Another incident with the alien virus." Anne sat down on the edge of Hollman's bunk.

Hollman was wide-awake now. "Where did they find it?"

"North Carolina. Specifically, Roanoke Island."

The name rang a bell with Hollman. "Why does that sound familiar?"

"You know, the lost colony of Roanoke Island. It was one of the first English settlements in North America. The colony vanished without a trace between the years of 1588 and 1590."

Hollman snapped his finger. "That's right, but what does this have to do with our virus?"

"We believe the virus was used to kill the original colonists of Roanoke Island. There could very well be dormant traces of the virus still there."

Hollman appeared confused for a moment. "How do you know?" Anne smiled, "Nothing *ever* vanishes without a trace."

Chapter Nineteen

Jake sat on the edge of his cot staring through the cell bars at the wall outside. He was still wearing his leather jacket, a rumpled white t-shirt and a pair of blue jeans. Jake kept running the day's events over and over in his head. *Did Alex really say that? Did she really say Major Griggs is alive?*

Jake thought about the man who had helped him rescue Alex and Christina Anderson from Area 51, then bring down Site-4. He had watched Griggs die in Alex's arms after General Perry, the previous commanding officer of Area 51, had shot him. Perry had received his own justice in the end, though. The alien device at S-4 had completely obliterated Perry's body when it exploded.

Jake and Alex had been lucky to get out of the base at all. Jake couldn't understand how a woman in such an injured state could've made it out of the base before it exploded. *Alex had shot Anne*, Jake told himself. *How then was she alive?*

A knock on the bars in front of Jake startled him. Two guards stood with weapons trained on Jake. "Stand up," they commanded him. "It's time to go."

Jake complied. He was too tired to resist. He hadn't had any sleep in over thirty hours. Lifting himself off the cot, he stood up and walked toward the cell door.

The first guard slid his key card through the slot, opening the door. "Now, step out slowly with your hands on your head," the first guard commanded him. He watched as Jake followed his instructions. "Turn around." Removing a pair of silver handcuffs from his belt, he grabbed Jake's right arm and pulled it down behind his back and slapped the cuff over his wrist. Repeating the process with Jake's left arm, the guard made sure the handcuffs were snapped securely around Jake's wrists before letting go. Lifting up his rifle, he pressed the barrel into Jake's back. "Now move. You've got a long journey ahead of you."

***

Durard stared at the black craft sitting ominously in the main hangar of Area 51. It was one of several triangle shaped crafts housed there. Turning his head, he saw five black Apache style helicopters sitting in the back of the building. The hangar was gigantic, looking as if it had been carved completely out of the side of the mountain. The walls and roof were bare stone, while the floor was highly polished steel. Huge lighting fixtures hung from the ceiling that cast a strange glare across the building as the light reflected off the silver floor.

Two soldiers were escorting Durard across the bay toward the black triangle. They had his hands cuffed behind his back and they were leading him toward it. Activity was buzzing around the strange craft. Several technicians were performing final flight checks, while two men in flight gear were walking around the craft inspecting it.

The two soldiers stopped Durard in front of the craft. Grabbing his handcuffs, the second soldier unlocked them. After pulling them off, they quickly spun Durard around to face them. The soldier again snapped the cuffs around Durard's wrists, this time, his hands were in front of him.

Two members of the flight crew dressed in dark blue jumpsuits approached the soldiers and Durard from the rear of the craft. Thick black goggles covered their eyes, giving them an ominous appearance. Both men drew their weapons and aimed them at Durard. "We'll take the prisoner from here." The two soldiers nodded, saluted, then turned to leave.

One of the men stepped toward Durard. He was a taller, well-built man, with tightly cropped brown hair. "It is my job to make sure you get properly loaded and situated on the Aurora." He spoke with a deep scratchy voice. "If I give you an order, you will comply, or I will drag your ass up to twenty thousand feet and then throw you out of the plane with no parachute. Do I make myself clear?" Durard nodded. "Good, now let's go."

The two members of the flight crew began to lead Durard toward the Aurora. As they drew nearer, the craft appeared even more immense. A large ramp led up to a wide rectangular opening on the hull. Durard studied the craft as he began to walk up the ramp. It seemed to be one continuous piece of metal with no seams. It had no squared edges, just curves on its black skin.

As the three men entered the hatch, Durard quickly surveyed the cabin. It was long, just like a 747's, but quite a bit shorter. He estimated only about twenty seats total. The interior was sparsely decorated with the craft's steel ribs still showing along the inside of its silver hull. The seats were designed around practicality, rather than comfort. At the back of the cabin, a large map hung on the wall next to a wide door. Hundreds of small, white LED lights dotted the map in various locations.

The two men led Durard to one of the center seats. Pushing him into a seat next to the center aisle, they began to strap him in. After buckling the harness around his chest, the two members of the flight crew exited the cabin, leaving Durard sitting in silence, but only for a moment.

The two men re-entered the cabin, escorting a second prisoner. Durard instantly recognized the prisoner. "Dr. Robinson!" Durard yelled across the cabin.

Alex looked up to see Durard. "Jim! Are you all right?"

"Yeah, I—"

Durard was cut off by one of the men. "Shut up!" The man pushed Alex down into a seat near the front of the cabin.

The two members of the flight crew quickly strapped Alex into her seat. Alex tried to struggle, but was easily stopped by the two men. "What are you doing with us?" Alex screamed. "You have no right to do this to us!"

One of the men stood straight up and smiled. "We have the right to do anything we want to you."

***

Anne stood between Jake and the entrance to the hangar. Having changed into full combat fatigues, she wore a black jumpsuit and a pair of boots. Her hair was pulled back into a ponytail behind her head.

Two soldiers were escorting Jake toward the

hangar. They stopped just short of Anne. The men snapped to attention and saluted. "Here's the final prisoner, Colonel. He's ready to board."

"Very well," Anne responded. "Dismissed."

"Colonel?"

"I'll take the prisoner from here." She looked at the two soldiers angrily, "Dismissed!" The two soldiers turned to leave. Anne stepped closer to Jake and smiled. "I'm very glad you could join us this morning."

Jake looked away.

"Don't you understand your importance in this?" Anne placed her hand on Jake's shoulder.

"I understand that you're a deranged bitch who's going to kill us all," Jake spat back at her.

"You are the key to *saving* us all, Jake," Anne ran her hand down Jake's chest. "Sure, you'll most likely die in the process, but you'll save millions of lives."

Jake was skeptical. "If I die," he lowered his tone, "you're coming with me." Anne slapped him hard across the face. "You should be honored to be a part of my plan to save humanity."

"Save humanity?" Jake asked laughingly. "You're the one who released this goddamned virus in the first place! It's your fault humanity is dying!"

Anne took a step back, "I had nothing to do with the virus."

"My ass." Jake smiled. "From the first time I heard a report about the virus, I knew Area 51 was behind it. This has your signature all over it."

Anne laughed. "You are seeing conspiracies where there are none. Area 51 neither created the virus, nor set it loose into the populace," she smiled

174

and walked behind Jake. Running her hands through his hair, Anne rested her chin on his right shoulder. "In fact," she whispered in his ear, "it was because of you the virus was released."

Jake quickly stepped away from Anne. "You're incredible. I had nothing to do with this virus. I know that because I've been on the run from you guys for the past year. If I had released a virus, I think I would've remembered it."

"I don't think you understand." Anne stepped around in front of Jake. "You see," Anne pulled a cigarette out of her pocket and placed it in her mouth. "Part of Site-4's duties was to research and store hazardous chemicals. One of these particular chemicals was of extra-terrestrial origin. So, when you decided to destroy S-4 with the help of that damn alien device, you released this virus."

Jake laughed. "You're so full of shit."

"Am I?" Anne lit the cigarette and took a long drag. "After this virus was released, it basically just laid dormant in the Southern Nevada desert." Anne took another drag off of her cigarette. "Then it found a friend. The extra-terrestrial virus combined with a fairly common strand of influenza, creating a kind of super flu. This new strain became very active and moved into the Southern United States."

"You're out of your fucking mind, Anne!" Jake was yelling. "I am at no fault for anything except stopping the government from abducting and experimenting on the citizens of this country!"

"You can believe whatever you want, Jake, but the facts stand. If you had never destroyed S-4, the virus would never have been released."

"I didn't destroy the base! The alien device you

175

found in Egypt did!"

Anne took another drag off her cigarette, "Yes, but you're the one who activated the device."

"We could go in circles like this forever," Jake admitted. "The bottom line is I didn't have anything to do with this damn virus, so don't lay any of this shit on me!"

"I'm sorry you feel that way, but it's the truth." Anne took one final drag off her cigarette and dropped it to the ground. She began to crush it with the toe of her boot. "You are responsible for the virus, both you and Dr. Robinson. You will be held accountable, and you will be instrumental in containing this virus." Anne pulled her pistol from its holster and pointed it at Jake. "Now we need to get on the Aurora. We're scheduled to leave in less than half an hour." Anne stepped around behind Jake, "Move."

Jake began to walk toward the hangar entrance. He remembered being in this very same place over a year ago with Major Griggs, Alex and Christina. He remembered watching the huge mother ship that had crashed in the desert, rise up and destroy the hangar in a brilliant flash of energy. Stepping into the hangar, Jake was awed at the sheer size of the rebuilt bay. Anne pressed her pistol into Jake's back, pressing him further inside.

Jake caught sight of several large, black triangle-shaped crafts resting in the hangar. He instantly recognized them as the fabled 'Aurora'. He knew this craft was instrumental in Area 51's abduction process. The craft was capable of high altitude supersonic speeds, and was completely undetectable by all radar systems. It had no markings on any of its surfaces, except a line of collision lights that ran along the front edges of the craft. Jake guessed these lights could probably explain a majority of the UFO sightings that described a line of lights moving in a 'V' formation. Jake remembered the pilots and occupants of the Aurora, when on an abduction run, dressed as gray aliens to deceive the abductees. Jake estimated the Aurora was at least as large as a 747, or bigger.

Two members of the flight crew quickly made their way down the ramp and met Jake and Anne at the bottom. "Colonel," the first man spoke. "Flight preparations are almost finished. We should be airborne in about twenty minutes."

"Very good. Have preparations been made for my special guest?"

"Yes, Colonel. All is standing at readiness."

"Good," Anne smiled at Jake. "Back to work."

"Yes, Colonel." The two men stepped back up the ramp and disappeared into the hull of the ship.

Anne poked the barrel of her weapon into Jake's back again. "Up the ramp, Silver." Jake spun around ready to light into Anne. Before Jake could start, Anne had her gun against Jake's temple. "I don't want to have to kill you. Now get on board."

Jake stared into Anne's icy green eyes. He knew she wasn't bluffing. Turning around, he made his way up the ramp. As he passed into the cabin, he quickly caught sight of Alex. Jake rushed to her side. "Alex! Are you all right?"

Alex nodded, "I'm fine, Jake." Her voice was weak. "What happened to your gunshot wound?"

"I don't know. I think they healed me."

"Why?" Jake asked.

"That's not important right now." Alex tried to lift her hands, but they were restrained. "Jake, Jason Griggs is alive."

Jake let his head drop. "I heard what you said in the cell block, but it can't be true. We both watched him die."

"I know, but I've seen him. He's here at Area 51!"

Anne grabbed Jake by the shoulder. "That's enough of this little reunion, get moving, Silver."

Jake stood up. "I'll get you out of here," he promised Alex. Turning, he began to walk down the aisle, but spotted another person in a rear seat. Jake didn't recognize him, but guessing from the way he was strapped in, Jake knew he was a prisoner as well. Moving toward the rear of the cabin, Jake stopped just short of a closed door.

Anne quickly stepped around him and pulled her key card out of her pocket. Sliding the card through a small black keypad next to the door, Anne punched in a five- digit password on its alphanumeric pad. The door slid open revealing a huge white room. Stepping aside, Anne pushed Jake past her into the room. Once inside, Anne turned around and pressed a button on a similarly placed keypad, sending the door hissing shut.

Jake glanced around the room. Every surface was a glossy, shimmering white. It looked to him like a hospital room, complete with operating tables and banks of medical oriented computer monitors. Several men and women in white lab coats scurried about the room, prepping for the upcoming mission.

A woman with blonde hair and blue eyes caught sight of Jake and Anne, then quickly rushed over to greet them. "Colonel," she acknowledged Anne.

"Dr. Cisan, what's our status?" Anne asked.

Cisan was a tall, extremely good-looking woman by Jake's standards. Her short blonde hair just barely touched the collar of her white lab coat, while her blue eyes sparkled against her tan skin. She was wearing a blue button blouse with a black skirt under her lab coat. "Everything is proceeding according to plan, Colonel. Dr. Hollman will be joining us in about five minutes." Her voice was soft and sweet.

"Very good, Dr. Cisan. I'm placing Mr. Silver in your capable hands." Anne smiled at Jake, "I hope you take very good care of him."

Cisan nodded. "I will." She took Jake by the arm. "He'll be very safe here."

"Now if you'll excuse me," Anne turned to leave. "I have other...guests to attend to." Anne stepped to the door and quickly entered her pin number. As the door opened, Anne gave Jake one final look before she entered the cabin.

Cisan turned to Jake. "Mr. Silver, my name is Dr. Heidi Cisan, and I'm going to be in charge of your stay here. Dr. Greg Hollman will be joining us shortly, and he'll be conducting several experiments confirming that your body chemistry will be suitable to the virus'."

"That's very comforting," Jake laughed.

"Now," Cisan motioned with her hand toward the back of the lab, "if you'll follow me over to this side of the Med Bay, we'll start prepping you for the trip."

Jake pulled away from Cisan's grip. "What if I

refuse?"

Cisan smiled and lifted open her lab coat, revealing that she was wearing a side arm. "Then I will kill you."

"Point taken."

"Please, this way." Cisan pointed toward an examining table. Jake walked with Cisan toward the table. "Please take off your coat." Jake stripped his worn brown leather jacket and handed it to Cisan. She quickly deposited the coat on a small rack next to the examination table. Cisan motioned for Jake to sit on the table. "Would you please remove your shirt?"

Jake slipped off his shirt and tossed it on the same small rack that his coat inhabited. "I hope you have warm hands," Jake said jokingly. "Nothing worse than a doctor with cold hands."

Cisan wasn't amused. Grabbing a small plastic thermometer off a nearby table, she pressed it into his left ear and tapped a button on its handle. Waiting for the thermometer to finish, she looked over Jake's chest. "Bullet wound?" She pointed to a white scar on Jake's shoulder.

"Yeah, forty-four at close range. One of the many reminders from my time in the FBI."

The thermometer beeped, signaling the completion of its cycle. Cisan pulled it from Jake's ear and checked the reading. "Your temperature is normal." Placing the thermometer aside, Cisan placed her hand in the middle of Jake's chest. "Please lay down." Jake complied, slowly lying down on the sterile white table. Cisan momentarily turned away from Jake toward a small table. "Are you allergic to any medications, Mr. Silver?" She began to prepare a syringe. Dipping it into a bottle of a powerful sedative, she took quite a bit into the needle.

"No, I'm not allergic to anything," Jake answered.

Cisan quickly spun around and jabbed the needle into Jake's shoulder. "Good, then this won't hurt a bit."

Jake struggled, but it was too late, the yellow fluid had been completely injected into his system. "What the hell?"

"It's just a light sedative so we can run a few various tests." Cisan checked Jake's pulse on his wrist. "Your heart rate is beginning to slow a bit, you should be fast asleep in moments."

Jake's eyelids started to become heavy. "Why are you doing this to me?" he asked groggily.

Cisan continued to check Jake's pulse. "I'm just following orders."

Jake felt his body succumbing to the sedative. A strange sense of peacefulness passed over his body. Slowly, his eyes began to close and Jake fell unconscious.

***

Captain Jannis stepped through the hangar bay door to meet Anne. She was standing on the edge of the tarmac watching the sun begin to set in the west. Accompanying her was a large man with long blonde hair in black army fatigues. Jannis didn't recognize the man. "Colonel?"

Anne spun around to face Jannis. "What can I do for you, Captain?"

181

Jannis snapped to attention and saluted Anne. Anne quickly nodded at Jannis. He stood at ease. "We are ready to board, Colonel." Jannis looked over at the tall blonde man and was prepared to ask who he was, but suddenly caught sight of the man's rank insignia on his collar. Snapping back to attention, Jannis saluted again. "Sorry, Major, I wasn't aware of who you were."

"Captain Jannis, this is Major Griggs. He's recently been assigned to Area 51." Griggs returned the salute, but was confused at what Anne had said. "Pleasure to meet you, Captain Jannis."

"Likewise," the gruff man responded. Jannis motioned toward the Aurora. "We can begin boarding now. We estimate about five minutes until launch."

"Very good, Captain. We'll be joining you shortly."

"Thank you, Colonel." Jannis nodded, then turned to walk back to the Aurora. Anne turned to Griggs. Placing her hands on his shoulders, she began to speak very softly. "This is going to be a very dangerous, but important mission, Jason. I need you to be operating at one hundred and ten percent during it. Do you feel capable of that?"

Griggs nodded, "I'm ready, Colonel. You can count on me." Griggs looked down at his black uniform. "I may have been out of service for over a year, but I am still sworn to follow the orders of my commanding officer and protect the integrity of this country."

"Good, I was counting on that." Anne took a step back from Griggs, but continued to look him in the eyes. "There are going to be two prisoners on

182

this mission who are going to try and confuse you by telling you lies about your death and previous deeds. You have to stay focused and loyal to me. Do you understand?"

"Yes, Colonel, but why would these people do this to me?"

"There are people in this country who think our government is unjust. These people want to destroy everything we've worked for. They are nothing more than radical terrorists."

Griggs understood. "What is the nature of our mission, Colonel?"

"We are on a mission of mercy. A virus is ravaging the Southern United States. Our job is to try and find an original sample of the virus and create a cure." Anne slid her hand over Griggs' cheek, "We're trying to save the lives of millions."

"We're going to do a very good thing." Griggs felt a sense of pride in this mission. He had always wanted to help people. He knew that's why he joined the military in the first place, but something still felt wrong. His memories were still unclear. Anne had told him that his memory would clear up in time. Moreover, she told him that his amnesia was just temporary, but something still felt off. Especially about the woman he had met in the detention area, and about Anne. Griggs' just couldn't put his finger on it, yet.

"We need to get on board now." Anne began to lead Griggs toward the awaiting Aurora.

Griggs walked slowly behind Anne as they approached the huge black triangle. This craft also seemed familiar. "Colonel, why did you tell Captain Jannis that I had recently transferred here?"

"It's just easier that way," Anne kept walking. "I don't understand," Griggs admitted.

Anne stopped and spun around. She had an angry look on her face. "How dare you question your commanding officer?"

"I'm sorry, Colonel, but—"

"I don't want to hear it! I told you it was just easier that way, and that's more explanation than you needed in the first place!" Anne leaned close to Griggs. "Now, you get on that damned plane and you shut your mouth. If you feel like asking any more questions, think about how you'll feel going through a court-martial, and then a little well spent time in federal prison. Do I make myself clear, Major?"

Griggs snapped to attention. "Yes, Colonel. Crystal clear."

Chapter Twenty

There were no windows in the cabin of the Aurora, but Alex could feel the great ship taxiing onto the runway. She glanced around. Anne, Griggs and another unknown soldier had seated themselves in the back row near the map. Another man dressed in a white lab coat had entered the cabin, but had exited through the doorway at the rear of the ship. Alex could see the four pilots sitting in the cockpit through the open door at the front of the cabin. Two men and two women sat at the controls.

Alex listened to the engines whine as they began to power up. The g-forces slammed her back into her chair as the pilot gunned the huge jet down the runway. Alex felt squashed as the nose of the craft began to rise up and off the runway. She gritted her teeth as the jet lifted into the sky. Alex wished she could see outside to understand where they were.

The mighty jet finally leveled off. Because they hadn't designed the cabin for comfort, no sound insulation was added allowing the wind and engines to roar in everyone's ears. Alex turned around to see Anne, Griggs and the other soldier pulling on flight helmets with ear guards. Alex muttered several profanities under her breath.

***

Jake started to come to lying flat on his back from an uncomfortable and listless sleep. His eyes refused to focus as the drugs ran the remainder of their course through his system. His head felt like it was swimming in a thick fog. Jake tried to lift his arm to rub the sleep out of his eyes, but found he had been restrained to the table with leather straps. Turning his head to the right, Jake caught sight of Dr. Cisan standing over a bank of computers.

Cisan turned to look at Jake and smiled in surprise that he was awake. She turned and began to walk toward him. "Why are you awake, Mr. Silver?"

"Why am I strapped to the table?" Jake asked.

"It was for all of our protection," Cisan responded coolly.

"What?"

Cisan placed two fingers on Jake's neck and checked her watch. "Colonel Caroll told us that you are a very dangerous prisoner. We were just taking certain," Cisan searched for the correct word, "precautions." She took her fingers off Jake's neck, satisfied with his pulse.

"How's the patient, Dr. Cisan?" A voice boomed out from behind Jake.

Jake turned his head to see a tall dark-haired man walking toward him. "What the hell?"

Cisan handed the man a clipboard containing Jake's chart. "Everything checks out, Dr. Hollman. He seems to be completely compatible with the virus. He has no pre-existing conditions that would alter the virus in any way. He seems to be in perfect health, except for a bit of dehydration and sleep deprivation. We should be able to pull a perfect sample when the virus is integrated into his system."

Greg Hollman smiled as he read over the notes on the clipboard. "Very, very good." He flipped through several pages, then set the clipboard down next to Jake. "I want this man in perfect health by the time we reach North Carolina. That means well hydrated."

Cisan nodded. She signaled to a nurse on the opposite side of the Med Bay. The small female nurse dressed in blue hospital scrubs quickly made her way over to Cisan. "I want a saline IV started on this man right away." The nurse nodded, then went to her task. "Anything else, Dr. Hollman?"

Hollman thought for a moment, "No, that should do it for now. Just make sure our patient is kept comfortable. Millions of lives are counting on him."

Jake was beginning to tire of everyone talking to him about saving the lives of millions. No matter what happened a year ago at S-4, he held fast to the idea that he was not responsible for the outbreak of the virus, although his conscience was beginning to weigh heavily on him. *What if it is really my fault this virus is running rampant?* Jake wondered. *Am I truly the one to blame for the deaths of all those lives in the Southern United States?* The image of the sick man he saw in Las Vegas kept running through his mind. The man was in agony as he died. *He drowned in the fluids accumulated in his lungs. What a horrible way to go.*

Jake was snapped back to reality by a sudden sharp pain in his right hand. He looked over to see the nurse inserting a long silver IV needle into one of the veins in his hand. "You could've warned me," Jake scolded the young nurse.

"Sorry, sir. Just following orders." The woman tucked an errant lock of brown hair behind her left ear. Apparently of Hispanic descent, she had a light creamy brown skin tone. Behind her wire rimmed glasses, she had big soft brown eyes, and full, well defined lips.

Jake shook it off. He had been through much worse. "I didn't catch your name." The young woman smiled, "I'm really not supposed to be talking to you."

Jake looked around the large Med Bay. Hollman and Cisan had moved off to a row of chairs in the rear and were apparently discussing Jake's chart. "I don't think anyone will notice."

"My name's Faith, Faith Marin." Her voice was still filled with the exuberance of youth.

Jake guessed she was only in her mid-twenties. She didn't seem like the kind of person that would work at Area 51. Jake lowered his voice, so their conversation wouldn't be noticed. "How did you end up here?"

"On the Aurora, or at Area 51?" Faith asked. "Both."

"GI Scholarship. I wanted to be a doctor, but couldn't afford college. The Air Force seemed like the logical alternative."

"It seems odd," Jake started, "that a rookie would be positioned on one of the most sensitive bases in the world."

"I really hadn't thought about it that way," Faith admitted. "I signed up, went through boot camp, went to college and then got posted here."

"You mean this is your first posting?"

"Yeah."

Jake knew the military cutbacks had been severe, but still, a green behind the ears rookie assigned to Area 51? "Do you like it here?"

Faith shrugged. "It's a job, just like any other. I don't have any family or close relatives, so I don't mind not being able to leave the base."

Jake began to understand. The brass that controlled Area 51 didn't want family oriented people. It was easier to send an unattached person to a top secret base in the middle of the desert, than a person with a family. The unattached person would have no reason to leave, whereas the attached person would always be distracted with thinking about their separated family. "I'm sorry to hear that."

"It's no big deal." Faith wrapped one final piece of tape over the IV needle and tubing to keep it in place on Jake's hand. "There you go," she smoothed over the edges of the white translucent tape. "All finished."

Jake looked down at his hand. "You do good work, Faith."

"Thank you," Faith smiled. "So, you know my name, but I don't know yours."

"My name is Jake Silver, and apparently, I'm the reason millions of people are dead." Jake then realized his guilt was worse than he thought.

Faith looked confused. "What?"

"I'm the reason the virus is loose in the southwest," Jake admitted.

"I don't understand. How can that be? Dr. Cisan said you were in perfect health."

"I didn't have it and spread it, but I was the cause of it." Jake looked away from Faith. "I helped destroy the facility that stored the virus. By destroying it, I inadvertently released the virus."

The information suddenly clicked in Faith's mind. "You're Jake Silver? One of the terrorists that annihilated Site-4?"

Jake laughed uncomfortably. "My reputation precedes me."

Faith took a step back, horrified. "How could you do something like that? Against your own government?"

"Faith, you don't know about the circumstances behind—"

"I don't need to know anything from you, Mr. Silver." Faith shook her head. "You are a terrorist and I will have nothing more to do with you. If you speak to me again, I will inform the guards." Faith turned and quickly walked away.

Jake let out a sigh of exasperation. *I am a terrorist,* he thought, *and the cause of millions of deaths.* Jake rested his head back on the white table. The more he thought about it, the more he began to question his own motives. *Why did we feel it was necessary to bring down S-4, along with Area 51? We only wanted to stop the abduction process and rescue Christina Anderson and Alex Robinson. All because of two fathers I got wrapped up in this whole mess.* Jake felt a bead of sweat begin to roll down his forehead. *Jonathan Anderson, Christina's father, wanted to blow the whistle on Area 51 because they had been abducting his daughter and experimenting on her. Likewise, General Tom Davis, Alex's father, had contacted me and asked me to also rescue his daughter from Area 51. Alex had been detained when she found the Alien Device under the Sphinx in Egypt.*

Jake suddenly realized why. The mother ship

had implanted the thought in his mind after it had reclaimed the Alien Spacecraft, and demolished the main hangar of Area 51. *It was the will of the aliens that S-4 be annihilated, and we were just doing their dirty work.* Jake began to think deeper. *Maybe this was part of their plan all along,* Jake reasoned. Jake thought back to the alien device at S-4 they had recovered in Egypt. Its only purpose was to destroy. *Maybe they knew this virus was being contained at S-4, and by destroying it, the aliens knew the virus would be released....* Jake shuddered at the idea.

Chapter Twenty-one

"Sir, could you come take look at this?" A thin man with dark hair sat in front of his radar screen. The screen was casting an eerie green glow over his face. He untwisted his blue tie and tried to make it lie flat over his white, short sleeve, button up shirt. Adjusting his headset, he turned and shouted again, "Mr. McCall?"

A stout, older man worked his way across the control tower to answer the young man. "What is it, Dan?" McCall ran his thumbs up his black suspenders as he stood behind Dan.

Dan Rollan pointed to his radar screen. "I'm getting a very strange signal, sir." McCall leaned over to get a closer look at the screen. "What is it?"

"Every so often, I get a strange blip on my screen. I've been tracking it ever since it entered Texas air space." A large light green blip appeared on the screen again. "There it is!"

"It's probably just a passenger jet," McCall replied coolly.

"I've contacted every flight on that screen. It's not any kind of passenger jet or military craft that I've ever seen."

The blip reappeared. "It looks like it's about to cross the flight path of that passenger jet! Get on the horn now! I want that jet notified and moved immediately!"

Dan keyed the mic on his headset. "Delta one-two-niner, do you copy?" Dan waited a moment, "Delta one-two-niner, do you copy?"

"Go ahead, tower." A male voice crackled over Dan's headset. "We read you."

"We're tracking a bogey heading your direction. Suggest you increase your altitude to avoid the craft."

"Roger, tower, increasing altitude."

Dan waited in silence for a moment. "Delta one-two-niner, do you have a visual on the bogey?"

"Negative. Don't see a damn thing up here. We have a thick cloud cover—"

"Delta one-two-niner?" Dan asked nervously.

"Wait a minute, tower," a more excited voice returned over Dan's headset. "We can now see the bogey."

"Do you recognize the bogey?" Dan waited, "Delta one-two-niner, do you recognize the bogey?"

"Nothing we've ever seen, tower." The voice now seemed a little frightened. "What does it look like, Delta one-two-niner?"

"Can't really tell, tower, just looks like a huge black triangle. It has what appear to be two rows of running lights trimmed to side of the craft." Static began to interrupt Delta's signal. "If I didn't see the outline of the ship, I would swear it was a group of jets flying in tight formation."

Dan and McCall gave each other looks of disbelief. "Delta one-two-niner, what's the bogey's attitude?"

More static began to fill the transmission. "Tower, the bogey is changing course."

"Affirmative Delta one-two-niner, unidentified craft is now on a collision course!

Evasive maneuvers now!" Static hissed over the speakers. "Delta one-two-niner, do you read me? Delta one-two-niner?"

The static gave way to choppy reception. "Craft

193

heading...for us...bright lights...intense...no time...turn...."

"Get them back! Get them back!" McCall shouted frantically, sweat dripping from his forehead.

Dan became frantic. "Delta one-two-niner! Delta one-two-niner, are you there? Do you read me, Delta one-two-niner?"

The static suddenly cleared. "...Intense white light passing, I'd say, within ten feet of the nose! Tower, do you read?"

"We copy, Delta, go ahead." Dan breathed a sigh of relief.

"It was the most incredible thing I've ever seen, tower," excitement filled the captain's voice. "We all saw it, tower. It was right in front of us!"

"Delta one-two-niner," Dan hesitated and looked at McCall. The large man nodded. They both knew the procedure. "Do you want to report an unidentified flying object?"

Silence ensued.

"Delta one-two-niner, do you want to report a UFO?" Dan repeated.

"I don't think so," Delta replied. "I wouldn't even know where to begin."

"Neither would I," Dan admitted. "Neither would I, Delta one-two-niner. Tower, out."

***

Anne keyed the mic on her flight helmet. "Captain?"

"Yes, Colonel?" The pilot's voice replied over the speakers in Anne's flight helmet.

Anne smiled. "You enjoyed that, didn't you?"

The pilot laughed. "That's an affirmative, Colonel."

Chapter Twenty-two

Less than an hour later, the Aurora was hovering over a small wooded area on Roanoke Island, North Carolina. This area was known as the Outer Banks. It was a string of islands that formed a barrier between the mainland of North Carolina and the Atlantic Ocean.

The pilot began to reduce the power to the engines, bringing the Aurora slowly down to Earth. Darkness hung over the island like a thick blanket. Ever since they had entered North Carolina air space, the pilot had been monitoring all civilian and military air traffic channels. No one had seen them land.

Anne unbuckled herself and stood. Griggs and Jannis quickly followed suit. She motioned for the two to join her in the Med Bay. Sliding her key card through the slot next to the door, the three stepped inside and were quickly met by Hollman and Cisan. She guided the groups over to a table on the far side of the bay.

"We need to determine our battle plan," Anne spoke with graveness that none of her crew was accustomed too. "The recovery of a sample of the virus should be relatively easy. Dr. Cisan can brief us on that."

Cisan stepped to the front of the group and addressed the men. "From what our research shows, a skeleton was found by John White on his second trip to Roanoke Island in 1580. This skeleton was preserved by the expedition and brought back to England for study, and possibly identification." Cisan flipped over several pages in her notebook, then continued. "This skeleton was later returned to America, and currently resides on display at Fort Raleigh, right here on Roanoke Island. Our researchers seem to believe this skeleton still contains traces of the alien virus in a dormant state."

"Getting to that skeleton will also be very easy." Anne turned to her right, "Captain Jannis."

Jannis stepped forward. "We've had operatives infiltrating Fort Raleigh for the past twelve hours. Security is generally low, with the exception of a few motion detectors scattered throughout the facility, but nothing I would deem as spectacular or impenetrable." Jannis turned to Anne, "We should be in and out before anyone even notices."

"Very good." Anne looked at Hollman. "Dr. Hollman, how much time are you going to need to extract a sample of the virus from the skeleton?"

A shocked look grew over Hollman's face. "Colonel Caroll, this isn't one of those run in and take a blood and urine sample missions. I'm going to need time to study the skeleton."

Anne didn't fully comprehend. "Well how long do you need, Doctor? Five minutes? Ten minutes?"

"No," Hollman answered sternly. "More like twenty-four to forty-eight hours."

"What?"

"I'm sorry, Colonel, but that's the best I can do. I need time to work on this."

"I can't give you twenty-four hours, Doctor. We're on a tight schedule here!" Hollman's face turned red. "Millions of lives are hanging in the balance here, Colonel. You'll give me the fucking time I need to complete my research!"

Scowling, Anne stepped toward Hollman. "You

197

son of a bitch! How dare you speak to me like that?" Anne turned to Major Griggs and snapped her fingers. "Kill him right now." Griggs pulled out his sidearm and pointed it at Hollman's head.

Hollman stumbled backward, shocked at the unfolding events. "Colonel?" Griggs looked at Anne. Shaking her head, Anne stepped out of the way. "I'm sorry, Dr. Hollman, but you fucked with the wrong woman this time." She placed her hand on Griggs' shoulder. "The order stands, Major." Griggs started to squeeze the trigger of his weapon, but began to struggle against himself. He couldn't do it.

"Kill him, Major Griggs! That's an order!" Anne was shouting in his ear.

Cisan quickly jumped in front of Hollman. "No! You can't kill him! He's the only one who knows how to create the vaccine!"

Anne grabbed Griggs' weapon and shoved the barrel into Cisan's face. "Get out of my damned way, Dr. Cisan, or I'll kill you both."

Cisan held fast. "Please, Colonel, rethink your action! This mission would be for naught without Dr. Hollman!"

Anne stared straight into the eyes of Dr. Cisan for what seemed to be an eternity. Anne finally lowered the pistol and handed it back to Griggs. "Seems you've gotten a reprieve today, Dr. Hollman." Anne pushed Cisan out of the way, and stood toe-to-toe with Hollman, "But if you ever speak that way to me again, Doctor, I will kill without hesitation." Anne spun around and walked back toward Griggs. "I've come to a compromise."

Hollman perked up his ears, "Yes, Colonel?"

"You may have the skeleton for as long as you like, if," Anne pointed a finger at Hollman, "If you figure out a way to create a convincing mock skeleton to replace the original."

"Consider it done, Colonel." Hollman was very pleased.

Anne turned back to Griggs and Jannis. She tried to hide her scorn for Griggs' actions before. "You two are going to be in charge of the infiltration. I want you two outside right now to recon the base. Report back to me when you're ready."

"Yes, Colonel." Jannis and Griggs saluted and turned to leave. "Hold tight for a second," Anne announced.

Griggs and Jannis stopped cold. "Colonel?"

Anne turned to look at Hollman. "How much time would it take to create your fake skeleton, Dr. Hollman?"

"Give me about an hour, Colonel," Hollman said with the utmost respect. "Captain, Major," Anne turned back to Jannis and Griggs, "Your mission has been delayed by one hour. I want you in full night-time combat gear and back here to collect Dr. Hollman's skeleton ASAP. Dismissed." Anne turned to Cisan. "You have a lot of guts, Doctor. I respect that in a woman."

"Thank you, Colonel."

Anne stepped close to Cisan and lowered her voice, "but if you ever do that again, no one will ever find your body."

"Yes, Colonel Caroll."

Anne turned and quickly walked out of Med Bay toward the cabin, while Cisan briskly strode away, shocked at what she had just been told. Just behind a row of cabinets, working on several blood samples taken from Jake, Faith stood quietly and in complete horror of what she had just seen and heard. She looked over at Jake lying silently on the table. *What the hell is really going on here?* Faith wondered nervously.

***

Tyler came to in total darkness. Reaching around himself, he found he was in the small coffin shaped room again. A moment of despair passed over him. The round device had been removed from his forehead, allowing pain and hopelessness to grip him.

Reaching down his body, he felt he was fully clothed. He reached forward to the small recess in front of him and began to press the center button, but stopped. The last time he had pressed the button, he had been dumped into a water-filled room. He didn't want to go through that again.

He thought about the aliens and the tests. *Why did they keep calling me the "savior"*, Tyler wondered. *What do I have to do with anything?*

"You will play a very important part in helping all of humanity," the voice once again sounded in his head.

Tyler had become very tired of the aliens having access to his thoughts. "Why me?"

"You were chosen very carefully."

"I don't understand any of this!" Tyler's mind became frantic. "One minute, I'm up looking at the stars, then I'm here being tested on!"

"Your importance has been predetermined, as was our role in this." The alien voice had taken on a more sympathetic tone, but it still sounded very mechanical.

"What do you mean 'predetermined'?" Tyler asked.

"We have looked into your future and ours. The events have taken place just as we saw them foretold. It is not our place to ask why, but to heed the call of fate."

"I don't believe in fate," Tyler stated solemnly.

"That does not matter. We have done what was required of us, now you must do what is required of you."

"I still don't understand. Why is—"

Tyler was cut off as a red light began to filter in, while a high-pitched squeal started to emanate from all sides of the coffin. Tyler tried to cover his ears, but the sound was too intense. Closing his eyes, Tyler began to scream in hopes he could drown out some of the noise. Looking down, he saw the bottom of the box begin to slide open. Suddenly, the bottom shot open and Tyler found himself falling quickly into the blackness.

Glancing down, he saw the ground shooting up at him at an incredible speed. Tyler began to fall end over end, out of control, but before he impacted, a cool, blue light enveloped him and slowed his descent. Rolling onto his back, he stared up at the huge extra-terrestrial saucer hovering above him. He watched as the treetops slowly rose around him, and the ground loomed ever closer. Tyler felt his body being manipulated into an upright position by the blue light. His feet softly touched the ground as the blue light disengaged. Quickly looking up, Tyler saw the UFO begin to rise, then shoot out of sight in a flash.

The night was silent around him. He listened as the leaves in the trees softly rustled, and crickets chirped in all directions. Immediately, his body was assaulted by the dense humidity. Living in a dry climate like Nevada, Tyler wasn't used to it.

Glancing around, Tyler didn't recognize where he was. He was standing in the middle of a worn two-lane road. The night sky was clear and the moon was shining brightly, giving him quite a bit of light to see by. Around the road, the foliage was thick and still very green although it was fall, or at least Tyler still hoped it was fall. *How long was I gone?*

Turning around, Tyler stared up the road. It took a sharp curve and went out of sight past a group of trees. In the other direction, the road took another turn into the distance. Looking in both directions one last time, Tyler set off toward the east. *There has to be a town around here somewhere. I need to call home. My friends and family must be worried sick about me.* Picking up his pace, Tyler broke into a brisk jog as he rounded the corner.

Chapter Twenty-three

An hour and a half later, Jannis and Griggs had made their way through densely layered woods and residential areas to find Fort Raleigh standing quietly in the light of the silvery moon. The fort, constructed in 1585, was built with logs from huge trees that were arranged vertically like a fence. The tops had been sharpened into a point to prevent attackers from climbing the walls. Inside, there were several small, one room barracks, and a large two story building that used to house the city's hall and local government, but now was a tourist information center and colonial museum. The massive gates, also constructed of tall vertical logs, had been closed for the night, to prevent thieves from doing exactly what Jannis and Griggs were here to do.

Both men were still dressed in their standard Area 51 black fatigues, but Jannis had a large black sack draped over his right shoulder. Neither man was carrying their assault rifles, but both had their pistols strapped tightly to their sides. Jannis had even secretly attached one grenade on his belt, just in case.

Stopping in a patch of brush just outside the front gate, Griggs pulled an infrared sensor out of a small pouch on his belt. Holding it up in front of him, he clicked a series of buttons with his thumbs and waited for the device to work. A small, full color LCD screen at the top of the rectangular device fluttered to life. He quickly swept the sensor over the fort. With this, he could see right through the walls and find out if there was anyone inside. He stopped, when he found a single heat signature.

"Looks like one guard in the main building," Griggs said as he analyzed the readings. "Seems like he's sleeping on the job," Griggs noted when he saw the red blur on the screen seem to put his feet up on a desk.

"Good. Shouldn't be a problem," Jannis responded in a whisper.

"Intelligence reports this place has a backdoor." Griggs pointed at the corner of the fort. "Let's move." Griggs stood and stowed the sensor back on his belt.

Briskly jogging around the edge of the massive wooden structure, Jannis spied a metal door. It had been cut into the middle of several logs to give employees access without having to enter through the front gates. Quickly signaling for Griggs to take a look at the door, Jannis stepped out of the way and dropped the sack on the ground. Griggs gave the door the once over. It had no visible signs of alarms or trip wires, it just seemed to be a plain, locked door. Grabbing the handle, Griggs pulled hard on the door to see how sturdy it was. To his surprise, the door burst open, it's wooden frame shattering into thousands of splinters. The two men stood silently outside the fort waiting for any alarms to sound. All was quiet.

Looking through the doorway, Jannis searched for the guard. He was sure they had at least set off some kind of silent alarm and the guard would be coming to check it out. Jannis waited a few moments longer, picked up his black sack of bones, then rushed inside the door. He found himself standing in the courtyard of the fort. The ground was still dirt covered with the occasional patch of hay. Apparently, they had tried to keep the authenticity of the base.

Griggs quickly joined Jannis inside the courtyard. Pulling the infrared sensor out of his belt pouch, he clicked it on and scanned the main building. "The guard is definitely on the second floor of the main building, and he hasn't moved since we entered. He's either asleep or incompetent," Griggs stated. Turning to Jannis, Griggs pointed at the black sack. "Where's the real skeleton located, Captain?"

"Second floor, main building," Jannis replied quickly.

"Understood." Griggs thought for a moment. "We're going to need to incapacitate that guard if he stands between us and our target."

"Why not just kill him? I could put a quick bullet in his brain, executioner style. He'd never make a sound," Jannis stated coldly.

"We need to avoid that kind of situation, Captain," Major Griggs responded quickly. "I want full safeties on this mission! Is that understood, Captain Jannis?" Jannis nodded. The two men began to creep toward the entrance of the main building.

***

Colonel Caroll?" Faith asked timidly.

Anne turned around from her position in the Med Bay. She had been overseeing a few of the numerous tests on Jake. "Yes, Nurse Marin?"

"May I ask you a question?"

"Yes."

"In private?" Faith wondered.

Anne sighed. She didn't have time to answer rookie questions. "Fine, if you make it quick."

Faith nodded and led Anne over to a secluded corner of the Med Bay. "Colonel, I just have a question regarding procedure."

Anne nodded impatiently for Faith to ask the question.

"Why are we stealing the skeleton?" Faith started off slowly. She knew she was treading on thin ice with Colonel Caroll. "It's officially the property of the US government, right? Couldn't we just ask for it? I mean, if the fate of millions is riding on this, don't you think the Federal Government would willingly allow us access to the remains?"

Anne turned and began to walk away. "I don't have time for this."

"Colonel, please! I deserve an answer!"

Anne stopped abruptly, then quickly spun around to face Faith. "You deserve nothing." She said scornfully to the younger woman. "I am the Commanding Officer on this mission and I alone deem what information you 'deserve' to know."

"I apologize, Colonel, but I've begun to question our methods." Faith was mustering all the courage she had. She quickly noticed her hands shaking.

"You're questioning my methods? What gives you the right?" Anne stepped behind Faith and began to shout in her ear. "Do you know how long it takes for Congress to approve an operation like this? It has to be officially sanctioned by the President! I am acting to save lives! I don't need

206

some fucking rookie questioning the way I conduct my missions!"

Faith began to tear up, "But, Colonel—"

"Do you not know when to quit?" Anne walked around in front of Faith again and clasped her hands behind her back. "The US Government is a dinosaur," Anne said calmly. "They couldn't pass legislature to pull their heads out of their asses! I know what I'm doing," Her tone turned darker, "And if I have to do that without the approval of the government, so be it." A strange look passed over Anne's face. It was a look of evil pleasure. "I can't wait to see their faces when I...." Anne let her sentence trail off.

Faith stopped cold as she stared at the bizarre expression on Anne's face. "Colonel?" she asked in a shaky voice.

Anne realized what she had just said. She quickly tried to cover her own tracks. "I am here to save lives. Are you going to be a part of that, or aren't you?"

"Again, I apologize, Colonel. I was completely out of line." Faith started to backdown. She knew this was a battle she couldn't win.

"Yes, you were." Anne leaned close to Faith. "I should bust you back down to Private First Class and send your cute little ass packing." Anne considered what Faith had heard and chose her next words carefully. "I won't, though. I need every member of this team working at peak capacity and that means you, too. I'm here to help, but I need everyone here to do that effectively."

"Yes, Colonel," Faith said eagerly. She was just glad she hadn't received the same treatment Dr.

Hollman did earlier.

"You have work, Nurse Marin?" Anne asked quickly. "Yes, Colonel."

"Then snap to it," Anne commanded. Turning around, Anne walked back to her position next to Dr. Cisan by the examination table.

Faith wiped the tears from her eyes. *Here to help my ass,* she thought as she returned to work. Pulling on a pair of latex gloves, she slipped a sample of Jake's blood into the separator. *I don't think we're here to help at all.* Faith hit the start button on the separator and stepped back. A question popped into her mind. *Why is a colonel in charge of one of the most sensitive bases on Earth? I thought only generals were responsible for them....*

***

Griggs and Jannis slipped easily through the front door to the main building. They had been standing outside for close to five minutes as Griggs checked his readings on the infrared sensor one last time. The inside was decorated rustically, with photos and trinkets from early settlers and colonists. The walls seemed to be made of wood paneling, as darkened knots in the wood were scattered about.

To the right side of the massive room stood a glass case with a cash register sitting quietly on top of it. The case was filled with stickers and souvenirs from Fort Raleigh and Roanoke Island. Griggs read one of the stickers. "I found the missing colony on beautiful Roanoke Island, North Carolina. Cute."

The rest of the room was wide open. To the left side, Griggs caught sight of two doors marked "restrooms", but to the rear through a small archway, was the door that led upstairs. Griggs motioned quietly with his hands for Jannis to check out the door. Griggs still wondered why he still hadn't heard any alarms. Looking up into the corner, he saw a small white box attached to the ceiling. He instantly recognized it as a motion detector. A small green LED light was glowing in the bottom right hand corner. Griggs reasoned they couldn't be active, since a guard was in the building.

Jannis returned and gave Griggs the "all clear" signal. The two men made their way through the arch and onto the stairs. Griggs began to breathe easier. Their mission was going off without a hitch.

***

A white and blue police car slowly pulled into the parking lot of Fort Raleigh with all its lights off. The cruiser rolled to a stop in front of the massive wooden gates. Two police officers dressed in black and blue uniforms quietly stepped out of the car. The driver keyed the radio he wore on his shoulder. "Dispatch, car twenty-six responding to the silent alarm at Fort Raleigh. We're just going to take a look around."

His radio crackled with static. "Roger that, twenty-six. You guys be careful," responded a female voice on the other end.

The driver, a tall black man with a mustache, grabbed a long black flashlight out of the car and closed the door. His partner, a slim white male that looked to be fresh out of the academy, did the same.

Clicking on their flashlights, they began to make their way around the rear of the Fort.

The younger man stopped and turned to his senior officer. "Lieutenant Shapp?" Shapp listened to the younger man as he continued to look around the fort.

"Yeah, Bobby?"

"Why would someone break into Fort Raleigh?" Bobby asked in a voice still maturing.

"Probably a prank, or some damn teenagers just looking for a thrill," Shapp answered in a deep voice.

Bobby nodded and quickly caught up with Shapp. "You don't think this could be dangerous?"

Shapp laughed. "You're a Goddamned officer of the law now, Bobby. Show some sack!" Shapp patted the younger man on the back. "This is probably just a case of vandalism, relax."

"Yeah," Bobby laughed nervously. This was only his third day on duty. He hoped someday soon he would be as knowledgeable and as comfortable on duty as Shapp.

He knew from just around the precinct that Shapp was a ten-year vet of the police force, and a well-respected officer at that.

Shapp was the first to notice the rear door open. He stepped closer and examined the frame. He quickly keyed his radio. "Dispatch, we have signs of a forced entry here at Fort Raleigh. Requesting backup immediately. The perps could still be inside."

***

210

Jannis and Griggs hit the top step and stopped. Poking his head around the corner, he saw the guard was indeed sleeping. The man had his hat tipped forward over his eyes, and his feet up on the display case in front of his chair. He was an older man, with silver hair and a slight beer belly developing. His tan security uniform was tight on him and his pants were one size too short.

Griggs cautiously stepped into the room and looked around. It was a long, thin room that seemed to him like attic space had been used to create it. Several display cases lined the walls. Each had an example of local wildlife in it. Jannis quickly joined Griggs in the room and moved over behind the guard. He began to pull a small bottle of chloroform out of his belt pouch, when a board on the floor creaked loudly as he stepped on it.

The guard shot straight up in his chair and stared at Griggs. Jannis dropped the bottle of chloroform and yanked his pistol out of his holster.

The aging security guard scrambled to his feet and grabbed his nightstick off his belt. He hadn't yet spotted Jannis. "Hold it right there!" He pointed his black nightstick at Griggs, "Just what do you think you're doing?"

Without warning, Jannis grabbed the guard by the back of the collar and pressed the barrel of his gun to the man's head. "Whatever we fucking want to, old man." Before Griggs could stop him, Jannis had pulled the trigger, sending the guard crumbling to the ground.

***

211

The two police officers quickly slammed their backs to the wall of the main building and pulled their weapons from their holsters. Shapp hit the talk button on his radio. "We have shots fired! Repeat, we have shots fired at Fort Raleigh. We need backup now!"

***

"Why the fuck did you do that?" Griggs yelled angrily at Jannis. "You could've just drugged him and been done with it!"

Jannis smiled. "What can I say? I love my work."

"You son of a bitch!" Griggs grabbed Jannis and slammed him against the wall with a strength even he didn't know he had. "He was an old man who didn't deserve to die! We're here to save lives, remember?"

Jannis tried to push Griggs off him, but was unsuccessful. Griggs was firmly holding him against the wall. "Colonel Caroll authorized deadly force at the start of this mission. I was just doing what I deemed necessary to complete this mission!"

Griggs stared angrily at Jannis. "We don't have time for this right now," Griggs admitted. Letting go of Jannis, Griggs took two steps back. "We need to finish the mission. Find the skeleton, Captain."

Jannis straightened his uniform and saluted haphazardly. Grabbing the black sack off the floor, he set off down the hall toward where the skeletal remains were being contained.

Griggs turned around and stared at one of the display cases. It housed a stuffed blue bird that was perched on a dry branch. The case was decorated as if the bird were still alive in the wild. Griggs stared at the bird, marveling at its blue feathers and rust colored breast. A strange light began to flash in the room. Quickly spinning around on his heels, Griggs ran to the window and looked outside. Several police cruisers were parked in front of the fort with their red and blue lights flashing. Several of them were using their spotlights to search around the fort.

"Shit," Griggs muttered to himself. He jumped away from the window just as a spotlight crossed it. "Captain, we've got company," Griggs shouted down the hall.

Jannis ran up the hallway to stand next to Griggs. "What?" Griggs pointed toward the window. "Silent alarm."

Jannis peeked out the window and saw all the police stationed outside the front gate. "Fuck! We need to get the hell out of here!"

"Are you finished?"

"Almost. Just a few more bones to switch, then we can get the hell out of here."

"Get to work," Griggs commanded. "It's way past time for us to leave."

***

Shapp keyed his radio again. "We're inside," he began quietly. "We're going to try and make it into the main building to take a look around."

"Roger, twenty-six. Caution is advised," a male voice answered back. Shapp tapped Bobby on the shoulder. "You ready, kid?"

Bobby nodded. "As ready as I'm going to get."

Shapp smiled. "This'll just be a walk in the park," he assured the younger officer. Holding his pistol tightly in his hands, Shapp slid a few inches closer to the front of the building along the wall. "Stay behind me," he instructed. Peeking his head around the corner quickly, he scanned for any signs of the intruders. Pulling his head back around, Shapp signaled for Bobby to follow his lead.

Stepping around the corner, Shapp moved swiftly toward the front door. Stopping short, he waved his hand for Bobby to stop. Listening for a moment, Shapp tried to pick out any noises that might indicate the suspects were still inside. The silence was deafening. An eerie stillness had passed over the fort, only being broken by the alternating red and blue lights flashing. Counting to three in his head, Shapp jumped in front of the door with his pistol aimed inside. Nothing.

Stepping inside the front door, Shapp pulled his large black flashlight from his belt and clicked it on. He quickly surveyed the room for any signs of damage or stolen product. He was suddenly startled by a dull thud. He knew it came from upstairs. Moving further into the main building, Shapp began to walk toward the main stairs.

***

Griggs had pulled the body of the old security guard into the corner and dropped it. He noticed a small gold band on the man's left finger. *Damn,* Griggs thought. *He was married.* Reaching into the guard's coat pocket, he pulled out a small brown leather wallet. Opening it, he saw several pictures of

214

the security guard and his family, and what looked like photos of either his children or his grandchildren. Griggs lowered his head and tossed the wallet onto the floor next to the man. "I'm sorry, old timer."

Standing up, he turned to see Jannis racing toward him with the black sack slung over his shoulder. "Finished, Major," Jannis reported.

"Good. Let's get the hell out of here." Griggs watched Jannis head for the door leading to the stairs and quickly followed. The two soldiers had reached the top stair when a bright light caught them both off-guard.

"Freeze!" Shapp yelled. "Don't move a muscle or I swear to God I'll shoot!"

Shapp took a few steps up the stairs. He still had his flashlight aimed into both suspect's faces and his gun trained directly on them. "Throw down any weapons you may have and put your hands up!" Bobby slowly followed behind Shapp.

Jannis turned his head toward Griggs. "We don't have time for this, Major." Before Griggs knew what was happening, Jannis had pulled his pistol from his holster and shot the first police officer on the stairs. Griggs wrapped his arms around Jannis and started to fumble for Jannis' weapon. In the chaos, Jannis and Griggs had spun around so Griggs' back was now to the staircase.

Shapp cried in agony as the bullet ripped through his upper chest. He fell to the ground and began to roll down the steps toward Bobby. Stopping at the bottom, he looked up at the younger man through bloodshot eyes. "Get out of here. Get back up."

"No!" Bobby cried. Without thinking, Bobby aimed his weapon recklessly and pulled the trigger. Shots rang out as the bullet careened off the wall. Pulling the trigger again, he heard one of the suspects slam into the wall and let out a moan of pain.

Jannis ducked back into the doorway and pulled Griggs with him. He quickly assessed the wound. The bullet had only grazed Griggs' neck, but had sliced through his carotid artery. Blood was spurting in all directions. Grabbing Griggs' hand, Jannis pressed it hard to the neck wound to try and stop the bleeding. He knew if they didn't get back to the Aurora within ten to twenty minutes, Griggs would bleed to death.

Peeking around the corner, Jannis saw the younger officer trying to pull the older officer's body off the stairs and out the door. He had dropped his pistol on the stairs. Standing up, Jannis quietly made his way to the middle of the staircase and trained his weapon on the younger man. "Hey, kid."

Bobby looked up to see Jannis standing directly over him. Tears were streaming down Bobby's face. "Don't kill me! Please don't kill me!" he cried.

"Sorry, but I've got orders." Jannis pulled the trigger.

***

Most of the police officers outside the fort had heard all the gunshots. They were all in ready positions with their weapons drawn, while they ducked behind the doors and bodies of their vehicles.

216

Two officers at the back were arguing over procedure. "I will not authorize the use of tear gas! I have two of my men inside!" The first man yelled. He was wearing a brown sport coat and black slacks with a brown tie. His brown hair was slicked back, and his badge was tucked into the breast pocket of his coat.

"It's not your decision to make, Detective," argued a man in dark blue fatigues. "I am the captain of the SWAT team, and I make the call in these situations!"

"Fine, but it's your ass on the line, Captain." The detective turned and retook his position behind his black SUV.

The captain whistled and pointed toward his men. "I want tear gas in there now!" Several officers, dressed in the same dark blue fatigues, quickly pulled canisters of gas off their belts. Pulling the pins, they tossed them over the tall walls of the fort and into the center of the compound. The noxious yellow smoke began to shoot out, filling the fort with gas.

***

Jannis had lifted Griggs to his feet. Using all his strength, Jannis led Griggs down the stairs. He knew Griggs was quickly going into shock from the massive blood loss. Griggs lost his footing, sending the two men stumbling down the steps. The two men and the black sack landed with a thump at the bottom. Standing up, Jannis lifted Griggs and the black sack off the floor. Griggs' left side and left hand were covered with a deep red blood.

Stepping over the two dead policemen, Jannis made his way toward the front door. Outside he saw the thick yellow smoke covering the courtyard. "Shit," he muttered under his breath.

Propping Griggs up against the wall, Jannis dropped the sack next to him and began to quickly search the room. On the far wall behind the cash register, he spotted a row of handkerchiefs hanging there. Grabbing the first two, he caught himself staring at the sewn in shape of Roanoke Island. "Why would anyone want to buy this crap?" he wondered.

Tying one around his mouth and nose, he did the same for Griggs. Grabbing a third off the wall, the tied it on Griggs' neck to try and stop some of the blood flow. Wrapping his arm around the other man's shoulders, Jannis began to lead them toward the front door. "They're using gas. Only take shallow breaths if you have to," Jannis instructed Griggs.

Stepping out into the courtyard, the smoke began to burn Jannis' eyes and throat. Pulling Griggs quickly, the two headed for the back door. He hoped no police officers had taken up shop outside. Peering through the still open door, he saw nothing out there. Going as fast as he could while pulling Griggs, Jannis made it outside the compound. Pulling the handkerchief off his mouth, he took a deep breath of fresh air.

Quickly, the two began to retrace their steps back to the Aurora. Jannis stopped at the front edge of the fort and looked around. All the police officers, including the SWAT team, had donned gas masks and were beginning to open the two massive front gates. Looking down, Jannis remembered he had one grenade attached to his belt. Removing the grenade, he pulled the pin with his teeth and lobbed the small black ball toward the police officers. The grenade slammed down on the hood of one of the police cruisers.

Two officers simultaneously spotted the device land and quickly began to run in the opposite directions. "Grenade!" they yelled loudly. "Grenade!" The other officers heeded the warning and began to scatter.

Jannis pressed himself and Griggs tightly to the wooden walls as the grenade exploded. The force from the explosion rocked the fort walls and the police outside. Turning around the corner, Jannis stared at the destruction that he had just wrought. Police cruisers were on fire and bodies lay everywhere.

Pulling Griggs with him, the two men disappeared into the brush on their way back to the Aurora. Behind them lay a smoldering battlefield.

Chapter Twenty-four

Jannis dumped Griggs onto one of the examination tables in the Med Bay. There had been of flurry of activity since they had returned from the mission. Doctors Hollman and Cisan quickly went to work on Griggs on Anne's orders, leaving the bag of bones lying unattended on a nearby table. Griggs writhed in pain as they began to operate.

Anne grabbed Jannis and took him aside. "What the hell happened, Captain?" Jannis snapped to attention. "We encountered unexpected resistance, Colonel."

"What do you mean?"

"The police arrived just as we were completing our mission at Fort Raleigh, Colonel."

Anne rolled the information around in her brain for a moment. "How was the local law enforcement alerted to our operation?"

"As far as we can figure, Colonel, we must've tripped some kind of silent alarm." That was the last thing Jannis wanted to tell Colonel Caroll.

"You tripped an alarm?" Anne threw her head back and laughed out loud. "You two are both members of Special Forces. You've trained for operations similar to this your whole career, and you tripped an alarm at a local tourist shop? That's damn funny."

Jannis began to laugh with Anne. "It is rather funny—"

Anne stopped laughing quickly and began to tear into Jannis. "No, it's fucking not funny! What the hell is the matter with you two?" Anne grabbed Jannis by the collar and pulled him close to her. "I

didn't send a couple of rookies out there, did I?"
Anne paused for a moment to let the question sink
in. "No, I thought I was sending a couple of
seasoned Special Forces veterans!" Anne let go of
Jannis' collar and stepped back. She tried to
compose herself. After all, she was talking to one of
her best men. "How did Major Griggs get
wounded?"

"There was a fire fight between us and the
police, Colonel. One of the policemen got off a
lucky shot that injured Major Griggs." Jannis kept
himself completely composed and at strict attention.

Anne's face filled with rage again. "Were any
of the officers killed?"

"Yes, Colonel."

"How many?"

Jannis took a moment to try and tally the totals.
"I am unclear on that, Colonel. I would say at least
ten to twelve police officers were killed in the
ensuing battle."

"Jesus Christ!" Anne shouted. Taking a step
back, she turned her gaze away from Jannis. "I can't
even look at you right now, Captain Jannis. Please
tell me that you recovered the skeleton."

"Yes, Colonel. The skeletal remains were
recovered." Jannis beamed with pride. Ann pointed
toward the door. "Get out of my sight."

"Yes, Colonel," Jannis responded, then made
his way out of the Med Bay.

Anne turned around to look at the commotion
in the Med Bay. Hollman and Cisan were still
feverishly working on Major Griggs. Taking a step
closer, Anne peered in on their work. "How's the
patient, Doctors?"

Cisan stopped for a moment to address Anne. "We're not sure how much blood he lost, but we'll try and stitch him up."

Faith stood at the rear of the Med Bay watching quietly as the events unfolded. She peered over at Jake, who was lying unconscious on a second examination table. No one was attending him. Making up her mind, she reached into a nearby drawer and palmed a small silver device and hid it in her hand. Picking up a clipboard, she walked over to Jake and began to conduct a routine exam on him. She stood with her back to the rest of the doctors and Med Bay personnel.

Lying the clipboard down on a table next to Jake, Faith pressed the end of the silver device against Jake's upper left arm. Tapping a small button on the end of the device, she heard a small snap followed by a quiet hiss. Jake's eyes suddenly shot open. Forgetting he was restrained, he tried to sit up on the table. Faith pressed him down, and quickly placed her hand over his eyes. "Hold still, Jake."

"What happened?"

"Dr. Cisan gave you a heavy dose of anesthetic to keep you asleep. I just used a stim to wake you up." Faith replied quietly, still acting as if she was completing the exam. "Pretend you're still unconscious.

Jake had plenty of experience in that department, so he knew his portrayal would be fairly accurate. "Why?" Jake asked.

"Let's just say that I have my own motives that don't coincide with the Colonel's." Faith began to loosen the straps that were restraining Jake. "I'm going to make you a deal. I'll do everything I can to get you out of here, if you take me with you when you escape."

Jake nodded slightly. "Deal."

"I'm only going to loosen the straps enough for you to slip out of them, okay?" Faith dug into the front pocket of her nurse's uniform and pulled out a small pistol. She slipped it into Jake's back pocket. "I've just given you a weapon." She turned around to check the progress of the doctors on Major Griggs. They were setting up an IV with blood packs on it to try and replenish his supply. "Now that they have the skeleton, they're not going to stay long here on Roanoke Island. They should begin preparing for take-off once they've stabilized Major Griggs' condition."

Jake shot opened his eyes. "Who did you say?"

"Major Griggs. He was apparently wounded on the mission," Faith replied, unaware of the two men's past history.

"Griggs?" Jake turned his head to try and catch a look, but saw only the back on the doctor's backs.

"You're unconscious, remember?" Faith turned Jake's head back to look at her and closed his eyes. "Listen to me, that's not important right now." Faith picked up the clipboard and began to check off items on a list. "When they take off, everyone will have to be cleared from the Med Bay into the cabin. That'll be your chance to get up and out of here. In the back, there is a hatch that leads to the cargo bay. Once inside the cargo bay, you'll be able to easily parachute out of the ship. I'll meet you there after take-off, understood?"

"Wait," Jake interrupted. "I have another friend

on this ship. She's strapped into a seat in the cabin. Her name is Dr. Alex Robinson."

"I don't know if I can save her."

"We have to. Without her, there's no reason to escape," Jake said sternly. Faith thought for a moment. "There might be a way—"

"There must be a way."

Faith placed the last mark on the checklist. "I'll see what I can do." She turned to walk away.

"Thank you, Faith."

Faith smiled and continued on her way. She had no idea how she was going to be able to get this woman back into the Med Bay. Placing the clipboard back in its place on one of the counters, she went back to work. Suddenly, an idea hit her.

***

Alex and Durard sat alone in the cabin, still strapped into their seats. They had not spoken a word or moved a muscle since they had arrived in North Carolina.

Alex had seen a soldier dragging Griggs onto the Aurora. Both men were covered with blood. She feared the worst for Griggs. *I don't want him to die again.* Alex was torn inside as she thought back to when she first saw him again inside Area 51. Alex felt as if all of her dreams had come true to see him standing there alive and well, but then he rejected her. She couldn't understand why. *Have they brainwashed him?* But then another more important idea troubled her mind. *How can he possibly be alive?* Alex was brought out of her thoughts when she felt a light touch on her shoulder.

"Excuse me," a pretty young Hispanic woman said. "Yes?" Alex answered.

"Are you Dr. Alex Robinson?"

"Yes," Alex replied, unsure of what to expect next.

"My name is Faith Marin, and I'm a nurse here on the Aurora." Faith leaned a little closer to Alex's ear, "And I'm here to rescue you."

Alex's eyes widened. "What?"

"I'm working with your friend, Jake. We've got a plan to escape, but time is critical, so please, just listen."

Alex nodded.

"I'm going to give you this hypo." Faith pulled a small silver tube out of her pocket and placed it in Alex's hands. "When the Aurora is ready to take off, give yourself an injection in the wrist. There is a chemical inside that will make you appear to have had a heart attack. During this, you're going to feel like hell, but you're going to be all right." Faith turned to see if anyone was listening. "I'll be sitting in the seat directly across from you, so when this takes effect, I'll be the first one to look at you and take you back to Med Bay. Once there, just follow Jake and I."

"What if one of the doctors wants to take a look at me?" Alex asked nervously. "That shouldn't be a problem. I've got everything all figured out," Faith smiled. That didn't make Alex feel any more comfortable with the plan. "All right, but what about Dr. Durard over there?"

"Jesus, what is it with you people? I'm sticking my neck out here and you want me to rescue everyone on the plane!"

"Please."

Faith turned to look at the man strapped into his seat a few rows back. "Okay." Faith stood up. "Remember the plan, okay?" Alex nodded.

Turning, she began to walk toward Durard. He looked up at her cautiously. "My name is Faith and I'm here to help. Follow my lead."

Durard nodded.

Faith rushed over to Durard and began to check his vitals. "I need help!" she yelled. "This man is very ill! Help!" Durard quickly understood and began to play along. He began coughing as loudly as he could and holding his throat. Faith began to unstrap Durard from his seat. "Someone, help me, this man is choking to death!"

Two members of the flight crew rushed into the cabin and began helping Faith lift Durard out of the seat. "What happened?" one man asked.

"I'm not sure," Faith said. "I was just walking by and this man started to choke! He could be having an allergic reaction to something. We need to get him back to Med Bay immediately!"

Alex, who was watching the whole thing, turned around in her chair and smiled. *Faith is a very brave and daring young woman,* Alex thought as she slid the small silver tube between her left leg and the seat cushion.

Chapter Twenty-five

Close to two hours later, all the doctors and nurses had made their way into the cabin and taken their seats. Griggs had been patched up the best they could within the limits of the technology on the Aurora. Durard had been strapped to one of the four remaining exam tables and given a dose of muscle relaxer to try and stop his throat from swelling shut due to his fake allergic reaction, and Faith had taken the seat directly across from Alex, just as she had promised.

Alex listened to the mighty engines begin to power up as the Aurora prepared for take-off. All the flight crew had taken their seats and the main hatch was closed. Alex knew it was now or never. Sliding the silver tube out from under her leg, she pressed it to her left wrist and tapped the button on the top. A warm sensation began to flow up her arm as the drug entered her blood stream. Quickly sliding the tube into one of the pockets on her black jump suit, she began to prepare herself for what was about to happen.

Beads of sweat began to roll down her forehead as she felt her heart begin to slow. Terror passed over her. *Maybe this wasn't such a good idea,* she thought, but it was too late. The drug gripped her body and pain shot from her heart. Alex keeled over in her seat.

Taking her cue, Faith quickly unstrapped herself and jumped to Alex's aid. Pressing her fingers to Alex's throat, she tried to detect a pulse. Her pulse was very weak. Faith began to unbuckle Alex. "Dr. Hollman, this woman is having a heart attack!"

Hollman looked up in surprise. "What did you say, nurse?"

"This woman is having a heart attack!"

Hollman began to unbuckle himself. "We need to get her back to Med Bay STAT!"

"There's no time, we're about to take off," Anne cut in.

"I'm already up, Colonel. I'll take her and begin emergency treatment," Faith offered.

Anne thought for a moment. "Very good. Make it so."

Faith tried not to smile. Her plan was working just as she had hoped it would. Lifting Alex out of her seat, Faith stumbled up the aisle toward the door to the Med Bay. Grabbing her key card out of her pocket, Faith slid it through a slot next to the door. Holding Alex up as they walked through the door, Faith pressed several buttons on the pad on the inside of the Med Bay. The door hissed shut. Grabbing a fire extinguisher off the wall, Faith slammed it into the keypad, effectively destroying it and locking the door.

Faith pulled a silver tube out of her pocket and pressed it to Alex's neck. Tapping the button, Faith sent the counter agent into Alex's blood stream. "You should be fine in about five minutes," she assured Alex.

Sitting Alex on one of the exam tables, Faith turned her attention to Durard. She quickly made her way over to him and began to loosen his restraints. "Are you good enough to go?"

Durard nodded as he sat up. "Just a little groggy, but I'm okay."

Faith ran over to Jake, who was already sitting up and undoing the restraints on his ankles. "Are you ready?"

Jake undid the last strap and stood up. "Ready as I'll ever be."

The four felt the mighty jet begin to lift into the air. Faith ran toward the back of the Med Bay. Sliding her key card through another slot, the door to the cargo bay hissed open. "We've got to hurry. If we take too long, we'll be too high to parachute out!"

Jake ran over to Alex and lifted her up. "Let's go."

***

Anne was sitting quietly in her seat next to Jannis. She was thinking about Alex's heart attack. Her eyes suddenly widened. All the prisoners were in the Med Bay. Anne keyed the mic on her radio. "Abort the launch!"

"Colonel, what's happening?" Jannis asked.

Unbuckling herself, she turned to Jannis. "Captain, the prisoners are trying to escape!"

Jannis quickly tossed off his harness and stood. Running to the door of the Med Bay, he pulled out his key card and slid it through the black slot next to the door.

Nothing happened. He tried it again with the same result. "Colonel, the door's been jammed!"

"Then force it open! I want those sons a bitches now!"

***

Faith stopped a moment while she was pulling on her parachute. "We're not lifting off. Something's happened!"

Jake dropped his parachute and ran toward the controls for the cargo bay hatch. "They're on to us. We need to make a break for it!" He slammed his fist into the open button. Yellow warning lights began to flash around the bay as the huge door began to slowly open.

Durard was standing next to Faith watching the door creep open. "Is it always this slow?" Durard moaned.

Faith shrugged. "Don't know. Never actually saw it open or close before."

"What?" Durard shouted.

Jake, still holding Alex around the waist, stepped in between the two. "That's not important now. We need to get off of this plane." The door suddenly stopped about half way down. "They must have an override in the cockpit." Jake watched as the door began to close. "We've gotta go now! Run!"

Alex shook her head. "Jake I can't do this. I'm not ready."

"We don't have a lot of time to get ready, Alex," Jake stated. "It's now or never."

"I'm still really woozy from the drug Faith gave me. What if I land wrong? I could break my leg, or worse, my neck!"

Jake held Alex tightly in his arms. "I'm not going to lose you, or let you get hurt," Jake said in a very sensitive voice. Jake thought for a moment, "We'll jump together. I'll be with you all the way

230

down."

Alex turned to watch the door slowly closing. She knew Jake was right. This could be their only chance to escape. It had to be now. "Don't let go of me, Jake."

Jake smiled. "Why would I do something like that?" Jake took Alex by the hand and turned toward the door. He looked at the two other members of his team. "Ready?"

Durard and Faith both shook their heads no. "Good, let's go."

All four hit a dead run onto the Cargo Bay door. Faith skidded to a stop at the end of the door. "It's too far to jump!"

"Do it!" Jake tore past her and flung himself and Alex into the air. Durard quickly followed suit.

Fear gripped Faith's body. She had always been afraid of heights. Taking a deep breath, Faith watched the door she was standing on come closer and closer to closing.

It was now or never. From behind her, Faith heard the cargo bay door hiss open. Turning, she saw Jannis and Anne charging inside with their weapons drawn. Jannis pulled the trigger sending a bullet careening past Faith's head. Without even thinking, Faith twisted around and leapt off the edge of the door.

Anne and Jannis reached the door just as it snapped shut. She turned to Jannis angrily. "Take every man you have. I want every single one of those prisoners found before dawn."

Jannis saluted. "Yes, Colonel." He turned and began to walk briskly out of the cargo bay.

Anne stared at the cargo bay door. Anger

welled up inside her and she felt like she was going to scream. *Think they can escape from me? I can't wait until I see the look on their faces when Captain Jannis brings them back.*

Chapter Twenty-six

The four hit the ground hard. Rolling onto his back, Jake looked up at the twenty feet they had all just jumped. Shaking his head, he lifted himself up on his knees. Looking around, he saw the other three members of his party scattered about. Durard, who was slowly lifting himself off the ground, had landed wrong and might have broken his left wrist. Alex had hit right next to Jake, and had only jarred her ankles a bit. Faith was quickly pulling herself out of a patch of bushes she had landed in.

Once all three were on their feet, Jake looked up at the Aurora. "They're not taking off, Faith."

Faith shook her head frantically. "We need to go! Colonel Caroll and Captain Jannis saw us escaping."

"That means they're sending a team to look for us as we speak," Durard interjected.

Jake agreed. "We need to stick together, and we need to get the hell off this island."

The foursome hastily made their way deeper into the woods and brush that surrounded the landing site. Weaving in and around the dense foliage, they tried to put some distance between them and the Aurora. Alex stumbled over a rock and fell.

Motioning for Faith and Durard to keep going, Jake quickly knelt down beside her. "Are you okay, Alex?"

"Yeah," Alex nodded. "It's just this damned humidity. I'm having a real hard time catching my breath."

After living in the south for so long, Jake

233

wasn't even affected by it. Helping Alex up, he patted her on the back. "You'll get used to it. Let's catch up with the others." Alex smiled as she stood up. Looking behind them, Jake spotted several searchlights coming their direction. "Damn. Run!"

Jake and Alex sprinted away from the lights. They caught up with Faith and Durard a few moments later. They had stopped to catch their breath. Jake snatched Faith and Alex seized Durard. "We just saw the search party. They're after us right now!" Alex shouted.

"Maybe I should've rethought this plan," Faith admitted as she ran.

Tree branches whipped across their skin, leaving long red welts as they ran. They weren't even trying to miss the bushes, just running right through them. Turning his head around, Jake again saw the searchlights still behind them. Tearing through the foliage, they found themselves standing in the middle of a two-lane road. Alex and Durard quickly crossed over, but Jake stopped. He saw a pair of headlights looming in the distance. *We needed an advantage to put some distance between us and the search party, and this could be it*, Jake thought.

Grabbing Faith, Jake laid her down on the highway. "Act like you're injured."

"What?" Faith asked, confused.

"I'm going to get us a ride. Lie still!" Jake stepped back into the brush and waited. He could hear the search party looming ever closer. The crunch of their footsteps became louder and louder. Pulling the small pistol that Faith had given him out of his back pocket, Jake readied himself.

A tan sedan screeched to a stop in front of Faith. The driver, a younger man in jeans and a T-shirt, jumped out of the vehicle to check on Faith. Kneeling down, he placed his hand on her wrist to check her pulse. "Lady, are you alive?" he asked in a distinctly southern drawl.

Moving steadily out of the brush, Jake lifted the small pistol high in the air. Once behind the man, he delivered a sharp blow to the back of the man's head. The man toppled over onto Faith, unconscious. "I'm sorry, buddy," Jake said as he pulled the man's body over to the side of the road. Helping Faith up, Jake motioned for the others to get in.

Durard and Faith climbed into the backseat, with Alex sitting shotgun and Jake driving. Grabbing the gear shifter on the still running car, Jake slammed the shifter into drive and mashed the gas pedal to the floor.

Jannis burst out of the foliage and saw the tan sedan peeling away. Lifting his rifle, he clicked off the safety and fired. A spread of bullets scattered over the rear of the car and shattered the rear windshield.

"Get down!" Jake yelled as shards of glass flew into the car's cab.

Three more men jumped out onto the road next to Jannis and began to fire at the fleeing vehicle. Jake tried to keep his head down as he piloted the car haphazardly along the road. Hitting the first corner, Jake skidded off the road. The passenger side hit a large tree, crunching in the side panels. Alex screamed as the jagged interior of the door cut along her leg. Faith, also on the passenger side, quickly leapt out of her seat and onto Durard's lap as the panel dented in.

Cranking the wheel hard, Jake pressed the gas pedal to the floor. The vehicle made a terrible screeching sound as it pulled away from the tree and back onto the road. Checking his rear-view mirror, Jake saw Jannis and his men approaching.

Durard turned to look out the window. "Go now!"

"I'm going!" Jake yelled as the car spun around the corner.

Jannis fired off a final shot as the battered tan sedan sped off. Jannis tossed his rifle to the ground in anger as he watched the two red taillights shrinking into the distance. "Damn!" he shouted. "Colonel Caroll isn't going to like this." Turning around, Jannis looked at his men. "Let's get back to the Aurora."

The foursome began to relax in the car as Jake put more and more distance between them and the search party. Jake checked his rear-view mirror again. There was nothing but darkness. Jake finally allowed himself to take a deep breath. "I think we're clear," he announced.

Alex placed her hand on her bleeding right leg. "Nice driving, Evil Knievel."

"How bad is it?" Jake asked.

"Just a little scratch," Alex stared at the at least one inch deep gash in her leg. She knew it was worse than just a scratch. "I think I'll still be able to walk just fine." She began to apply pressure to the wound. "I need to get to a hospital to be sure, though."

Jake nodded, "Everyone else okay?" Durard

236

laughed. "Yeah, fantastic."

Faith was still sitting in Durard's lap. She had wrapped her arms around his neck and was smiling broadly. "Well, I think my plan worked!"

"I think your plan was a major disaster, Faith." Jake snickered, "But it worked."

"Jake, look out!" Alex screamed.

Jake snapped his head forward just in time to see someone standing in the middle of the road. Cranking the steering wheel hard to the left, Jake sent the car skidding off the road. Turning off the engine, Jake jumped out of the car and ran toward the middle of the road. Jake's eyes widened when he saw a teenager lying flat on his back. "Are you okay, son?" Jake knelt down next to him.

Lifting himself onto his elbows, the young man shook his head. "Yeah," he began to rub the back of his head. "I guess I shouldn't have been walking in the middle of the road at night."

Jake stood up and helped the young man up. "What's your name?"

"Tyler."

"Well, Tyler, do you live around here?" Jake asked, dusting his back off. Tyler shook his head. "I don't even know where here is," he admitted. "What happened?"

"Nothing I want to talk about." Tyler's mood turned very dark as he turned and began to walk away.

"Wait, Tyler!" Jake reached out and grabbed the young man by the shoulder. "Are you sure you're okay?"

"No, man. I'm not okay." Tyler stepped close to Jake. "You're going to think I'm insane, but,"

Tyler stopped to consider his next words. "I was abducted by aliens."

"What? I thought we ended that program!" Jake stamped his foot on the ground. Turning around, Jake motioned for Faith to join him on the road. Placing his hand on Tyler's shoulder, Jake looked into the young man's eyes for any signs of stress.

Faith joined Jake at Tyler's side. "What is it?"

"Are the brass at Area 51 continuing with the 'Uber-Soldier' Project?" Jake asked. "How did you know about the project?" Faith asked.

Tyler looked confused. "What project? What does Area 51 have to do with this?"

"Tell me, Faith! Are they continuing with the project?"

"I don't know," Faith admitted. "The last thing I heard about the project is that it died about the same time General Perry did."

"Who is General Perry, and what the hell is this 'Uber-Soldier' Project?" Tyler yelled.

Jake turned to Tyler. "The 'Project' was designed to harvest the best genetic samples and use them to create a kind of super soldier. They used the whole UFO phenomenon to their advantage," Jake explained.

"They would come in the middle of the night and use high tech equipment and aircraft and abduct people," Faith continued. "They made it seem like these people were being abducted by aliens, when in truth, the flight crew would just wear rubber alien masks, and dose the abductee with a chemical that would give them hallucinations. The combination of the hallucinogen, masks and the advanced technology on the Aurora made a very convincing encounter with aliens."

Tyler shook his head. "No. That's not what happened to me! The aliens, the UFO, the experiments, they were all real!"

Jake nodded. "Aliens do exist, Tyler. I've seen them, but they don't go around abducting people. The US Government does."

Faith stepped in. "There hasn't been an actual alien since the 1940's."

"How would you two know?" Tyler asked.

Jake laughed. "I've been abducted by aliens and she works at Area 51," Jake said while pointing at Faith. "My name's Jake, and this is Faith. Over there in the car is Dr. Robinson and Dr. Durard."

"Do they work for Area 51 too?" Tyler asked.

"No, Dr. Durard works for the Federal Emergency Management Agency, and Dr. Robinson is an Archaeologist and UFOlogist." Jake said as he looked at the beaten tan sedan.

"I'm sorry to break this up," Faith interjected, "but we really need to keep moving."

"You're right. Let's get going." Faith turned and began to walk back to the car.

Jake turned to Tyler, "You need to come with us, kid."

"Why should I come with you?" Tyler asked.

"Because there's a lot of weird shit happening here, and I have this strange feeling that you're a part of this somehow." Jake took a step closer to Tyler. "We can help you understand what happened to you, and you can help us."

Tyler didn't respond.

"Come on, what do you say?" Jake asked with his hand outstretched.

Tyler didn't know what to think, but at least he had someone who understood what he was going through. "All right, I'm in."

"Let's get going." Jake said. Turning, the two strode back to the car. Tyler had to climb in the back seat between Durard and Faith. The crunched in door on the passenger side reduced the back seat by about a quarter, so all three were packed in very tightly.

Kicking the car into gear, Jake piloted it back onto the road. He looked over at Alex, who was still cradling her wounded leg. "Are you all right?"

Alex nodded in obvious pain. "I need to get to a hospital, Jake."

"I know. We're going." Jake said as he flattened the gas pedal to the floor.

Chapter Twenty-seven

Anne slammed her fist against the bulkhead in the cargo bay. Pacing back and forth, she stared angrily at the group of soldiers standing at attention in front of her. She walked near the men pointing her finger, then stopped. Turning around, Anne walked away and began to pace again. The soldiers remained at attention, unblinking.

Anne spun on her heels and charged toward the men. "What the fuck were you doing out there?" she screamed. "I could've sworn I only had professionals with me!" Anne began to pace again. "You let all three of our prisoners escape with one of our nurses!" Anne walked over to Jannis, who was standing on the far left of the group. "Captain Jannis," she started in a harsh tone. "Do you have any explanation for this?"

"The prisoners had commandeered a vehicle, making it impossible for us to pursue on foot, Colonel." Jannis answered matter-of-factly.

"Well, how did they get the chance to get a vehicle?" Anne sneered. "If you had been on their asses like I had commanded, Captain," she leaned close to Jannis, "then they wouldn't have had a chance to commandeer a fucking vehicle!"

"Yes, Colonel. Sorry, Colonel."

Anne took a step back and looked at the rest of the men. "I want the prisoners found. Dismissed." All the men turned to leave the cargo bay. "Not you, Captain Jannis. I would like a word in private with you."

Jannis stopped and quickly snapped to attention. "Yes, Colonel?"

Anne stepped behind Jannis and leaned her mouth close to his ear. "This is the second time in about as many hours I've had to reprimand you for failing. Why is that, Captain?"

"I don't know, Colonel."

"I think I know why." Anne moved around to face Jannis. "I think it's because you're a fuckup." Anne delivered a swift upper cut to Jannis' midsection. Jannis doubled over, but quickly tried to regain his composure. "Why do I keep placing my trust in you, when I know you're a fuckup?" Anne kneed Jannis in the groin, dropping him to the floor. "Why can't you do anything right?"

"I'm sorry Colonel," Jannis moaned from his knees.

"Stand up," Anne commanded him. Reaching down, she grabbed Jannis by the collar and lifted him up. "I said, stand the fuck up, Captain!"

Jannis tried to pull himself to attention. "Yes, Colonel."

"I'm going to give you one more chance, Captain Jannis."

"Thank you, Colonel Caroll."

"Don't thank me yet, Captain." Anne pulled her sidearm from its holster and cocked back the trigger. "Do you see this, Captain?"

"Yes, Colonel," Jannis swallowed hard.

"I'm giving you a very specific mission, Captain Jannis. It's your job to track down Jake Silver and Faith Marin and kill them. Do you understand? I want you to kill them on the spot."

"Yes, Colonel."

"If you fail," Anne pressed her weapon to Jannis' head, "I will hunt you down and kill you with this very gun." Anne uncocked the hammer on her pistol and returned it to its holster. "I don't want to see you again until you can tell me that Jake and Faith are dead. Is that understood?"

Jannis nodded. "Yes, Colonel. I won't fail you again."

"I hope not for your sake, Captain Jannis. Dismissed." Anne watched as Jannis saluted, turned, and exited the cargo bay. Walking over to the bulkhead, Anne slammed her fist into it in anger. *Jake Silver will not make a fool of me again,* Anne swore to herself. Lifting a small black radio off of her belt, she keyed the talk button. "Captain Mathen?"

"Yes, Colonel?" Mathen answered back.

"Prepare the Aurora for take-off. I want us in the air within the hour."

"Yes, Colonel. Destination?" Mathen asked.

"Take us back to Area 51. Dr. Hollman has a lot of work to do with the skeleton."

"Understood, Colonel. Mathen out."

Anne slid the black radio back onto her belt. Walking toward the cargo bay hatch, she pulled out her key card and slid it through the slot next to the door. The door hissed open revealing a bustling Med Bay. Stepping inside, she swiftly made her way to the side of Griggs' exam table. He was still asleep. Dr. Cisan was busy checking his vitals. "How does it look, Doctor?"

Cisan shook her head. "I won't be sure until I get him into Medical back at Area 51. His condition seems to be stabilized, but he has lost a lot of blood."

"What about the transfusion?" Anne asked.

"It's like filling a bottle that has a hole in it with water." Cisan checked the white bandages around Griggs' neck. "We've patched him up the best we could, but Dr. Hollman and I still think there's some internal bleeding. The bullet did strike the major artery in his neck."

"Is he going to live?" Anne asked nervously. "I can't say," replied Cisan.

"Damn," Anne muttered under her breath. Running her hand over Griggs' chest, Anne turned and walked away. Torment passed over her body. *Jake just keeps hurting me. Soon though, I will exact my revenge.*

***

Jake ran his fingers through his brown hair as he sat in the lobby of the University of North Carolina's Hospital. They had arrived in Chapel Hill about an hour ago and gone straight to the hospital. Jake knew there were perfectly good hospitals in Raleigh and Durham, but Alex had insisted she be taken to the University of North Carolina. Jake hadn't wanted to argue with her.

Looking across the plush waiting area, Jake noticed Faith and Tyler talking softly while Durard was trying to get some sleep. Durard had slipped down onto the couch so his head was resting on the back of it and his feet were sprawled out across the floor. Jake wondered what Faith and Tyler were talking about.

Standing up, Jake stretched his tired body as a yawn escaped his mouth. He couldn't remember the last time he had gotten a good night's rest. *Probably well over a year ago.* Turning around, he took a step out of the waiting room. There was a long hallway that led right to left in front of him. He could see the doors on both sides, but it still seemed very long to him. Across from him stood the check-in station. Jake had carried Alex in his arms through a pair of double doors and up a flight of stairs to that spot. They had admitted her immediately when they saw the condition of her right leg. There was no one currently inside the station.

Turning back around, Jake noticed a coffee machine sitting in the corner of the waiting room. Stepping across Durard's outstretched legs, Jake made his way over to it. Grabbing a small white Styrofoam cup off the table, he lifted the hot pot of coffee and poured the thick black liquid into his cup. Placing the cup to his lips, Jake sipped at it, slowly feeling the warmth flow through his chest. Taking another sip, he felt the caffeine begin to energize his system.

A doctor suddenly pushed past Jake while making his way to the coffee pot. The doctor, a scruffy looking man with medium length brown hair and a brown beard, poured himself a tall cup.

"Don't you guys have a coffee maker back in your offices?" Jake asked, just trying to make conversation.

"Yeah," the doctor said in a nasally voice, "but mine's all the way up on the third floor, and I really didn't want to go that far." The doctor turned around and walked out of the waiting room.

Jake suddenly had a sinking feeling about the doctors here. Shaking it off, he took another sip of his coffee. Looking over to a row of four chairs on the far side of the waiting room, he saw that Faith and Tyler were still talking. Curiosity overwhelmed him. He took a seat next to Faith. "So, do you mind if I butt into this conversation?" Jake asked cordially.

"No, not at all," Faith responded cheerfully. "We're talking about Area 51 and alien abductions."

Jake suddenly lost his interest.

"It seems that Tyler here is quite the expert on such matters," Faith added. Tyler was beaming with delight that an older woman was talking to him, and seemed interested. "Did you know," Tyler started, "that there's a system of tunnels that connects every military base on this continent?"

"That's preposterous." Jake said. "Why would the US Government need a system of tunnels, and what would they be used for?"

"That's the thing. The US Government doesn't use the tunnels." Tyler smiled. He loved discussing conspiracy theories.

"Then who does?" Faith asked.

"The aliens," Tyler stated matter-of-factly. Jake groaned.

"Seriously. Have you guys ever wondered why aliens can abduct someone right out of their own house in the middle of the night and no one sees anything?" Tyler asked.

"Probably because aliens don't really abduct people," Jake answered.

"Bullshit!" Tyler stood up and pointed at Jake. "I was abducted by actual aliens, and let me tell you, it wasn't a pleasant experience."

Faith grabbed Tyler by the arm. "Lower your

voice, Tyler, and sit down."

"I will not!" Tyler ripped his arm away from Faith's grasp. "You all claim to be witnesses to the extent the government will go to cover up the existence of a secret base in the Southern United States, but you won't acknowledge the existence of aliens!"

"That's not what I said at all, Tyler. I do believe in aliens. In fact, I have seen them myself, but they don't go around abducting people! The US Government does that!" Jake argued.

"You have no idea what I've been through! I saw the aliens with my own eyes! They did horrible things to me while they conducted their tests!" Tyler took a step back from Jake and Faith. "They kept telling me it was for the good of mankind, but I didn't like what they were doing to me!"

A small group of patients and visitors had gathered outside the waiting area. They were intently watching Tyler's tantrum. Jake spotted the group and tried to calm Tyler down. "You're attracting attention to us, Tyler. Please sit down and be quiet."

"I will not!" Tyler yelled.

"Please, Tyler," Faith pleaded. "People who are on the run from the government don't make it very far by attracting large crowds."

"I don't care! I'm not on the run from the government!"

"Goddamn it, Tyler!" Jake said. "Sit down and shut up!" Jake stood up and tried to grab Tyler.

"You fucking leave me alone!" Tyler shouted at Jake. Stepping back, Tyler tripped over Durard's legs and tumbled to the floor. "Don't touch me!"

247

Tyler screamed. Lifting himself up, Tyler began to push his way through the crowd frantically.

Jake hung his head. "Faith, go bring him back."

Faith stood up and nodded. "He's just a kid, Jake. We need to give him a break."

"I know he's just a kid, but that doesn't make him any less important to us."

"Why is he so important?" Faith asked.

"I don't know," Jake answered. "I just know he is."

Faith nodded as she turned to leave. "I'll find him and bring him back." Jake smiled. "Thanks, Faith."

"Mr. Silver?" a voice asked from out of the crowd.

Jake looked at the crowd that had now begun to disperse. "Yes?"

A doctor stepped through the crowd into the waiting room. He was wearing a long white lab coat, blue shirt and red striped tie. His dirty blonde hair was closely cropped to his head. "Mr. Silver, my name is Dr. Black."

Jake reached out and shook Black's hand. "How's Alex?"

"She's fine. The cut on her leg wasn't as bad as it looked. We put in twelve stitches, and prescribed some painkillers."

"That's great news, Doc," Jake smiled. "Can I see her?"

"Yeah, just follow me. She's resting comfortably in the ER."

***

248

"Tyler!" Faith yelled as she ran out the two double doors and onto the sidewalk. It was empty outside, except for a row of cars that lined the curb in front of the hospital. The dawning sun was casting a golden light across the trees and grass surrounding the hospital. Faith, still wearing her blue hospital scrubs from the Aurora, charged down the sidewalk. "Tyler? It's Faith. Where are you?"

Tyler stepped out of the shadows cast by a tall oak tree. "I'm right here, Faith," he spoke in a quiet voice.

"Why did you run out like that?" Faith scolded the young man, then took him into her arms and hugged him tightly. "We need you, Tyler."

"To make fun of?" Tyler asked spitefully, pulling away from Faith. "You have no idea what I've been through the past few days!"

"No I don't," Faith admitted, "but I do know one thing."

"What's that?"

"That you're a person with a good heart, and that deep down you want to help us." Faith wrapped her arm around Tyler's waist. "You just need to find a way to cope with what's happened to you."

Tyler sunk down to his knees. "How can I do that?"

Faith shook her head. "I don't know. That's an answer you need to find for yourself." Sitting on the grass next to Tyler, she laid her hand on his shoulder. "Tell me a little about yourself."

"Like what?" Tyler asked.

"Let's start with how old you are and where you're from."

Tyler watched the morning light make Faith's

249

eyes glitter. He felt safe with her. "I'm eighteen, and I'm from Nevada."

"You're eighteen?" she asked delightedly. "Yeah, why?"

"I could've sworn you were older than that. I thought you were around my age."

"How old are you?" Tyler asked.

"Twenty-three," Faith replied. "Really?"

Faith nodded. "Really."

"Where are you from?" Tyler started to become more comfortable.

"I was born in New York, but when I was very young, my family moved to Los Angeles."

"Why did you enlist in the military?" Tyler wondered.

"I wanted to be a doctor, but my family was a little on the poor side, so this was the only way I could follow my dreams." Faith turned her attention to the sunrise. "Look at that."

Tyler had seen many sunrises in his young life, but he couldn't remember any before now, nor did he want to. "It's wonderful." He stared at the mixture of yellows and reds that comprised the eastern sky. The glowing tip of the sun was barely visible above the horizon.

"Yes it is." Faith leaned her head on Tyler's shoulder.

***

Alex spread her arms as soon as she saw Jake step into the emergency room. Grabbing her, Jake squeezed Alex tightly in an embrace. Alex's black jumpsuit was gone, replaced with a light blue

250

hospital gown. She was sitting on a gurney with her right leg propped up.

Stepping back, Jake stared at the bandages around her wound. "How are you feeling?" he asked.

"Good," Alex replied in a calm tone. "The doctors here are wonderful. They took very good care of me."

"Are they going to release you?"

"I'm not sure."

"We need to get going." Jake stated solemnly.

"Where are we going?" Alex asked.

Jake shook his head. "I don't know, but as far away from Anne Caroll and Area 51 as I can get."

"We're running again, Jake."

"I know," Jake sighed. "What else are we going to do?"

"Make a stand," Alex said sternly.

Jake was surprised at Alex's response. "How do you propose we do that?" Alex spun to face Jake. "We need to take what we know to the press."

"They'll label us as crackpots!" Jake complained. "You remember that guy that came out and said he was an employee of Area 51? What was his name? Dan Lazarus? They've done entire documentaries, just to discredit him."

"I think it was Bob something, but that's not the point." Alex argued.

"It is the point, Alex. We'll just be another couple of whackos talking about aliens and government conspiracies!"

"I don't care, Jake! I want this to end." Alex brushed her hair out of her face. "Don't you want to go back to having a normal life?"

"Sure, but that's all irrelevant now," Jake answered. "Why is it irrelevant?"

"It just is." Jake stated.

"That's not any kind of answer," Alex grabbed Jake's arm and pulled him close. "I lost my father and Major Griggs to this damned crusade. I don't want to lose anybody else." Alex wiped a tear away from her eye. "We need to stop this, Jake."

Jake thought for a moment. "All right, we do need to stop this." He waved a hand in front of Alex to dismiss her smile, "but going to the media isn't the way to do it. Not at first. We're going to need proof if we want anyone to believe us."

"How do we get proof?"

Jake smiled. "That's easy. We just need to get a sample of the virus they let loose in the southwest."

"How will that be easy?" Alex asked. "It's a highly contagious agent that, from what I've heard, kills within twenty-four hours of contracting it."

"Then we'll just have to be careful, now won't we?"

"Yes we will," Durard said from behind Jake.

Jake spun around to see Tyler, Faith and Durard standing together inside the emergency room's door. "I'm going to warn you all, this is going to be extremely dangerous. Last time we attempted an operation like this, Alex and I watched two of our teammates die, and there was nothing we could do," Jake stated gravely.

"We're well aware of the risks, Jake," Durard replied coolly. "I can't speak for anyone else, but I want to repay the sons a bitches that held me hostage and killed my friend, Steve."

"I just want to know the truth," added Tyler.

"The truth is a very subjective thing," Jake interjected.

Alex nodded. "What the truth is for one man, isn't necessarily the truth for another. I, we," Alex corrected, "just want you to be prepared for the possibility that the truth you find may not be the truth you wanted."

Tyler understood. "I want the truth, whatever that may be."

Jake turned away from the group to hide his worry. He was taking an eighteen and a twenty-three year old into one of the most dangerous areas in the world, on what most would consider a suicide mission. He wasn't sure he was ready for the burden of their deaths. Jake tried to shake this feeling of guilt.

Turning back to the group, he put on his best poker face. "Okay, we need to get back on the road. Let's go." Jake watched the group stroll out of the emergency room. Still standing next to Alex, Jake closed his eyes. Alex placed her hand on Jake's chest. Grabbing Alex tightly in his arms, he thought about her father, General Davis. It was his last request that Jake watch over his daughter. At the time, Jake was beginning to see a blossoming relationship between Alex and Griggs. Jake knew Griggs would've taken very good care of her, but Jake wasn't sure if he was doing a good job. Running his hand through Alex's long hair, Jake lifted his head up. "God forgive me for what I'm about to do."

Chapter Twenty-eight

The Aurora touched down softly on the tarmac at Area 51. The mighty black jet quickly taxied into the awaiting main hangar. Four men began to pull the massive bay doors closed. They all knew it was against procedure to have the Aurora out in daylight.

The main hatch on the Aurora popped open and a ramp folded down to the floor of the hangar. Anne briskly stepped out, followed by Hollman and Cisan. Jannis was one of the last to exit the craft.

Major O'Connell was standing at the entrance to the base with his hands clasped behind his back. He saw Anne approaching him. "Good morning, Colonel Caroll."

"Did the spy bird see us?" Anne asked quickly.

"No, Colonel. By our calculations, the Russian spy satellite Gregov should just now be passing overhead. It shouldn't have seen the Aurora at all," O'Connell reported.

"Good, at least one of my men isn't ignorant," Anne spitefully announced. "Colonel?"

"Never mind." Anne had turned around to see several men carrying Griggs off the Aurora on a stretcher. Cisan was at the bottom of the ramp barking orders. Anne turned back around to O'Connell. "I want you back up in command right now, Major. I have a feeling we'll be paid a visit very soon."

"Yes, Colonel." O'Connell saluted, then left.

Anne stepped aside as Cisan approached the door with Griggs on the stretcher. "Excuse me, Colonel," Cisan said as she walked by.

Anne watched as Griggs lay silently on the stretcher, a bag of blood lying on his chest attached to a tube and an IV needle still inserted in his arm. Anger welled up inside Anne. Her creation was dying and it was her fault.

"Colonel Caroll?"

Anne spun around. "Yes, Dr. Hollman?"

Hollman was walking toward her with the black bag of bones slung over his back. "We need a new patient to test the vaccine on."

Anne hadn't thought that far ahead yet. "You start creating that vaccine, and I'll make sure you have a warm body to test it on."

"Thank you, Colonel." Hollman stepped past Anne into the doorway and stopped. "Colonel, may I speak freely?"

Anne wasn't in the mood for this. "Maybe another time, Doctor. I have a lot to attend to."

"Please, I just need a moment." Hollman pleaded.

"You have one minute, Dr. Hollman," Anne stated firmly.

"I'm beginning to question our motives, Colonel," Hollman started. "Jesus Christ, not you too. I really don't have time for this."

"What?" Hollman asked.

"Back on the Aurora, Nurse Marin was expressing the same opinions to me," Anne admitted. "We're trying to save lives, Dr. Hollman."

"You've told that lie so many times, you're actually starting to believe it yourself, aren't you?" Hollman asked venomously.

"How dare you?"

"Don't give me that crap, Colonel Caroll."

255

Hollman interrupted. "You're not talking to one of your brainless lackeys here. I am well aware of our true plans in this matter." Hollman took a step closer to Anne. "We started this project together, and we're going to finish it together."

"Then what's your problem?" Anne said spitefully.

"A lot of people are dying out there because of us!" Hollman yelled.

"That's the point now, isn't it?" Anne asked. "We released this virus to show the world we had one of the most potent chemicals ever to be used for warfare. We expected people to die."

"I know, but we went ahead and released it without having a vaccine prepared." Hollman argued.

"Acceptable losses for the project, Doctor," Anne replied coldly. "You've got to start looking at the bigger picture here. Sure, a few people die, but we have effectively demonstrated the efficiency of this killer."

"How are we going to sell this virus to other countries if they don't have an inoculant to use on their own soldiers?" Hollman asked.

"Well, looks like you have a big job to do, Dr. Hollman. Better get to it," Anne said almost cheerfully.

Hollman stared at Anne in awe. He was about to continue the argument, but changed his mind. "Yes, Colonel." Turning, Hollman disappeared through the doorway.

Anne calmly strode toward the Aurora. Looking around the hangar, she marveled at the job the workmen had done in rebuilding it. Anne

256

thought back to that day when she saw the hangar utterly annihilated by the alien mother ship. The roof had collapsed, sending tons of rock raining down on all the aircraft and personnel inside. Flames caused by loose electrical wires and ruptured fuel tanks were licking the walls. Billions of dollars in experimental aircraft were lost that day, along with all the recovered alien saucers and technology.

Stopping, she turned around and began to walk toward the doorway. She needed to check up on Captain Jannis before he left on his mission. She had a new task for him to complete first.

**

Jannis stood quietly in his modest quarters. The walls were the standard concrete gray. A small bunk sat in the edge of the room with a green footlocker at the foot of it. He had been squaring away his gear, preparing for his mission. He had decided to go out in plain clothes, rather than in full uniform, to be more inconspicuous. He was wearing a white t-shirt, a black leather jacket than hung just a little past his hips, and a pair of worn blue jeans with his black combat boots. His black forty-five sat alone in the middle of his bunk. A knock on his door startled him. "Enter," Jannis announced.

Anne strode into his room. "Captain Jannis."

Jannis snapped to attention. "What can I do for you, Colonel?"

Anne smiled. "You become a completely different person when you're out of uniform." Anne walked over and sat down on the edge of Jannis' bunk. "At ease, Captain."

Jannis nodded. "Why am I being paid this visit, Colonel?"

"I have an extra assignment for you," Anne crossed her legs. She was still wearing her black fatigues.

"What's that, Colonel?" Jannis asked as he moved over to his footlocker and sat down on it.

"Look, Captain," Anne brushed a single lock of her brown hair out of her face and tucked it behind her ear, "I want you and I to get along. I think you're a damn fine soldier and I know your career is on the fast track."

"Thank you, Colonel," Jannis spoke softly, as if embarrassed.

"We've come to a very critical junction in our plans, and I need everyone on my team on the same page. We can't afford any screwups now," Anne stated.

"Understood, Colonel."

"Now," Anne uncrossed her legs and stood up, "with that out of the way, we need to discuss your new assignment."

Jannis stood up in front of Anne. "Yes, Colonel."

"Dr. Hollman needs a new test patient."

A worried look crossed over Jannis' face. "You don't mean me, do you, Colonel?"

"Hell no," Anne laughed, "Although the thought did cross my mind. We need you to get us one."

"Yes, Colonel," Jannis sounded relieved.

Anne tried to compose herself and stop laughing. "I need you to go into Las Vegas and try

258

to find a person who hasn't been infected by the virus, and then bring them to us." Anne began to leave the room. "The chopper leaves in fifteen minutes."

"Yes, Colonel," Jannis saluted.

Anne turned her head as she left the room. "Oh, and Captain Jannis?"

"Yes, Colonel?"

"You might want to take a gas mask with you, Captain." Anne laughed again as she left the room.

***

Nine hours had passed since the group had left Chapel Hill, North Carolina. They were currently passing through Arkansas, the third state on their trek back to Nevada. It was getting close to four o' clock in the afternoon now, and dusk was beginning to fall over the wooded countryside. A light fog had begun to develop and was hanging close to the ground.

Halfway through Tennessee, Jake and Durard had switched positions in the car. Durard had felt obligated to take his turn driving. Alex was sitting in the backseat with Faith and Tyler, her still bandaged leg stretched across both their laps. Jake was trying to catch a quick nap in the passenger seat of their beat-up tan sedan. The whole time in the car, Alex had been regaling Faith and Tyler with her stories about aliens and UFOs. Faith had, for the most part, lost interest just outside Chapel Hill, but Tyler had been hanging on every word.

"So it turns out," Tyler started, "that your dad, General Davis, was actually in charge of Area 51?"

Anne nodded. "He had actually signed the approval for my abduction from Egypt."

"He didn't know it was you?" Tyler asked.

"No, they just wanted to protect the alien device buried beneath the Sphinx."

"I don't understand," Tyler admitted. "If the US Government knew the alien device was buried under the Sphinx in Egypt the whole time, why didn't they just go in and get it? Why would they leave it there?"

"That's easy. They couldn't go in and get it. It was the Egyptian Government's jurisdiction."

"Why?"

"Well, I don't know any of this for certain, but during my research, I uncovered evidence of a secret pact between all the major powers of the world. From what I can tell, this pact was referred to as the 'Moscow Convention', due to the fact it was held in Russia in the 1960's. The Moscow Convention states that any government to recover alien entities or technology are to destroy them on the spot." Alex adjusted her leg, trying to find a more comfortable resting position. "The funny thing is, none of the governments that agreed to this pact follow it, except when it comes to the jurisdictional aspect."

Tyler shook his head. "That would mean the United States has been violating this agreement by recovering and studying alien technology at Area 51."

"Right, but we're not the only ones. The Egyptian Government wanted to keep and study the device, but they just hadn't had a chance to get out there and recover it. With all the recent digs and discoveries in Gaza and the Valley of the Kings, they couldn't risk it," Alex explained.

"That still doesn't cover how the US ended up with the device that blew up S-4."

"The US seized the opportunity when my father signed the order to abduct me.

The Egyptian Government had already been in contact with the brass at the Pentagon about me. They discovered I'd been using falsified papers and work orders at my dig."

Tyler laughed. "What the hell were you thinking?"

"Most governments won't approve your visa if you tell them you're there to dig up alien artifacts. I had to use a little bit of misdirection to get the job done." Alex lifted a small ice pack off the floor and handed it to Tyler. "Would you hold that on my leg for a little while? It should reduce the swelling."

"Yeah, sure." Tyler grabbed the pack and laid it gently on Alex's bandages. "Anyway, our government instructed the team going in to retrieve me, to also pick up the alien device. That way, the US could say the people responsible for breaking into the Sphinx had unfortunately gotten away with the device."

"Oh," Tyler said, finally beginning to understand. "They got what they wanted by using you as a scapegoat!"

Alex smiled. "Now you're catching on."

"So what was the alien device for?" Durard asked from the front seat.

"Jake's really the one to answer that question, but from what he's told me, the device was created just to destroy things." Alex answered. She began to speculate, "I think it could probably be equated to an alien wrecking ball. After the aliens who had built these fantastic bases and landing ports were finished with them, they would leave one of these devices to eliminate any trace they were ever there."

"So this alien race had colonized the Earth some time in the distant past?" Durard asked again.

"As far as we can tell," Alex confirmed. "From artifacts we've recovered, we think they were here around the same time as some of the earliest human civilizations. We think this alien species even helped shape some of those civilizations, such as the Egyptians."

"What do you know about the virus we're after?" Tyler asked.

"I don't know much," Alex admitted. "From what I've heard, the virus is a deadly strain of influenza."

Durard began to put the facts together in his head. "If this is the same strain as the one we found at the S-4 dig, then this isn't just the flu virus," Durard cut in. "Steve and I found traces of what could best be described as a bacteria in the soil surrounding S-4. Steve thought it was extra-terrestrial in origin."

"Why is that?" Alex asked.

"He found a code contained within the DNA strand that he couldn't identify," Durard said still facing forward.

"That's incredible," Tyler admitted. He had been researching UFOs and Aliens his entire life, and now he was sitting and talking with people who had actually been inside Area 51, people who knew the truth.

262

Jannis was sitting uncomfortably in one of the rear seats of the helicopter. The pilot and co-pilot were busily working the controls in the cockpit, navigating the helicopter toward Las Vegas. Jannis had been strapped tightly into the rear seat by the co-pilot just moments before the chopper was scheduled for take-off. He had rushed to gather the necessary equipment after Colonel Caroll had informed him of his new mission. The mighty rotor blades of the helicopter were already spinning when Jannis had walked through the hangar bay's door.

He had packed a small black duffel bag with a multitude of different equipment. Lifting the duffel off the floor, he set it on his lap and began to check through it, trying to forget about how uncomfortable he was.

Inside the black bag, he found his rubber gas mask. Using the corner of his black shirt, he began to wipe off the large visor. Jannis had rummaged through the equipment room at Area 51 until he had found the most powerful filters to put on the mask. In hindsight, he realized he should be wearing a level four decontamination suit.

Placing the mask in his lap, Jannis pulled out a long, flat, black taser. Hitting the trigger with his thumb, he watched the blue spark jump across the two silver prongs on the front of it. He needed this to immobilize the subject. Placing the taser in his jacket pocket, he set the black duffel back on the floor.

"Captain, we're about two minutes out of Las

Vegas," the co-pilot reported. Jannis nodded. Reaching up, he pulled the bulky flight helmet off and set it beside him. Grabbing the gas mask, he pulled it over his face and tightened the rubber straps. The mask covered his entire face, so only his eyes were visible behind the thin visor. Two circular filters sat on either side of the lower part of the mask, giving Jannis a very ominous look.

Pulling his forty-five out of its holster on the inside of his jacket, Jannis clicked a button dropping the clip into his hand. He quickly made sure it was full of rounds. Slamming the clip back into the pistol, Jannis cocked the weapon, sending a shell into the chamber. He knew he was as ready as he was going to get.

"Thirty seconds, Captain," the co-pilot reported.

Jannis looked out the open cargo door at Las Vegas sitting quietly below them. Most of the lights in the city were black, including those of the casinos. Jannis considered this. *It's probably the first time in fifty years all the lights have been off.* He couldn't see anyone on the streets, not even a vehicle.

Jannis was lurched sideways as the helicopter banked down toward the ground. He felt the chopper's momentum stop as the skids touched down. Unbuckling himself, Jannis walked behind his seat to the open cargo door. Stepping off the chopper, he heard the rotors begin to whine as they slowed. Looking back at the helicopter, Jannis gave the co-pilot the thumbs up to signal his readiness. The co-pilot returned the gesture, and Jannis was off.

Jannis scanned the area with his eyes. It looked like they had landed in the middle of a golf course. Breaking into a brisk jog, Jannis began to move away from the helicopter. Finally coming to the edge of the course, Jannis found himself standing in the middle of Sands Avenue. Running along the road, he stared at the huge casinos looming in front of him. He knew he was almost to "The Strip". There was a stillness that seemed very eerie to Jannis on this hot Nevada day.

Coming around the corner, Jannis skidded to a stop and stared down The Strip. Casinos stood magnificently in all directions casting huge black shadows across the quiet street. Trash was being whipped around by the harsh Nevada winds, making it appear to be a ghost town.

He began to quickly walk north on The Strip. Casino widows had been broken by vandals and storefronts were smashed, their wares scattered haphazardly about the sidewalks. A fire hydrant on the left-hand side of the street had been knocked over by a car and was now sending gallons of water shooting into the air. Jannis caught sight of the driver of the car slumped over his steering wheel, a crusty yellow substance covering his face. Two more corpses were lying awkwardly in the doors of a casino; their bodies apparently trampled by a massive group of people trying to get out. Their faces were also covered with thick yellow foam. Jannis knew it was the virus.

Pushing their bodies aside with his foot, Jannis stepped into the casino. It was pitch black inside, except for an occasional emergency light on the walls. Retrieving a small black flashlight from his pocket, he clicked it on and shone it around. Bodies were everywhere. He found an elderly woman crumpled in front of a group of slot machines, a bucket of coins still clutched tightly in her hands.

Turning away, Jannis saw a blackjack dealer lying dead on his table, the green felt stained by the yellow foam. Two more bodies, a young woman and man, were wrapped in each other's arms on the craps table. Jannis saw the wedding rings on their fingers. He guessed they were on their honeymoon when this tragedy struck.

Making his way quickly through the gaming area, Jannis moved toward the elevators. He knew they would be out, but he also knew that's where the stairs were. Jannis decided his best bet was to look up inside the hotel rooms.

Stepping into the cove that held the elevators, Jannis grabbed the handle of a door that was marked emergency stairs. Pulling the door open, he gazed into the empty stairwell. A few emergency lights were also turned on, casting strange shadows over the stairs. Jannis didn't want to be here. He didn't want to be around all the dead bodies, and he certainly didn't want to be exposed to the virus.

Climbing up the first flight of stairs, Jannis encountered another body, a middle-aged woman dressed in business clothes, she was lying on her back at the bottom of the second flight of stairs. Her head was twisted unnaturally to the side, and her mouth and eyes were wide. Jannis assumed this poor soul had fallen down the stairs and broke her neck. Traces of the yellow foam were still present on her nose and mouth.

Stepping over her broken corpse, Jannis sped

up the second flight of stairs. He reached a door marked second floor, and opened it. The halls were done in a red and white floral pattern wallpaper, and the carpet was a deep red. Doors stood about every ten feet along the hall. Passing the first four doors, Jannis stopped when he heard cries coming from inside the fifth door. Looking down at the handle, he saw that it required a key card, much like the ones used at Area 51. Pressing his ear to the door, he listened intently for several moments. He heard another soft whimper from inside.

Rearing back, Jannis kicked the door hard, sending it crashing open. Stepping inside, he saw two dead bodies lying on the bed, and a teenage girl curled up in the corner crying. She was wearing a pair of blue jeans and a white shirt, and her short blonde hair was dirty and matted. She looked as if she hadn't eaten in a few days.

Jannis realized the dead bodies were the girl's parents. The girl looked up at Jannis with terror in her eyes.

Jumping up, she ran to Jannis and threw her arms around him. "Thank God, you're the first live person I've seen in days!"

Jannis pulled away from the girl. "You need to step back. I don't know if you're infected."

"I don't care!" the girl cried. "I need to get out of here!" She grabbed on to Jannis again with her frail body.

"Stop it!" Jannis pushed her to the ground. "I'll get you out of here if you stop!" Tears were welling up in her eyes again. "I'm sorry."

Pulling a flat silver object out of his pocket, Jannis knelt down beside the girl. "I need to run a quick test. Give me your hand."

The girl gingerly lifted her left hand up. "Is it going to hurt?"

Jannis grasped the young girl's hand. "It shouldn't, just hold still for a moment." Jannis pressed the end of the silver object to the girl's hand. "This device will take a quick blood sample, then test it to see if you've been infected by the virus."

Jannis pressed a small blue button on the back of the device, sending a small needle plunging into the girl's hand. The girl was startled by the pinch. She let out a gasp and quickly pulled her hand away and began to rub it. "That hurt," she complained. "This'll just take a moment to run the sample." Jannis said.

The girl was still rubbing her hand. A trickle of blood had run down her hand from the puncture mark. "Who are you anyway?" she asked, her voice trembling.

"It's not important who I am, but I'm with the Air Force," Jannis admitted. He stared at the disheveled young woman. "What's your name?"

"Theresa," the young girl said.

"Do you live here in Vegas?" Jannis asked curiously.

"No, my family's from Kansas. We were just here on vacation." Theresa looked over at her dead parents. Tears began to roll down her face again. "We haven't been on a family vacation since I was very little. My dad had to work extra shifts all summer just so we could go."

Jannis shook his head. "I'm very sorry, Theresa." The silver device began to beep

268

interrupting him. Jannis lifted it up and stared at the square LCD screen. "Good news, the test was negative. You haven't been infected."

Theresa breathed a sigh of relief. "So that means you're going to get me out of here?"

Jannis smiled. "Yeah, get some of your stuff together and we'll go."

Theresa quickly moved to one of the dressers in the room and pulled open the drawer. She suddenly stopped and looked over at her parents. "What's going to happen to my parents?"

"After a vaccine is created for this virus, the Federal Emergency Management Agency will be sent in to clean-up. Families will be contacted and funeral arrangements will be made. Your parents will be fine." Jannis was lying.

"Thank you." Theresa began to pull clothes out of the drawers and place them into a small blue suitcase sitting next to the dresser.

"We need to hurry. Pack lightly," Jannis instructed her.

Theresa nodded and tossed the last piece of clothing into the suitcase. Closing the top, she ran the zipper around making sure her suitcase was closed securely. Lifting it, she walked toward Jannis and stopped. Jannis stepped out of the doorway to allow her to pass in front of him.

Putting his hand into his pocket, he grabbed the taser and pulled it out. Slipping his arm around Theresa's neck, Jannis pressed the taser to her neck and thumbed the button. Electricity surged through Theresa's body paralyzing her. "I'm sorry, Theresa," Jannis said quietly as he lifted her limp body over his shoulder. Stepping into the hallway,

Jannis started the trip back to the helicopter.

270

Chapter Twenty-nine

The Med Lab was dimly lit. There were only a few sparse work lights on in the far corner illuminating a small workspace occupied by Hollman and Cisan. Hollman had arranged the bones of the skeleton on top of one of the examination tables. He glanced around the Med Lab. This room had always sent shivers up his spine. Behind him, there were four rows of tubes that used to contain the bodies of abducted subjects. It held them in a thick green fluid in a sort of stasis. The tubes still had an eerie luminescence about them that cast a peculiar blue light across the lab. Hollman tried to return his attention back to the task at hand.

Cisan was hovering over the examination table, her blonde hair tied behind her head as she took samples from the bones with a scalpel. Reaching up, she seized an overhead light and tugged it a little closer to her work. Pushing the scrapings into a small plastic bag, she turned around and placed it on the workstation next to Hollman. The workstation was a long, metallic table with two microscopes and three computers sitting on it. Every tool they could conceivably need was located there.

"Thank you, Dr. Cisan," Hollman said without turning around. Adjusting the magnification knob, he stared into the microscope at a sample from the bones. "This sample is negative, too," Hollman said in exasperation. He pulled the small glass slide from the tray and tossed it onto the table. Pulling off his latex gloves, he dumped them into a large bin next to the workstation. Crossing his arms, Hollman leaned up against the table in frustration. "We've run fifteen different tests and all have been negative. I don't understand."

"We need to keep trying. We'll find a sample," Cisan reassured Hollman as she pulled her safety goggles off. "We haven't taken samples from all the bones yet."

"Why would it make any difference?" Hollman turned around and placed his palms flat on the table.

"This isn't helping, Greg. We need to get back to work. There are people counting on us," Cisan argued.

"You're right, Dr. Cisan." Hollman straightened up. "We need to continue." Pulling another pair of latex gloves out of a box on the table, Hollman snapped them on. "Let me have the next sample."

Cisan reached for two glass slides and placed them side-by-side on the table. Opening the small plastic bag, she carefully removed a scraping and placed it on the glass. Grabbing an eyedropper, she put one small drop of water on the sample, then laid the second piece of glass on top of it. Lifting it carefully, she handed it to Hollman.

"Here we go," Hollman said as he gently took the slides from Cisan. Sliding them onto the tray of the microscope, Hollman leaned over and looked into the lenses. Adjusting the magnification, he suddenly straightened up. Stepping to the side, he tapped a series of buttons on the keyboard. The monitor flashed to life with a detailed image from the microscope. "I think we have a winner," Hollman said excitedly.

Cisan leaned close to the screen. "I don't see

272

anything."

Hollman pointed to a small yellow glob amidst a sea of gray in the upper left- hand corner of the screen. "It's right there. It's just a few cells, but it's enough to work with!"

Cisan smiled. "We've done it, Doctor."

"Yes we have." Hollman pulled a small black radio from his lab coat. "Commander Caroll?" he said while keying the talk button.

"Yes, Dr. Hollman?" Anne responded quickly. This was a secure frequency only Anne used. She had given it to him to report directly to her.

"Dr. Cisan and I have found an intact sample of the virus!" Hollman excitedly reported.

"Very good. I also have good news, Doctor."

"What's that, Colonel?" Hollman asked.

"Captain Jannis has found you a new test patient. He should be here within the hour."

"Thank you, Colonel. Dr. Cisan and I will get to work on synthesizing the virus immediately," Hollman responded eagerly.

"Good. I want regular progress reports, Dr. Hollman," Anne stated firmly. "Yes, Colonel," Hollman said.

"Caroll out."

Static hissed over the radio for a moment before Hollman turned it off. Hollman looked at Cisan. "You heard the boss, we need to get back to work."

Cisan nodded. "Yes. Doctor."

***

Anne was sitting alone in her office staring out

273

the window at the setting sun. She had removed her black jumpsuit and had slipped into her blue uniform. Her jacket was draped over the back of her chair and her white blouse was only buttoned up halfway. Running her hand along the back of her head, she slipped her fingers around her hair tie and pulled it off her ponytail. Anne tossed the tie on her desk and ran her hands through her hair while she leaned back in her leather chair. Taking a deep breath and slowly exhaling it, she kicked off her shoes and relaxed. Lifting her legs, she crossed them as she rested her feet on the lip of the windowsill. Her brown eyes became lazy as they watched the horizon fade slowly from the fantastic reds to a deep black. A sprinkling of stars began to pepper the sky.

A knock at her door interrupted her. Anne quickly began to button her blouse as she spun around in her chair. "Come."

Her door opened and Major Griggs cautiously stepped inside. "Colonel?"

Anne smiled and stopped buttoning her blouse. "How are you feeling, Jason?" Griggs took a few more steps into the room and stood at attention. "Very good, Colonel. After we returned to Area 51, it was just a matter of the doctors patching me up." Griggs still seemed pale due to the massive blood loss he had experienced. "Have a seat," Anne motioned to the chairs in front of her large metal desk. Griggs slowly moved toward the chair and seated himself. His posture remained very rigid and uncomfortable. "Colonel, may I speak frankly?" Anne nodded.

"Colonel," Griggs searched for the words to

express what he was feeling. "Something's wrong with me."

"In what way? Didn't Dr. Hollman give you a clean bill of health?" Anne asked.

"Not physically, Colonel," Griggs seemed to be struggling with what he wanted to say.

"Then what, Major?" Anne asked impatiently.

"Mentally," Griggs admitted.

"I don't understand."

Griggs tried to put his thoughts in order to properly articulate them. "When you brought me out of stasis, you said I would begin to regain my memories, that I was suffering from a mild case of amnesia."

"Yes, I recall, Major." Anne started to button her blouse again. Slowly, she pulled open her top desk drawer revealing a small silver pistol inside. She slowly placed her hand inside the drawer and around the handle of the gun, all the while keeping eye contact with Griggs. Anne had hoped this day wouldn't come.

"Well, it's coming back, and I'm remembering things that don't seem to coincide with what you've told me, Colonel," Griggs stated solemnly.

Anne slipped her finger around the trigger and began to lift the pistol. "What do you need me to do to help?" she asked in her most pleasant and sincere voice.

Griggs leaned forward on Anne's desk. "I was hoping you could help me try and straighten them out."

Anne smiled and nodded. Letting go of the gun, she slowly closed the drawer. "Sure, I'll help you, Major." Anne smiled deviously. She knew it would be easier to control Griggs if he was still under the impression they were friends. Anne knew he would snap if he knew the truth.

"That woman I met in the detention area before we left on the mission, she seemed very familiar to me, like I knew her." Griggs was struggling to lift a heavy fog from his thoughts. He felt as if every so often he got a break in the storm and his mind would clear, but just as quickly as clarity came, it left again.

Anne thought quickly. "She was one of the terrorists who infiltrated Area 51 and S-4 and helped destroy them. You were on the team assigned to stop them."

"That still doesn't make sense, Colonel. If I was there to stop her, why do I have vivid memories of her giving me CPR?" Griggs asked.

"They shot you during their escape. I'm assuming they didn't want to be charged with murder, so they tried to save your life in order to save their own asses." Anne knew the lie was thin, but it was all she had.

Griggs sat back in his chair. Anne could see the wheels turning in his head. "That makes sense, but if they shot me and S-4 was destroyed, how did I get back here to Area 51?"

Anne leaned back in her chair. She wasn't prepared for that question. "Just before the explosion, a group of officers encountered our bodies lying unconscious in the hallway and pulled us to safety."

Griggs shook his head. "That's not the way you stated what happened in your report."

Anne stood up. "How did you get a copy of my

276

report?" she hissed.

Griggs continued undaunted. "You stated in your report that I died at S-4 from complications due to a bullet wound I received from General Perry, and that you barely escaped the explosion at S-4 by yourself!" Anne began to pull open her top desk drawer, when Griggs pulled out his pistol and brought it to bear on her. "Don't move, Colonel. I don't know what you did to me, but I know it wasn't right." Griggs stepped around Anne's desk and placed his weapon to her head. "I remember everything now," he whispered. "I wanted to see if you would lie to me."

"Major Griggs, stand down! That's an order!" Anne screamed.

"I'm sorry," Griggs said, "but I'm not taking orders from you anymore. I want to know the truth!"

"Fine, you want to know the truth?" Anne asked maliciously.

"I think that's what I asked," Griggs said, pressing the barrel of his gun harder into her head.

Anne thought for a moment. Turning her eyes toward Griggs, she could see that his hands were shaking. Anne knew he hadn't fully recovered from his ordeal, and she could use that to her advantage. "Major Griggs, you're dead."

"What?"

"What you read in my report was true. You died in that hallway at S-4," Anne told him in a very stern tone.

"Then how am I here?" Griggs asked.

Anne stared at him for a moment. "I don't think you want to know."

"Tell me," Griggs replied.

Anne smiled. "You are the first successful clone designed from the 'Uber-Soldier' Project. We took the DNA sample we had here at Area 51 and a tissue sample I cut from your body as I escaped from S-4 and grew a new Major Griggs in a tube." Anne watched Griggs' eyes widen in horror. "I made you, Major Griggs. I watched you develop from ooze in the bottom of a test tube, to a full-grown adult male in almost a year. You were so cute when you were just a little baby—"

"Shut the fuck up!" Griggs took a step back from Anne. "How can that be? I have all my memories, I know I'm Jason Griggs." His mind was swimming in confusion.

Anne knew this was her only chance. She quickly reached down and retrieved her pistol from the drawer and shot from her hip. Anne watched as Griggs crumpled to the floor of her office. Stepping over to his body, she saw he was still breathing. "How dare you do this to your maker?" Anne hissed. "I created you!" she roared.

Griggs rolled over onto his back. The bullet had entered his upper chest and had shattered his collarbone. He was in a great deal of pain. "Why did you do it?" Griggs asked with a weak voice.

"I needed the one weapon that could crush my enemies," Anne said as she knelt down over Griggs. "Jake Silver and Alex Robinson would be killed by the very man who helped them escape from Area 51 and they would be powerless to stop it." Anne smiled again. "It's almost poetic, isn't it?"

Griggs sneered at Anne. "You brought me back to life just so I could be a pawn in your sick little

278

games?"

"I didn't just bring you back to life, Griggs," Anne was enjoying this, "I gave you a whole new life. You could've used this new life any way you wanted, but you chose to go back to your old candy ass ways." Anne reached down and pinched Griggs' cheeks just as a grandmother would. "You have really disappointed me."

Griggs shook loose of her hands. "Fuck off."

Anne reached to her desk and grabbed her radio. "That's not a very nice thing to say to a woman." Lifting the radio to her mouth, she keyed the talk button. "This is Colonel Caroll, I need a full security detail to my office on the double."

Griggs suddenly lifted and tossed Anne off him. Anne landed awkwardly next to Griggs, smacking the left side of her face against the cold gray wall. "I'm not going to let you kill me again." Scrambling toward where he dropped his pistol, he picked it up and aimed it at Anne, but she had already made it to her feet. She pulled the trigger again, hitting Griggs in the right shoulder. He fell to the floor instantly in agony.

Anne walked over and stood above Griggs, rubbing her left eye. "I don't want to kill you, Major. I need you to help me finish my plans." She knelt down and rolled Griggs over onto his back. Placing her hand over his bullet wound, she pressed as hard as she could. Griggs cried out in pain. "Do you see what you get when you fuck with God?"

With her other hand, Anne scooped up Griggs' pistol and tossed it away from him.

A team of five security guards burst through Anne's door and stopped. "Colonel Caroll?"

Anne stood up. "I want this man arrested and taken to the brig."

"On what charges, Colonel?" one of the security guards asked. "Mutiny and treason."

The security guards paused for a moment. They knew this was a very serious offense. "Yes, Colonel." They moved over to where Griggs was lying and lifted him up. "This man is wounded, do you want us to take him to Medical, Colonel?"

"No, I want him to suffer for a while longer."

"Yes, Colonel." The five guards escorted Griggs out of Anne's office.

Slumping down into her chair, Anne grabbed the radio off of the floor and held it to her mouth. "Dr. Emmerson?"

"Yes, Colonel?" Emmerson's crusty voice answered back.

"How long would it take you to do a complete mind wipe?" Anne asked.

Chapter Thirty

After passing through Oklahoma, Kansas and making a quick stop in Boulder, Colorado to pick up a change of clothes for Alex, the group had finally made it into Utah. Faith was sitting in the driver's seat with Durard sitting next to her, and Jake, Alex and Tyler were crammed tightly into the back seat.

Faith had been driving since Kansas, and she estimated that was over ten hours ago. After Faith had taken over driving, no one had really been talking. The closer they got to Nevada, the closer they all knew they were to whatever fate held for them. Most everyone had decided it was best to try and get some rest before they made it into Nevada.

Faith gripped the steering wheel tightly as she kept the battered car moving down the long, straight stretches of highway that were common in Southern Utah. The headlights of other cars and trucks shone brightly in her eyes as they passed. Night had fallen over eight hours ago and the stars were shining brightly overhead. It was a very clear night, not a cloud in the sky. The stars were one thing she never got tired of looking at. Being from Southern California, the smog was usually too thick and the towering buildings too bright for her to get a good look at the stars, so Faith enjoyed every minute of it.

She was beginning to regret her decision now as she stared at the stars. Faith wondered if she would have much time to gaze into the heavens when she was on the run from the government. It was strange, but she was following her dreams while in the military. She was training to become a doctor, just like she had always wanted, but on a whim, she had decided to throw it all away and help these three strangers she hardly knew, and for what?

Faith cleared the doubts from her mind as she led the vehicle gradually around a corner. It was too late to go back. She had made her decision and now she had to deal with the consequences, whatever they might be. Faith checked her rear-view mirror. She noticed a pair of headlights behind her, but paid no attention to them. It was probably just another car on this long and lonely stretch of highway.

Reaching down, Faith clicked on the radio and began to scan for radio stations. She had no idea where the closest town was, or even if she could get a signal, but at least this would keep her mind occupied. Static filled the car speakers, as Faith hurriedly turned down the volume so as not to wake anyone. Hitting the 'seek' button, the dial began to filter through the static. Faith watched it run through the dial four times before she turned off the radio. There was nothing out here in the middle of the desert.

Faith checked her rear-view mirror again. The pair of headlights behind her was drawing nearer. *Wow,* she thought, s*omebody's in a rush.*

Faith's eyes widened as a bright light shone straight at her. Cranking the wheel to the right, she narrowly avoided the skids of a helicopter that had swooped down in front of her. Mashing the gas pedal to the floor, she sent the car accelerating away from it.

"What the hell is going on?" Jake yelled from the backseat, sitting up.

Faith turned her head around and stared out the back window. The helicopter was fast approaching again, its searchlight shining on the back of the car. "We're in trouble," Faith announced. A white jeep had sped up behind them and was trying to maneuver around the battered sedan. The windows were tinted, but Faith knew who was inside.

Pulling alongside, the jeep veered to the right and slammed into the driver's side of the sedan. Faith twisted the wheel to the right, trying to pull away from the jeep. Looking to her left, she stared at the tinted windows. Fear began to well up inside her. She saw the jeep turn toward her again, and ram into the car. Everyone in the car was thrown hard to the right.

Faith was having trouble seeing because of the bright spotlight from the helicopter. "They found us!" Faith screamed.

Jake pulled his pistol from his jacket pocket. "Apparently," Jake nodded. He cocked back the hammer on his gun. "Get us alongside."

Faith tried to keep the car on the road as the jeep smashed into the side again. "I don't think that's going to be a problem, Jake!"

Jake turned to Tyler. "You keep an eye on that helicopter behind us. If it starts to make a move toward us, yell!"

Tyler nodded.

Jake returned his attention to the jeep next to them. Reaching down, he grabbed the window handle and tried to roll down the window, but couldn't. The door panel had been impacted. Lifting his elbow, he slammed against the window. Nothing happened. "Damn." Jake turned to Alex, "close

283

your eyes." Jake pointed the gun at the window and pulled the trigger. The glass shattered as the bullet broke through it. Leaning out the window, Jake took aim at the other vehicle. It veered to the right, and then began to swerve back again. Jake pulled himself back in through the window just before the jeep hit. He listened to the terrible grinding noise as the two metal beasts tried to pull apart.

Aiming his gun, Jake fired a shot into the rear window of the vehicle, sending shards of glass spraying in all directions. Jake cocked the gun and fired again, this time, hitting the passenger window. Jake saw two men dressed in black fatigues sitting inside the vehicle. The passenger sneered at Jake through the open window.

Lifting up his gun, Jake pointed it out the window at the passenger in the jeep. "Pull over right fucking now!" Jake yelled. With an extremely quick movement, the passenger reached out and slapped the gun from Jake's hand. Jake watched in horror as the silver pistol went skittering along the ground below them. Jake lifted himself out of the window and grabbed onto the soldier's jumpsuit and began to haul him out of the car. Jake pulled his arm back and sent his fist into the soldier's mouth.

"Jake! Get back in the car!" Faith screamed frantically.

Still grappling with the soldier, Jake turned his head to the right and looked up the road. He could see the headlights of a large semi-truck bearing down on them. He estimated he had close to twenty seconds before the truck hit. Turning his attention back, he sent another barrage of punches into the soldier's face. Pulling hard, Jake tipped the soldier out of the window and sent him to the asphalt. The back tires of the jeep hit the soldier with a sickening crunch of bones.

Pulling his head back inside the window, Jake stared at the lights of the oncoming truck. He suddenly grasped what Faith was trying to do. "Steady, Faith."

"In chicken, it's all about who turns first." Faith's knuckles were white, she was gripping the wheel so hard. Checking her rear-view mirror, she saw the helicopter was still only flying about ten feet off the ground as it followed the chase. Faith turned her head to glance at the driver of the white jeep. He was terrified. There was nowhere for him to go. On his side of the road was a sheer rock wall; on Faith's side was a small shoulder. He was motioning wildly for Faith to get out of the way.

Durard was in a panic. "What the hell are you doing? Turn!"

Durard began to reach for the wheel, when Jake stopped him. "Trust her. She's got a plan," Jake said in a very calm voice.

Durard sank back into the passenger's seat. "I hope so."

Faith had focused all her attention on the truck. She knew the impact was imminent now. Cranking the wheel hard to the left, she sent the car skidding out of the path of the truck. Jake and Durard turned to look behind them. The white jeep crashed headlong into the front of the semi sending the driver through the front windshield. He slammed into the grill of the truck killing him instantly. A massive fireball erupted as the truck tore through the jeep.

Seeing the accident, the helicopter tried to pull up, but clipped its landing skid on the cab of the truck, sending it careening wildly toward the ground. Its rotors hit the pavement and splintered into a thousand pieces. Chunks of the rotor blades shot off in all directions at a deadly speed. The hull of the helicopter impacted next and skidded along the asphalt. Its nose caught the road and flipped the helicopter end over end, destroying the tail assembly and demolishing the craft.

Everyone in the car cheered as smoke and flames reached high into the sky. Jake patted Faith on the shoulder as she slowly brought the car to a stop. "Nice work, Faith," Jake said commending her.

Faith sat motionless in the driver's seat, her knuckles still white and the color flushed from her face. "That's not what I had planned at all," she admitted.

"What?" Durard asked astonished.

"I just wanted to split us away from the jeep," Faith said quietly. Jake leaned back in his seat and began to laugh. "I'll be damned." Alex and Tyler looked at Jake. "What's so funny?" Alex asked.

"I'm just enjoying the fact I'm still alive," Jake laughed.

Durard reached down and grabbed the door handle and pushed the door open. Getting out of the car, he walked around to the driver's side and opened the door. "I think you need a break for a little while," he told Faith.

Faith nodded and slowly began to pry her fingers off the steering wheel. Sliding out of the car, she tried to stand up. Her whole body was shaking.

"I think the adrenaline is starting to wear off," she said with a smile.

"I'll help." Durard slid his arm around her waist and walked her slowly to the passenger side. He watched Faith slowly sink down into the seat. Closing the door, Durard walked back around to the driver's side. Taking one final look at the wreck behind them, Durard climbed in and shut the door.

***

Jannis had enjoyed the journey back to Area 51. It had been, for the most part, a quiet one. Once back on the helicopter, he had administered a mild sedative to Theresa to keep her unconscious during the trip.

Stepping off the helicopter, Jannis was met by two lab technicians with a gurney. They quickly loaded Theresa onto the gurney and wheeled her into the bay. Jannis grabbed his black duffel bag and started to walk into the mighty hangar. He spotted a row of vehicles along the back wall. The row mainly consisted of white Jeep Cherokees, but there were a few different models and colors intermingled amongst them. Pulling a set of keys out of his pocket, Jannis moved toward one of the white Cherokees. Sliding the key into the door lock, he turned it over and heard the lock pop. Opening the door, he tossed his black duffel into the passenger seat and jumped in. Jannis had the key in the ignition when the radio on his belt crackled to life. "Captain Jannis?"

Pulling the radio off his belt, Jannis held it to his mouth. "Yes, Colonel Caroll?"

"Good work," Anne's disembodied voice said over the speaker. "I need to speak with you in my office. It's urgent."

"On my way, Colonel." Jannis tossed the radio on top of the duffel and pulled his keys out of the ignition. Lifting the bag onto his shoulder, Jannis stepped out of the jeep and made his way toward the door on the far side of the hangar.

***

Hollman watched the lab techs slide the gurney into the dimly lit lab. He rushed toward the two men. "Dr. Cisan and I will take it from here." The two techs nodded and exited the room. Grabbing the bar at the back of the gurney, Hollman led it toward their workspace. "How's the sample coming?" he asked Cisan.

Cisan checked her findings one more time. "The virus has been perfectly synthesized, but I have taken the precaution of taming it down a bit. We don't want it to kill the patient before we've had a chance to run all our tests."

"Good thinking, Dr. Cisan." Hollman wheeled the gurney to an open spot between the workstation and the examination table that held the skeleton. Hollman began a cursory examination of his test patient. "Subject is female, and approximately fifteen years of age," he said into a small black tape recorder. Grabbing a tape measure, Hollman stretched it over the length of Theresa's body. "Subject is five foot one inch and weighs close to one hundred and ten pounds. She looks to be a bit dehydrated and malnourished, but we don't have

288

time to worry about that right now." Lifting a thermometer off the table, he pressed it into Theresa's ear. "Temperature is ninety-eight point two degrees, appears about normal." Laying the thermometer down, Hollman began to remove the white blouse Theresa was wearing. "I want a blood sample taken."

Cisan grabbed a needle off the workstation and moved toward Theresa. Tapping her two fingers against the inside of the young girl's arm, Cisan watched a vein rise to the surface. Holding Theresa's arm, Cisan plunged the needle into her vein. Reaching for a glass tube, Cisan pressed the end securely into the needle. Blood immediately began to flow into the tube. Pulling it out, Cisan pressed a cotton ball against the point of entry and removed the needle. "She's all yours, Dr. Hollman."

Hollman nodded. "Dr. Cisan, can you prepare the virus for injection?"

"I'm on it," Cisan reported. Grabbing another syringe off the table, she inserted the needle into a small vial filled with yellow fluid. Pulling up on the plunger, she took the yellow fluid into the syringe. Turning around, she carefully handed it to Hollman.

Accepting the syringe, Hollman carefully set it down on the gurney next to a bottle of rubbing alcohol and a few cotton swabs. Taking one of the cotton balls, he dipped it in the bottle and began to swab her shoulder. Tossing the cotton ball aside, Hollman picked up the syringe and held it over Theresa's arm. "Cross your fingers," he muttered under his breath. Pushing the needle into Theresa's shoulder, he pressed the plunger and delivered a large dose of the virus into her system. Pulling the needle out, Hollman took a step back. "We need to wait for the virus to take hold of her system before we can start testing the vaccine." Hollman pulled off his white latex gloves and tossed them in the trash.

***

"Thanks for coming, Captain. Have a seat."

Jannis walked into the room and sat down. He immediately noticed two large bloodstains on Anne's floor, and a black bruise forming over Anne's left eye. "What happened, Colonel?"

"You could say that Major Griggs and I had a bit of a falling out," Anne said, trying to hide her new bruise the best she could. "That's not what's important right now, though. There has been a change in plans."

"Yes, Colonel?"

"Our operatives have encountered the escaped prisoners on a stretch of highway in Southern Utah. They're apparently heading this way," Anne informed Jannis.

"Do you think they're going to try another assault on Area 51?" Jannis asked. Anne shook her head no. "I don't think they're that brave, or foolish."

"Then what are they doing?" Jannis wondered.

"We're really not sure, but we've speculated they may be trying to accomplish the same thing we are."

Jannis' eyes widened. "You think they're going to try and create a vaccine for the virus?"

Anne nodded. "That seems like the only logical

reason they would be heading toward Southern Nevada. They need a sample of the virus to create their vaccine." Anne stood up and walked around her desk. "I will not allow this to happen."

"What are your orders, Colonel?" Jannis asked as he snapped to attention.

"We're going to form a little raiding party. I want to head them off at the pass, Captain," Anne said smiling. "No more fucking around with these three. I'm authorizing the use of deadly force. I want them all shot on the spot. No questions asked."

"Yes, Colonel."

"I want you to head up the team, Captain. I want personnel assigned and all gear squared away within the hour. Advise me when you are ready to leave, and I will join you in the hangar bay." Anne returned to her chair and sat down. "Dismissed."

Jannis stood up and saluted. As he walked out of Anne's office, an evil grin grew across his face.

Chapter Thirty-one

"Dr. Hollman! Come quickly!" Dr. Cisan shouted into the dark of the Med Lab. Cisan was standing over the convulsing body of Theresa trying desperately to hold her down. With her hands on Theresa's shoulders, Cisan pressed down with all her strength to keep the girl from injuring herself.

Hollman burst into the room with a lit cigarette still burning in his mouth. Tossing it down, he quickly made his way through the rows of tubes that littered the Med Lab. "What happened?" he shouted.

"I don't know! I was just taking another blood sample and she started!" Theresa's arms began to flail wildly. Her right arm shot up and caught Cisan in the middle of the face. Cisan stumbled back toward the workstation, a trickle of blood running from her nose.

Hollman stared down at Theresa. Her eyes had begun to roll back in her head, and he feared she was in danger of swallowing her tongue. Grabbing her, Hollman flipped Theresa over onto her side. Theresa began to gag as yellow foam started to ooze from her mouth and nose. Hollman stepped back in horror. "Jesus!" He pressed his hand over his mouth. Then, as suddenly as it had begun, it was over. Theresa lay silently on the table, her unblinking eyes still wide with fear.

Cisan stood up and looked at the body. "Damn. I thought we were really close with this one." She wiped the blood from her nose on to the white sleeve of her lab coat.

Hollman slowly walked around the table and

joined Cisan. "How much time had elapsed from the point when we gave her the virus until the moment she died?"

Cisan checked her watch. "About an hour," she said grimly.

"This isn't good. The virus that's on the loose right now is killing people within twenty-four hours. This one did it in less than an hour." Hollman thought about the ramifications of his statement. "If this virus were to get loose into the population, we could conceivably see the total annihilation of the human species."

"Christ." Cisan leaned up against the workstation. Her knees had suddenly become weak. "We've been standing in the same room with an infected patient. We could have contracted the virus."

"We didn't," Hollman tried to reassure Cisan.

"How do you know, Greg? Our subject didn't show any symptoms of the virus until she began having a seizure and yellow foam started flowing from her mouth!" Cisan argued.

"First off, we have no idea if this strain of the virus is airborne. It's entirely possible that the virus needs to be contracted through the exchange of bodily fluids, or by ingestion. It's possible the virus in the southwest has become airborne because of its mutating with the common flu," Hollman argued.

"Yeah, but what if it's not?" Cisan asked with fear in her voice.

"Then we damn well better find a cure," Hollman responded seriously. The two doctors sat in silence for a long moment. just staring at the corpse on the table in front of them. "You said you took a blood sample before she began to seize?"

"Yes, but I didn't get a whole lot," Cisan admitted. "She started when the needle was still in her arm."

"It'll just have to do then." Hollman turned his gaze away from the body. "I want a total work up of that blood done immediately. It may give us a bit of insight into the nature of the virus." Hollman turned and began to walk away. "I also want you to perform a full autopsy on the body. I want to know what every cell in her body was doing before she died."

"Where are you going?" Cisan wondered.

"I need to go speak to the Colonel. We're going to need a new test subject," Hollman replied as he strode through the door.

***

Griggs was still reeling from his surgery. Two soldiers had moved him from the Med Bay to a separate sterile white room. Inside the room, there were two banks of computers surrounding what looked to Griggs like the electric chair. It was a high backed silver chair with black padding on the arms and seat. Sprouting from the top was a long arm with two metal tentacles hanging from it.

The two security guards that had escorted Griggs quickly pushed him into the chair and proceeded to strap him in. There were thick straps that went around both his wrists, his ankles and around his chest. Once they felt Griggs was securely in place, they turned to leave.

He felt a twinge of pain in his right shoulder.

Griggs knew they had repaired his wounds, but he swore he could still feel the two bullet holes. Rolling his shoulder around, he could still feel a few stray shards of bone pressing into the flesh of his chest.

Pushing the thought of the pain away, Griggs quickly scanned the room. He had been here before. It was small and looked like it could only hold about five people at a time. Behind him, he could see rows of hi-tech equipment lining the wall. In front of him, sat a small silver tray with several needles and surgical tools on it. In the middle of the tray, he spotted a scalpel, but it was too far away for him to grab.

The door opening and a lab tech walking in startled Griggs. He was a short, bald man with a gray beard. Griggs suddenly remembered him. "You were there when I was taken out of the tube, weren't you?"

Emmerson nodded. "Yes I was, Major, and we all had such high hopes for you. I guess since your sitting in the 'sizzle chair', our project has failed."

"The 'sizzle chair'?" Griggs asked.

Emmerson picked up a syringe already filled with a clear liquid. "Ah hell, I guess I can tell you, since you're not going to remember any of this in a minute." Emmerson walked around to Griggs' right. Grabbing Griggs' head, Emmerson pressed it firmly against the chair and wrapped another thick strap across his forehead. "This is the mind wipe chamber, Major. We mainly use it for removing the memories of the abductees, but since the 'Uber-Soldier' Project is dead, it hasn't seen much use. We call it the 'sizzle chair' because the amount of

295

electricity we pump through a subject kind of makes them sizzle like a piece of bacon."

"Nice," Griggs said with disdain.

Emmerson lifted the needle and with one quick stroke, pressed the needle firmly into Griggs' temple, then into his brain. Griggs cried out in pain and tried to break free of the straps. "Sit still, Major. The more you struggle, the more this is going to hurt." Emmerson pressed down on the plunger, sending the clear liquid into Griggs' brain.

After the last of the fluid had been injected, Emmerson removed the needle and set it on the small silver tray.

"Get the fuck away from me!" Griggs shouted, trying to break free of his restraints.

"I'm afraid I can't do that," Emmerson said sympathetically as he pulled the tray closer to him. Lifting the scalpel off the tray, he quickly cut a hole in the shoulder of Griggs' uniform. Setting the scalpel down, he lifted another needle and pressed it into Griggs' shoulder. "This device not only erases memories, but with it, I can create new one's for you. Fantastic little machine," Emmerson said with a smile.

Griggs felt the chemical Emmerson had injected into his brain spreading like a fire. "I need my memories!"

"You'll never even miss them," Emmerson responded. Turning away, he began to work with several of the computers in the room.

Griggs carefully grabbed the scalpel with his fingers and slid it between the arm of the chair and the restraint. He quickly began to work the scalpel around, cutting the strap. "I'm not going to let you do this to me," Griggs said very seriously, trying to keep the older man distracted.

"I'm afraid you have no choice in the matter." Emmerson returned to Griggs' side and reached up for the spider-like device above the chair. Pulling it down, he positioned the arm just above Griggs' head. Grabbing one of the tentacles, he pressed it to Griggs' temple and pressed a small, blue button on it. Griggs heard a snap at the same time as pain shot through his head. "I've just patched one of the memory arms directly into your brain. One more, and we're ready to go."

Griggs began to saw frantically on the strap as Emmerson moved around to his other side. "If you do this, you'll live to regret it," Griggs warned as he felt the scalpel cut through the final bit of the restraint. His left hand was free.

"Oh, I don't think so," Emmerson said as he attached the second memory arm to Griggs' head. "I think I'll be very safe indeed." He made his way to a hanging console in front of Griggs and keyed several commands into it. "So, what do you want to be when you wake up?" Emmerson joked. "I can make you a sixteen year old girl, if I want."

Griggs could feel the electricity charging on the ends of the memory arms in his head. He knew he had to do it now. Griggs smiled. "Come here and I'll tell you what I want."

Emmerson walked to Griggs' side and stopped. "What do you want? Tell me."

"Closer," Griggs whispered.

Emmerson leaned in a little nearer. "What?"

Griggs' left arm shot up and grabbed Emmerson around the throat. "I want all my

297

memories intact." Squeezing hard, Griggs watched the color begin to drain out of Emmerson's face. Using all his strength, Griggs tossed the old man away from him. Emmerson hit the wall hard and crumpled to the ground. Wasting no time, Griggs began to undo the straps around his head and arms. Once his hands and head were free, he yanked the memory arms from his temples. His head was shooting with pain. Reaching down, he pulled the restraints off his ankles. Griggs slowly stood up and walked toward Emmerson. "I told you I wouldn't let you do this to me." Lifting up the old man, Griggs tossed him in the silver chair and began to strap him in.

Emmerson was frantic. "What are you doing?"

"Just returning the favor, Doc." Griggs grabbed the two memory arms and pressed them into Emmerson's head. "I need everyone to think I've been wiped, so either you cooperate, or I'll rearrange your memories."

"I will do no such thing!" Emmerson shouted in defiance.

"Fine, have it your way." Griggs pulled the computer over in front of the chair. He noticed the system was already primed to activate, he just had to input the amount of memory he wanted to erase, and the replacement memory he wanted to implement. Griggs quickly set the mind wipe to erase the last three minutes of memories, and began to type in a suitable replacement memory. "Are you ready?" he asked Emmerson.

"You can't be serious! You don't even know what you're doing there! You could kill me if you activate that!" Emmerson screamed.

"I think that's a risk I'm willing to take." Griggs pressed the enter button on the keyboard. The machines around the room whirred to life. The sound was almost deafening. Emmerson's body was instantly flooded with electricity as the lights in the room momentarily dimmed. Every muscle in his body began to tense as the memory wipe began to take effect. Griggs looked down at the screen. It noted it was nearly eighty percent complete. "Almost done, Doc." Griggs heard a chime from the computer as it registered one hundred percent complete.

Walking over to Emmerson, he realized why they called it the 'sizzle chair'. He could smell Emmerson's slightly burned flesh. After unbuckling his restraints, Griggs lifted the unconscious man out of the chair and carefully propped him against the front wall. Griggs had no idea how long Emmerson would be out for. Slipping into the chair, he reattached his restraints and the memory arms the best he could. Slumping down into the chair, Griggs began to play possum.

Emmerson suddenly shot to consciousness at the front of the room. "What the hell?" Looking around, he saw Griggs still sitting in the chair. Moving over to the monitor, he saw that the process had been completed. *Must've fallen asleep for a minute while the machine ran its course.* Stepping over to Griggs, he began to remove the straps and memory arms. "Griggs," he shouted. "Name and rank!"

Griggs slowly lifted his head and opened his eyes. "Major Jason Griggs, United States Air Force," he said groggily. Looking around, he tried

299

to feign ignorance. "Where am I?"

"My name is Dr. Emmerson. You were injured during a routine combat drill and we had to bring you to the Med Bay," Emmerson said to Griggs. "You hit your head pretty hard, so we were worried about any kind of memory loss."

Griggs tried to hide his smile. The wipe on Emmerson had worked. "How am I, Dr. Emmerson?" Griggs asked coyly, playing along.

"You're fit for duty, Major," Emmerson reported pleasantly.

"Good, I need to get back to work," Griggs said as he stood up. "Thank you, Doctor."

Emmerson nodded as he watched Griggs walk out the door. Picking up a small black radio off a nearby table, he tapped the talk button and held it to his mouth. "Colonel Caroll?"

"Yes?" Anne's voice answered back.

"I've just completed the mind wipe on Major Griggs, as you requested. He doesn't remember anything about his involvement with the destruction of Area 51 and S-4, or being cloned."

"Good work, Dr. Emmerson. Where is he now?" Anne asked.

"I think he might be heading your direction, Colonel Caroll." Emmerson answered.

"Thank you, Dr. Emmerson. I knew I could count on you. Caroll out." A short hiss of static erupted on the radio, then died.

Setting the radio back down on the table, Emmerson smiled. He felt a great deal of pride in the job he had just done. He just couldn't figure out where he had gotten this severe headache.

***

"Come in," Anne replied to the knock on her door.

Hollman stepped inside. "I have bad news, Colonel. Can I have a minute of your time?"

Anne nodded. "Sure, but I'm in a bit of a rush, Doctor." She was leaning over and lacing up her black combat boots. She had changed from her blue uniform back into her black fatigues. She had also pulled her hair back into a ponytail.

"Thank you." Hollman made his way into the room and sat down in one of Anne's chairs. "We lost our test subject about ten minutes ago."

"What?" Anne exclaimed, sitting up.

Hollman sank down into the chair. "We don't exactly know what happened, Colonel. We gave her an injection of the virus, then less than an hour later, she died," Hollman explained. "The virus sample we found on the skeleton we recovered from North Carolina was an untainted one. It was the virus in pure form."

"So what you're saying is the virus on the loose in the southwest isn't pure?" Anne asked.

"No. What we think happened is that it mutated itself with a strand of the common influenza virus, and this mutation has, in effect, slowed it down. It kills within twenty-four hours, instead of the one hour the pure sample kills in."

"My God," Anne gasped. "We need to get more samples of the pure virus. They could make an awesome weapon."

Hollman was astonished at what Anne had just said. "That's not really the point right now,

301

Colonel."

Anne pulled herself away from her vision and looked crossly at Hollman. "Then what is the point, Dr. Hollman?"

Hollman began to feel very uncomfortable under Anne's gaze. "The point," he started, "is that we didn't have time to run the proper tests on the subject, therefore, we didn't come up with a vaccine."

Anne slammed her fist onto her desk. "What is it with you, Hollman? First, you need a test subject, so I provide that. Then, you need a new pure sample of the virus, and I provided that. Then you needed a new test subject, and again, I provided that. Now you need another new test subject? You need to learn to play with your toys more carefully, Dr. Hollman. I am getting very tired of getting you new ones."

"I'm sorry, Colonel, but if this project is to succeed, we need a vaccine, and to create a vaccine, I need a new test subject," Hollman explained.

"Very well," Anne said in an exasperated tone. "I'm heading up a mission into Las Vegas, and you have just become part of the team. This time, you can get your own guinea pig."

"But, Colonel, I'm not a field op."

"That doesn't really matter to me, Dr. Hollman. If you want a new test patient, you have to go get it yourself." Anne stated forcefully. A knock at her door pulled her from her rage. "Come."

Griggs briskly walked into the room, snapped to attention, and fired off a salute. "Good afternoon, Colonel."

"Did you go see Dr. Emmerson, Major?" Anne

asked, feigning ignorance.

"Yes, Colonel," Griggs responded unemotionally. "He said I was fine and cleared me for duty."

"Good. I want you to get with Captain Jannis and assemble a team. We're heading into Las Vegas in about an hour," Anne commanded.

"May I ask the objective of this mission so that I may put together a team accordingly, Colonel?" Griggs asked, still at attention.

"The nature of the mission is top secret, but I can tell you that we've received information that there are a group of known terrorists heading there as we speak." Anne stood up. "Now get to it, Major."

"Yes, Colonel." Griggs snapped off another salute, then turned to leave. Hollman watched Griggs leave before he turned back to Anne. "Do you really think he can be trusted with this mission?"

"Why not?" Anne asked curiously.

"I heard you over the radio asking for a mind wipe on this character." Hollman leaned forward toward Anne. "I'm just saying I wouldn't send him back out into the thick of things so soon after a mind wipe."

"That's why you'll never make it to the rank of Colonel, Dr. Hollman," Anne said sarcastically. "Now get out of my sight. I want you and whatever you need to get your new test subject on the tarmac in forty-five minutes."

Chapter Thirty-two

St. George, Utah was utterly decimated. It seemed like it had suffered the same fate as Las Vegas. Not a soul could be found on the empty streets, not even a corpse. Cars had been abandoned, and buildings and storefronts had been boarded up.

Jake had only been here one time before, on a retreat from the FBI. A buddy of his had convinced him to take up golf, so they had come here to use the plentiful courses. Jake never liked golf, or St. George. It was too hot for him. The landscape was flat and desolate. Temperatures here in the summer reached a high of one hundred and fifteen. Luckily, it was fall, and temperatures had cooled to only ninety-five degrees in the shade. Jake looked down at his watch. It read ten forty-five am. They had been driving for thirty-eight hours straight.

"We need to stop and rest before we head into Vegas," Alex said from the backseat.

"I agree," Faith added. "We've been driving for a long time."

Durard looked in his rear-view mirror at Jake in the backseat. "What's it going to be, boss? Continue on, or rest for a while?"

Jake shrugged. He was as tired as the rest of them, but he kept longing for this whole ordeal to be over. "It's up to you guys, but just remember, the longer we stay in one place, the more of a risk we run being spotted by Anne's goons."

"Understood," Durard pulled the car over. Shutting off the ignition, he pulled out the keys and stuffed them into his pocket. "I need some rest," Durard said wearily. He pointed to the building they were next to. "I'm going into this hotel, and I'm going to take a nap. You're all invited to come along."

Faith opened her door and got out. "I'm with Durard. I could go for a little rest. Most of us have been operating with little or no sleep for the past four days, and we all need to be in top form when we head into Las Vegas."

Jake nodded. "You guys are right." He looked down at Alex's leg. "Plus we need to change Alex's bandages."

"Then it's settled," Tyler said, opening the door. "We're staying here for a while."

"Yeah," Jake opened his door and stepped out. Reaching back in, he helped Alex out of the car. "Let's go in and take a look around before we get settled." Jake looked at the outside of the hotel. It was a tall brick building with gray trim, and a black iron fence that ran all the way around it for decoration. He glanced up at the sign and read it. "The St. George Super Seven Motel." Jake and Alex followed the other three into the lobby of the hotel.

"Hey, this isn't bad," remarked Durard.

"They must be going for that glitzy Las Vegas look," Jake said while glancing around. The hotel was still in very good condition. A few lamps and tables had been knocked over, but for the most part, it was clean. The lobby's interior was mainly white with a dark blue carpet. The front door led into a wide area that had the check-in desk on the right, and a large staircase at the rear. In the middle of the room, there was a small empty fountain and several comfortable chairs arranged along the walls. A bank

305

of elevators stood quietly to the left of the wide room. Tyler slowly made his way over to the check-in desk. Reaching over, he rang a gold bell that sat on top. The ding of the bell echoed through the entire hotel.

"I don't think there's anyone here to answer that bell," Faith commented.

"I know," Tyler hit the bell again. "I just want to make sure." As Tyler turned away from Faith, he spotted two black barrels of a shotgun slowly sliding out from a partially opened door behind the desk. "Get down!" Tyler leapt and tackled Faith just as the gunshot rang out in the lobby.

"Get the hell out of my hotel, you looters!" A male's voice shouted from the same direction as the shot had come from. "I'll kill you all if I have to!"

Jake, Durard and Alex had pressed themselves to the floor behind the stone fountain. "We're not here to rob you!" Alex yelled. "We just need a place to stay!"

Another blast from the shotgun echoed through the lobby. The spray of buckshot hit the ceiling, sending dust and bits of drywall raining down on Faith and Tyler. "I don't care!" The man yelled. "If you think you're going to come in here and spread that damned virus, you've got another think coming!"

"We've got nowhere else to go!" Alex cried.

"I don't have any vacancies," the man shouted again.

"Stop shooting and we'll leave!" Tyler screamed.

"Fine, go!" The man yelled while cocking his gun. "If you're not all out of my hotel within ten

306

seconds, I'll shoot every single person I see!" The man warned in an angry tone.

Jake quickly turned to look at Durard and Alex. In that moment, they all knew they had to run. Nodding, Durard and Alex prepared to go. Peeking around the edge of the fountain, Jake spotted Faith and Tyler cowering behind the check-in desk. Jake snapped his fingers to get their attention. He mouthed the words "let's go now". Crawling toward the fountain, Faith looked behind her to see the door behind the counter wide open. She began to panic. The man had taken position on the counter. A wicked smile crossed his bearded face as he brought his double barrel shotgun to bear on Tyler and Faith. He was wearing a brown suit and had a pair of glasses with white tape wrapped around the center. One of the lenses was also broken. He was balding on top, leaving only a small band of hair that ran around the back and sides of his head.

His suit was ripped and torn, and his tie hung crookedly off to one side on his white shirt. It looked like this man hadn't seen anyone in a while, and wanted to keep it that way.

Thinking quickly, Durard grabbed a handful of loose change out of the fountain and tossed it at the man. The coins pelted the man, sending him staggering backwards off the counter. They heard him hit, and at the same time, his gun went off. "Now!" Jake yelled. The five jumped up and raced toward the door. Bursting out into the heat of the day, the five all raced toward the car and climbed in.

Jake stood outside trying to catch his breath. "I feel more rested already."

"Get in the car, Jake!" Alex yelled as the front door to the hotel burst open and the man charged outside.

Diving into the backseat, Jake landed on the laps of Alex and Tyler as Durard smashed the accelerator to the floor. Alex screamed in pain as the sedan tore away from the curb awkwardly. Behind them, the man was able to snap off one shot with his gun. The buckshot ricocheted off the back of the car. Once well out of distance of the weapon, Jake lifted himself apologetically off Alex and Tyler and seated himself.

"We need to get into a different vehicle," Durard said. "This one's beat to hell."

"I think we can take our pick," Faith said looking at all of the abandoned vehicles scattered about the road.

"That one," Tyler said pointing to a small black Porsche.

"I don't think so. We wouldn't all fit in that," Alex was coddling the wound on her leg. She was bleeding again. She knew Jake had broken open her wound and probably a few stitches when he landed on her.

"There." Jake pointed at a blue, four door SUV. "That's our new ride."

Durard pulled the battered tan sedan over to the SUV. Stepping out, he looked inside the tinted windows. "Seems okay," he said while opening the door. Looking inside, he couldn't see any sign of the driver. Checking the steering column, he found the keys still dangling in the ignition. Climbing inside, Durard twisted the keys and listened as the vehicle roared to life. "We're in business here."

Anne was staring out the window as the Southern Nevada landscape passed by the window in a blur of yellow and brown. She listened to the radio chatter on her headset. Looking up front, she watched the pilots maneuvering the black helicopter along the gray road below. She had decided not to ride with the troops, instead, opting to take a helicopter to Las Vegas. She glanced over at Hollman and Cisan in the seats next to her. They were rummaging through their bag of gear, making a final check of what they had brought.

"Major Griggs?" Anne said into her headset. "Yes, Colonel?" Griggs answered.

"Are your men ready?" Anne asked.

"Yes, Colonel. We'll be ready to roll once we hit Las Vegas." Griggs responded with confidence.

"Very good, Major. I want a full gear check before we reach Las Vegas, understood?"

"Yes, Colonel."

"Caroll out." Anne turned off the mic in her headset and sat back in the seat of the helicopter. Something seemed wrong here.

***

Down below the helicopter, Jannis and Griggs sat in the front seats of the green bus that was barreling down the road. Behind them sat fifteen of the men Griggs had handpicked to be on this mission. He knew they were loyal to Anne and the Air Force, but he also knew they weren't the best on

309

the base. He had picked these men hoping they could eventually be defeated.

It was a quiet trip to Las Vegas. All the men on the bus were sitting quietly, either looking out the window, or just staring at the back of the seat in front of them. The only sound was that of the bus bumping and jostling along the dirt road that led away from Area 51. The various squeaks and creaks of the bus sounded loudly in the men's ears.

The driver, a young man in black fatigues with a goatee, carefully applied the brakes on the bus and brought the mammoth to a stop. "Major, we're at the turn onto the highway."

Griggs stood up and looked out the windows. He could see no traffic on the highway. Standing in the aisle, he addressed the troops. "These will be your final instructions before we reach Las Vegas. Once there, I want gas masks on and safeties off. This is a search and destroy mission." Griggs turned to the driver. "Let's go." Griggs felt the bus rumble onto the highway. Steadying himself with his hands, he looked over the faces of the men. He saw fear in the eyes of some of them. "You will report directly to myself or Captain Jannis, understood?"

"Sir, yes, sir!" The men yelled in unison.

"Good. I want a clean and quick dispersal once we reach Vegas. Weapons and gear check in five minutes." Griggs returned to his seat, and wiped the sweat off his forehead.

Jannis looked over and caught sight of Griggs' discomfort. "Feeling all right, Major?"

"Fine, Captain," Griggs said as he dabbed his face.

Jannis stared at him with an uneasy feeling in

310

his gut. He knew something was wrong here; he just couldn't put his finger on it. Turning back around, Jannis glanced out the front window and saw the black helicopter had taken the lead. He wondered if Anne had the same feeling.

Chapter Thirty-three

Close to an hour later, Durard saw Las Vegas looming ominously in the distance. The shimmering mirages on the road from the heat cast a kind of mythical quality over the city, as it seemed to appear out of nowhere. Durard felt like an archaeologist laying eyes on a lost city for the first time in thousands of years. Following an off-ramp, he piloted the SUV down onto the city streets. It looked the same way St. George did, empty, silent and foreboding.

Slowing the vehicle down, Durard glanced around. There was nothing left here except the buildings. The population seemed to have vanished. "Where do we go?" Durard asked almost nervously.

"I don't know," Faith replied from the passenger's seat. "I wouldn't have any idea where to start looking." Faith felt her skin crawl as she looked at the empty stores and casinos.

"Just keep looking around. At least we know a few people have survived the virus, we just have to find them." Alex was sitting in the backseat applying pressure to her leg.

"Yeah, our friend at the hotel in St. George proved that," Tyler joked.

Durard kept his speed low as they cruised around the vacant city streets. His hands firmly grasped the black steering wheel while he scanned for anything that might lead them toward their prospect. "This is like looking for a needle in a haystack."

"A haystack of more needles," Jake commented. "We just need to keep going...." Jake trailed off as he caught sight of something. "What was that?" He pointed toward an alley.

Faith stared hard at the alley. "I don't see anything."

"Stop!" Jake yelled as he threw open the door. Jumping out, he sprinted toward the alley and stopped just outside of its mouth. Squinting his eyes, he peered into the shadowy space. "I could've sworn I saw a person duck into this alley," he admitted to himself.

Tyler and Durard had joined him at the front of the alley. "I don't see anything Jake," Durard confessed.

"Neither do I," Tyler said, still searching the alley.

"Wait," Jake pointed to a man emerging from a door at the end of the alley. "There he is!" Jake began to walk quickly down the alley toward the man. "Sir?" He called out. "Sir, can we talk to you for a minute?"

The man turned around to see Jake, Durard and Tyler walking toward him and froze dead in his tracks. "What do you want?" he asked in a weak and fearful voice. He was dressed in a white lab coat and blue hospital scrubs. His short, brown hair was arranged messily on top of his head.

"We just want to ask you a few questions," Durard said calmly as he took a step closer to the man.

"You mean you're not the same vultures that have been looting in this neighborhood?" the frightened man asked.

"No, we're not really from around here," Jake explained. "Are you a doctor?"

"Yes," the man said, a little more at ease now. "My name's Doctor Rossdale, *uh*, Ken Rossdale."

"Pleased to meet you, Doctor Rossdale." Jake reached out and shook Rossdale's hand. "My name's Jake, and these are my friends Jim Durard and Tyler Mitchell." Jake turned to Tyler. "Why don't you go and get the girls?"

Tyler nodded.

"What are you guys doing out here? Don't you know about the virus?" Rossdale asked.

"As a matter of fact," Jake smiled. "That's why we're here. Is there some place private where we can talk, Doctor?"

"Yeah," Rossdale pointed toward the door he had emerged from. "Why don't we step into the clinic? We can talk in my office." Rossdale began to lead Jake and Durard in the door, when Tyler came running around the corner. "Jake!" Tyler screamed. "They're gone!"

"What?" Jake said stopping.

Tyler came to a stop right in front of Jake and tried to catch his breath. "They're gone! Alex and Faith are gone!"

"Shit!" Jake yelled. Turning around, he took a few steps away from the door. "Doctor Rossdale, can we come by a little later? We need to go find our friends."

"No," Rossdale said, pulling a gun out of his lab coat. "I really think you need to come inside."

Jake spun around to face Rossdale. "What the...?"

Rossdale's soft green eyes had hardened as he kept the pistol trained on all three men. "Everyone inside right now!" He motioned at them with the

314

gun.

Jake scowled at Rossdale as he walked past him into the door. Inside, the clinic was as empty as the rest of Las Vegas. Exam rooms lay in disarray, probably from the last few patients they had seen here. Files, folders and broken bottles of medicine lay scattered about the floor.

Rossdale pressed his pistol against Jake's back. "Keep moving."

Jake spun around quickly and got in Rossdale's face. "You better ease up with that, or something bad is going to happen," Jake warned.

Rossdale didn't even flinch. "Get the fuck out of my face," he pressed the gun to Jake's head, "or something bad will happen to you right now." He cocked back the hammer on the weapon. Jake knew he wasn't fast enough to disarm Rossdale. Rossdale would surely pull the trigger as soon as he saw Jake making a move. Reluctantly, Jake turned around and began to follow Tyler and Durard. "Take a right at the next door," Rossdale yelled at Durard.

Looking to his right, Durard spotted the door. Reaching down and grabbing the handle, he carefully opened it. The door led to another hallway and a set of stairs leading up at the end. Looking through the windows in the hallway as he passed, Durard realized these must be the offices of the doctors. For the most part, they seemed to be abandoned. Glancing to the left, he caught sight of a man in a white lab coat sprawled out over his wooden desk with yellow foam still oozing from his mouth. On his chest, the doctor was grasping a frame with a photo of his family inside. Quickly looking away, Durard tried to calm the wave of nausea and hatred that had passed over him.

"Up the stairs," Rossdale said again. "Go all the way to the top and open the door."

Durard, Tyler, Jake and Rossdale began to make the slow trek up the stairs. After they had walked up all four flights, Durard came to a gray metal door at the top. Slowly reaching out, he grabbed the door handle and cracked open the door. Sunlight flooded in, temporarily blinding him. Covering his eyes, Durard saw the doorway led to the roof. Stepping out onto the roof, Durard noticed several shadows to one side. Jake and Tyler followed immediately with Rossdale right behind them.

"So nice of you to join us," a female's voice boomed. "Why don't you come over and say hello to a couple of old friends of yours?"

Jake's eyes gradually adjusted to the light. Looking across the rooftop, he saw Anne, Jannis and Griggs standing amidst fifteen soldiers in black. Cisan and Hollman were hovering quietly at the back. "Where's Alex and Faith!" Jake shouted angrily.

Anne took a few steps forward toward Jake. "They're somewhere very," Anne smiled, "safe." She turned and pointed toward a metal tower that was on one side of the roof.

Jake's eyes widened when he saw Alex and Faith tied to it. "What the fuck are you doing, Anne?" Alex and Faith were both bound and gagged about halfway up the tower. Anne had placed them both in the positions of the crucifixion, their arms spread wide.

"Just leveling the playing field, Jake," Anne

laughed while pointing to a bomb at the bottom of the tower.

"Leveling the playing field?" Jake asked. "You have at least fifteen armed men standing over there with you."

Anne shrugged. "Do you have any last requests before I kill you and your friends?"

Jake took a step forward. "I just—"

"Whoa, stop right there," Anne said, lifting her assault rifle. "That is close enough."

Jake stopped. "I just want to know the truth before I die."

"The truth? What makes you think you're entitled to the truth?" Anne asked spitefully. "I don't owe you anything. In fact, you are the one who has taken everything from me. I think it is you who owes me, Mr. Silver. You and your little bitch Alex Robinson." Anne turned and shot a smile toward Alex on the tower. "Why?" Jake yelled.

"Because you killed my CO, General Perry, and you tried to kill me!" Anne screamed.

"We were protecting ourselves! You and General Perry were trying to kill us! You killed Major Griggs!" Jake felt strange saying that with Griggs standing less than ten feet away from him. "You received exactly what you deserved, Anne."

"Bullshit!" Anne screamed angrily. "I didn't deserve to wander through the desert for days with a gunshot wound in my chest." Jake shifted his eyes behind Anne to look at Griggs. He was motioning to Jake while slowly pulling his pistol out of its holster. Jake quickly turned his eyes back to Anne, unsure of what Griggs was doing. "I had no water, no food and no idea where I was going! The only

317

thing that saved me was my years of military training!" Anne took a step closer to Jake and pointed her rifle at his head. "You did this to me, and I will kill you because of it!"

"That's it, you're just going to kill me?" Jake was just trying to keep her talking long enough to see what Griggs was planning. "You're not going to slowly torture me to exact your revenge?"

"Nope." Anne clicked the safety off on her weapon with her thumb. "I'm just going to kill you right where you stand," Anne suddenly reconsidered, "but first, I'm going to let you watch your two bitches die." Anne took a few steps back and handed her weapon to a nearby soldier. She pulled a small black box out of her pocket and showed it to Jake.

It had two buttons on it, a green and a red one. "This beautiful little device was designed by our demolition experts. When I press this little red button, it will start a two-minute countdown. Once started, you get the pleasure of waiting for them to die." Anne smiled. "Hell, I guess I do want to watch you suffer for a little while before I kill you, Jake." Alex and Faith were struggling against their bonds as they tried to free themselves. Jake could see the terror in their eyes.

"Don't do this, Anne." Jake made a quick decision in his mind. "If it's me you want, then take me and let everyone else go."

"Interesting offer," Anne mused, "but no. I not only want to kill you, but Alex also." Anne pressed the red button.

"No!" Jake began to charge Anne, but was stopped short when two soldiers jumped forward with their weapons trained on him.

"You have less than two minutes, Jake. Better make your peace with Alex and Faith," Anne reminded him joyously.

"You bitch. I will kill you. I promise you that," Jake growled angrily. "As do I," a voice boomed from behind the group.

Anne spun around. "What the fuck? I thought you were dead!"

General Foster pulled himself up onto the rooftop. Standing up, he dusted himself off and pointed his weapon at Anne. "You tried to kill me, but failed miserably, just like you do everything else. I will have you court-martialed for this, Colonel Caroll. You can count on that." Several of Anne's soldiers spun around and pointed their weapons at Foster. "Tell your men to put down their weapons or I'll blow your fucking head off, Caroll."

"What do you think they'll do to you then, General?" Anne asked, delighted another player had come into the game. She quickly hid the detonator behind her back.

Jake was in awe of the events unfolding before his eyes. He had no idea who this Foster person was, he was just happy the man was on his side, although Jake knew the clock was still ticking on the bomb.

"Yes, but you'll be dead." Foster took a few steps closer to Anne. "Tell them to put their weapons down right now!" Foster looked like hell. His blue uniform was in shambles and his jacket was hanging open, revealing several blood soaked bandages wrapped around his midsection. A light beard had grown on his face and his brown hair was a mess.

Anne stared into Foster's tired eyes. "Put them down." She waited for her soldiers to respond. "I said, put your fucking weapons down!" All her soldiers quickly replied by kneeling down and dropping their rifles.

"Now tell them to step back!" Foster commanded. The men did so without any order from Anne.

"I don't understand. I shot you." Anne said.

Griggs found himself standing between Anne and Foster. He carefully looked down at his watch. One minute had passed. Only sixty seconds left on the clock.

"I wandered through the desert for days until I reached a highway," Foster explained. "From there, I was picked up by a trucker and brought here to Las Vegas, where I received some much needed medical attention. I almost bled to death in the desert from my bullet wound."

"What a great story, General Foster, and you tell it so well, too," Anne smiled deviously, "but this whole roof is going to turn into a giant ball of fire and rubble in about, oh," she checked her watch, "forty seconds."

"What?" Foster asked.

"She's got a bomb strapped to that tower." Jake pointed out.

"Then stop the countdown!" Foster yelled.

"I'm afraid I can't do that, General," Anne said, pulling the black detonator from behind her back.

"Why won't you turn the Goddamned thing off?" Foster yelled.

"I've got a mission to complete." Anne checked

her watch again. "You now have less than thirty seconds left to live."

Jake steeled his nerves and charged Anne. Anne turned just in time to see Jake a step away from her. Her eyes widened as Jake slammed into her, knocking them both to the ground. Griggs and Foster both took the opportunity and ran toward Jake and Anne. Durard and Tyler watched in horror as the minutes ticked away. Several soldiers turned and began to make their way toward the stairs as the four wrestled around on the roof. Watching his CO on the ground, Jannis charged and began trying to pull the men off Anne.

Anne held the detonator tightly in her hand as Jake, Foster, Jannis and Griggs all ripped at her trying to get to it. Jake pulled back and sent a punch into her face knocking Anne's head back. Her grasp loosened. Foster tried to grab the black box, inadvertently sending it skittering away from all of them. All four stopped and stared at the remote sitting close to four feet away from them.

Griggs was the first one to move. He leapt over the top of the pile and landed on his hands and knees. Foster was the next to go, diving for Griggs and slamming him flat to the rooftop. Foster crawled over the top of Griggs and reached for the detonator, only to be stopped by Jake holding on to his legs. Anne quickly sent a hard elbow into Jake's sternum knocking the wind out of him. Foster took the opportunity and slipped away from Jake's grasp. Pulling Jake back, Jannis sent several punches into Jake's kidneys. Jake moaned in pain.

Griggs rolled onto his side and held on to Foster. "Let go of me!" Foster yelled. Jannis tossed

Jake to the ground and leapt toward the detonator. Crawling over Foster and Griggs like a snake, Jannis inched closer to the detonator. Jake quickly caught his breath and rolled forward, latching onto Jannis' legs. Jannis tried to kick Jake, but he was being held too tightly. Jannis stretched out his hands. The tips of his fingers just barely brushed the edge of the black detonator. Jannis cursed under his breath.

Tyler stared at the detonator. Foster's hands were only inches from it. He glanced over at Faith and Alex on the tower. Tears were streaming from their eyes.

Faith had always been the nicest to him. Tyler quickly made up his mind. He couldn't let any of the men who were close to it get it. Breaking into a dead sprint, he raced toward the detonator and scooped it up off the ground out of Jannis' grasp. Looking at the small device, his eyes widened when he read the number on the counter: six seconds. Tyler panicked. He wasn't sure what to do. He had seen Anne press the red button, but he didn't know if he should press the green button. Would that detonate the bomb instantly, or turn it off? Three seconds. Tyler had to make a split decision. Two seconds. Sweat rolled down his forehead. One second. Closing his eyes, he pressed the green button. Relief passed over him as the counter stopped. He looked up at Alex and Faith. He was confused. Their eyes were still wide open, but the bomb had been defused. Tyler snapped his head to the right to see Hollman and Cisan charging him.

They knocked Tyler to the ground. "We need a new test subject, and you've been elected," Hollman sneered.

Tyler kicked hard at Hollman hitting him in the face. "Let me go!" Hollman stumbled backwards, his nose bleeding. "You little shit!"

Cisan pressed Tyler's shoulders and chest to the ground. "I've got him. Run the test!"

Hollman wiped the blood from his nose onto the sleeve of his uniform. Opening a pouch on his uniform, Hollman pulled out the same silver device that Jannis had used on Theresa only a day earlier. "Keep him still," Hollman commanded. Holding the silver device to Tyler's arm, Hollman pressed the button. A sharp pain shot through Tyler's upper arm as the needle was inserted. The silver device beeped, signaling the completion of its test. Hollman pulled it off and stared at the LCD display. "How can this be?"

"What?" Cisan asked as a dark form rising behind Hollman interrupted her. "Look out!"

Hollman spun his head around to see Durard standing behind him. Durard lashed out and kicked Hollman in the ribs. Hollman stumbled to the ground, holding onto his side.

"You backstabbing piece of shit!" Durard said as he kicked Hollman in the ribs again. "How could you do that to me! You sold Steve and I out! Now Steve's dead!" Durard kicked at Hollman again. Hollman rolled onto his side and intercepted the kick. Holding on to Durard's foot, Hollman twisted hard, sending Durard crumbling to the floor.

Climbing over to Durard, Hollman rolled him onto his back. He threw a quick punch into Durard's nose. "I had a job to do." He punched him again, "And I never liked Steve anyway."

Durard blocked the next punch with his arm and retaliated with a jab to Hollman's chin. Quickly standing up, Durard grabbed the back of Hollman's head and slammed it into his knee at full force. Hollman fell backward, his nose now broken. Stumbling to his feet, Hollman stared Durard down, then charged. Hollman hit Durard in the midsection, knocking both men to the ground.

***

Anne rolled onto her knees and pulled a knife from her belt. Diving at Jake, she grabbed him by the hair and pressed her knife against his throat. She leaned her mouth close to his ear. "You know, Jake, I always had a thing for you." She dug the blade into his neck sending a trickle of blood dribbling to the ground. "If things had been different, we could've been together."

Griggs turned around and saw Anne's actions. While still trying to hold Foster and Jannis, Griggs sent a kick into Anne's face knocking her away from Jake. Her knife fell to the ground. Scooping up the knife, Jake dove on top of Jannis. Returning the favor to Griggs, Jake stabbed the knife deep into Jannis' back. Jannis screamed in agony as the blade dove deep into his body. Standing up, Jake lifted Jannis off Griggs and tossed him easily aside. Griggs then lifted Foster and delivered a brutal head butt to him. Griggs watched Foster's eyes roll back as he passed out.

Rolling Foster off, Griggs sat up and looked at Jake. Jake took an uncomfortable step back from Griggs. He still wasn't sure what to expect. "Jake, it's me. Jason Griggs."

"I know who you look like, but I don't know what you are. Jason Griggs is dead," Jake said gravely.

"I'll explain everything later." Griggs stood and stretched out a hand to Jake. "Right now, we need to get the girls down and get the hell out of here."

Jake looked up at Griggs. Grabbing his hand, Jake stood up. "Right. Let's move."

***

Hollman delivered a second punch into Durard's chin. Durard reeled back from the blow, but quickly regained his balance. Stepping back toward Hollman, Durard sent a punch into Hollman's midsection, doubling him over. Grabbing the back of Hollman's head, Durard slammed Hollman's face against his knee. Pulling back, Durard sent one final uppercut into Hollman, knocking him to the ground.

Durard wiped the blood off his face from a cut just above his left eye. "Why did you sell us out, Greg? I've worked with you ever since I entered FEMA."

"Well then, you're well aware of what the government pays us. I wanted more, much more, and Colonel Caroll offered that to me." Hollman said.

"So your only motive is that you're greedy?" Durard asked amazed.

"No, you idiot." Hollman quickly pulled a small glass vial out of his pocket and held it up. "With this, we could rule. No one would be able to stop us without the fear that we would release the virus upon their country." Durard took a step toward Hollman and reached out to grab the vial. "Hold it right there, if you take even one step closer, I'll break this."

"Okay, okay," Durard took a step back. "Don't drop that, Greg."

Hollman stood up and looked at Durard. "I did what I had to do. I'm sorry that Steve had to die. I truly am, but we couldn't let anything stop the project."

"I don't understand, Greg." Durard took a step closer to Hollman. "You are a doctor. You took the Hippocratic oath to protect and save life, and now you're destroying it."

Hollman smiled. "That's not my problem anymore. We have created a weapon so severe, no government on Earth will be able to stop it. Colonel Caroll and I will be rich beyond our wildest dreams."

"Do you mean you're planning to blackmail the entire world?" Durard asked. "No, we're going to sell the virus to the highest bidder."

"Is there a vaccine or cure for it?"

Hollman smiled. "I'm afraid that's classified information."

Durard was startled at the crack of a rifle. He watched Hollman fall to his knees and grasp an ever growing red stain in the middle of his chest. Durard watched in horror as Hollman's hand let go of the vial. Leaping, Durard sailed toward Hollman. Landing flat on his stomach, Durard caught the glass vial gently in his outstretched hands. Holding the vial tightly, Durard stood up and searched for the shooter. He saw Anne standing directly behind Hollman's body with her weapon still smoking in her hands.

"I didn't pay him to tell everyone our plans," Anne said while a trickle of blood ran down from her lower lip. "Now give me the vial."

"Why should I? You'll just kill me like you killed Hollman," Durard said, holding up the vial.

"You're right, I will." Anne aimed her rifle at Durard's chest.

"Put it down, Colonel," Foster's voice echoed around the rooftop. "I will shoot you."

Anne turned her head and glanced behind her. Foster was standing with his pistol aimed at her head. "You don't understand, General. I have to continue with the project."

"The only thing I need to understand is that you're guilty of treason and mutiny, and I will see you prosecuted to the fullest extent of the law." Foster fired a warning shot over Anne's head. "Put it down, Caroll."

Anne made a bold decision. Spinning around, she fired her rifle toward Foster, hitting him in the shoulder. On his way down, Foster fired, sending a bullet shredding through Anne's chest. The two warriors fell silently to the ground.

Taking the opportunity, Durard ran over to Tyler and helped him off the ground. Cisan moved easily out of the way. She didn't want any part of this battle. He noticed a small silver device lying on the ground next to Cisan. Scooping it up, he slipped it into his pocket. "Come on, let's go get the others and get the hell out of here." Durard looked over to see Griggs and Jake helping Alex and Faith down off the tower. Running up, they stood together amidst the carnage.

Jake looked at Alex. "Are you okay?"

Alex nodded. "Yeah, I'll be fine. I just want to go home."

"I hear that," added Tyler.

Faith looked over the rooftop. It was empty except for the three bodies of Foster, Anne and Jannis. "Wow, this was incredible."

"Just another day in my life," Jake said jokingly. He turned his head to see Alex staring at Griggs. "Why did you help us, Major?"

Griggs looked at Jake. "You are my friends. I fought with you at Area 51 and at S-4."

"You died at S-4," Alex said with tears in her eyes. "I held you in my arms while you passed away."

Griggs smiled. "I remember." He quickly removed the thought from his mind. "You're right. I did die that day in the hallway of S-4."

"So you're a ghost?" Tyler asked amused by his own joke.

"Not quite, I'm a clone," Griggs answered. "I was the first successful result of the 'Uber-Soldier' Project. I was made from a sample of my DNA they had at the base and another sample that Colonel Caroll took from my body when she escaped from S-4. They didn't expect me to have any memories of the original Jason Griggs, but I did. I know everything he knew. Basically, I am Jason Griggs."

"That's too wild," Tyler said.

"I know it's a stretch," Griggs agreed, "but I am Jason Griggs."

Alex smiled and threw her arms around Griggs.

"I don't care how you came back to me, but you did and that's all that matters."

Griggs graciously returned the embrace. "Thank you."

Jake turned away and began to walk toward the door. "Let's get out of here."

"Hold it right there." Jake spun around to see Foster standing behind them with an assault rifle in his hand. "Hands up, you're all under arrest." Blood was running down his chest and arm from his new wound. He looked as if he was barely standing.

"Come on," Jake said in frustration. "We all just want to leave."

Foster stumbled closer to the group. "I don't think so," he said with a wheeze. "You're all wanted by the Federal Government. It's my job to bring you in."

"Why don't you take her in?" Faith asked pointed to Anne who was still lying unconscious. "She's the one who released the virus!"

"She will be dealt with," Foster assured. "Right now I think it's more important that I secure the prisoners."

"I'm not going back!" Alex screamed. Before anyone knew what was happening, Alex had pulled Griggs' pistol from its holster and was taking aim at Foster.

Griggs snapped his head around to see the events unfolding. "No!" He tried to reach for the gun.

It was too late. Foster had seen her grab the gun. Squeezing the trigger, Foster felt the weapon recoil as a bullet exited the barrel. Events seemed to be moving in slow motion. Jake could feel his heart pounding in his throat. He made a split decision. Springing off his heels, Jake leapt in front of Alex and Griggs. Pain shot through Jake's body as he felt the bullet pierce his chest. Alex screamed and pulled the trigger.

Chapter Thirty-four

There was nothing on TV. Clicking the power button on the remote control, he set it down on the stand next to his bed. Pulling up the covers, he tried to relax and catch a nap. He had the room all to himself. There had been no other patients since he had arrived over a week ago. Sunlight was streaming in through a large window on the far side of the room. Outside, he could see the vast cityscape of Las Vegas. The doctors had told him that he had been unconscious for the past three days, but they expected him to make a full recovery.

"Jake?" a female voice asked from across the room. "How are you feeling?" Jake rolled over in his hospital bed to see Alex and Griggs standing in the doorway. A large smile crossed his face. "Hey, come on in, guys!" Both had changed out of their black fatigues into more comfortable clothes. They were wearing jeans and t-shirts.

Alex was first in. She quickly moved to the side of the bed and leaned over Jake. She kissed him on the forehead. "We've been worried sick about you, Silver."

Griggs strolled in holding a large yellow vase with white flowers in it. It had a big black smiley face on it. "This was all Alex's idea," he confessed as he set the vase next to Jake's bed.

"It's the thought that counts, I guess," Jake said with a smile.

"I'm so glad you're okay," Alex said as she took a seat on the edge of the bed. "The doctors said the bullet just missed your heart."

"Yeah, but I'm feeling much better now. Where

are Tyler, Faith and Durard?" Jake asked.

"Durard took them back to FEMA with him." Alex rested one of her hands on Jake's leg. "Why?"

"This is incredible," Alex became very excited, "but Durard found the device Hollman was using to test subjects for the virus, and the readings showed Tyler has a natural immunity to it. Durard thinks he can create a vaccine from Tyler."

Jake allowed relief to wash over his body. "So the virus is being contained, that's outstanding."

"On a lighter note," Griggs interjected with a smile, "we think Tyler and Faith have grown very fond of each other."

Jake laughed. "Kids today."

All three laughed together for the first time ever. Alex stopped and stood up. Walking toward the door, she turned to Jake. "Well, we just stopped by to make sure you were okay."

Jake studied Alex for a moment. "There's something you're not telling me, isn't there?"

Alex reached behind her and slowly closed the door. Staring at Jake, she couldn't make up her mind to tell him or not. "Jake," she started, "we've got a bit of a problem."

"What is it?" Jake asked, sitting up in bed.

"As soon as we dropped you off here at the hospital, we went back to check on Colonel Caroll."

"And?" Jake asked impatiently.

"She wasn't there when we returned," Alex admitted.

"What? Where could she have gone?"

Griggs took a step closer to Jake. "We don't know." Jake felt his heart begin to race. "What about Foster?"

"His body was still there." Griggs placed his hand on Jake's shoulder. "Alex's shot hit him in the head."

Jake balled up his fists in rage. "She's going to come after us again, isn't she?"

"We don't know that," Alex started.

"The hell we don't. She almost killed all of us, and she brought Griggs back from the dead just so she could kill him again." Jake looked up at Griggs. Sadness had passed over his face. "I'm sorry, Griggs. I'm still not used to you being...well, alive."

"Neither am I," Griggs confessed.

Jake looked at Alex and Griggs for a long moment. "So what are we going to do to stop Anne?"

"We're not going to do anything, Jake," Alex declared. Jake looked confused. "What do you mean?"

"I'm getting on with my life, Jake. I'm going back to archaeology." Alex stepped closer to Jake. "I've signed on with a dig in Egypt, and our flight leaves this evening."

"Our?" Jake asked with a hint of spitefulness in his voice. "Jason is going with me."

"Alex," Jake reached for her hand. "Anne found us before. She'll find us again, no matter how far we run from Area 51."

"I don't care, Jake," Alex wrapped her hands around Jake's. "I want my life back." She looked up at Griggs. "I really feel like I've been given a second chance here. I'm not going to let this pass me by." She gently laid Jake's hand down and stood. "I hope you can understand." Walking toward the door, Alex reached out and slowly opened it. "Thank you for everything, Jake. You've saved my life more times than I can count."

Jake didn't even look up. He was staring blankly off into space. Alex waited for a response, but none came. "Goodbye, Jake." Alex and Griggs stepped through the door and were gone.

Jake sat quietly in the middle of his hospital bed contemplating what had just happened. The woman who wanted to kill him was still alive, and the woman he loved was gone. Grabbing the small black remote off the table next to his bed, Jake clicked on the television. After surfing through the channels again, he decided there was still nothing on TV. Rearing back, Jake threw the remote as hard as he could against the wall.

THE END